I0549708

Resolution

RESOLUTION

Her Sweet Revenge Series - Book #3

Mimi Barbour

Sarna Publishing

This is a work of fiction. Names, characters, places,

and incidents are either the product of the

author's imagination or are used fictitiously,

and any resemblance to actual persons

living or dead, business establishments, events, or locales,

is entirely coincidental.

"Resolution"

Her Sweet Revenge Series – Book #3

No part of this book may be used or

reproduced in any manner whatsoever

without written permission of the author except in the case

of brief quotations embodied in critical articles or reviews.

Contents

Dedication

I'm dedicating this series to my father, who we lovingly refer to as Papa John. This man has been a huge influence throughout my life. He's a smart, energetic, affectionate and very wise ninety-two-year-old man who is still going strong – likes to brag that he's only taking one pill a day. He's legally blind, but no one can tell from the way he gets around. Whenever he appears in the dining room at his lodge, people light up, and the jokes start flying.

This man brightens the day for everyone around him, and it thrills me to be his very fortunate daughter. To dedicate this new series to him is my way of telling the world that without his calm guidance and constant example, I'd never be the writer, the wife, the mother or the successful, happy woman I am today.

I love you, Papa John!

*Sadly, I lost my wonderful Papa John in 2018, and in his memory I wrote a book using him as one of the characters. It's called Special Agent Charli.

So far, he seems to be reaping the best comments in the book's many reviews.

Amazon Universal link: http://mybook.to/ SpecialAgentCharli

Praise

"The third book in the series, and they just keep getting better. Mimi Barbour continues the Series with another great story that sees Cassie continuing with her quest to find her brother's killer. The deeper Cassie gets involved with the underworld of Las Vegas while seeking her revenge and resolution, the harder it is for her to stay the sweet girl she once was. Sweet Resolution is another great read by Mimi Barbour that you won't want to miss. Once you begin reading the first page, you won't want to put it down until you have read the whole book. ~ *Reviewed by Laura*

"I have never rated Ms Barbour lower than 5 stars. But this time I am trying not to make it 3 stars. Other authors I have left 1 star for a cliff hanger. That being said she weaves a wonderful story. Her characters come to life. This is quite possibly her best story yet." ~ *Reviewed by Janine*

"What a fantastic third book in this riveting series. We see our heroine develop further both in her own self and her relationship with hot police detective Trace, and we also see some of the supporting characters grow. There are a few plot reveals that will shock you, and there is an almighty cliffhanger at the end! A highly compelling story that has me anxious about the ending." ~ *Reviewed by Bella*

Also author of...

All my books are available for FREE in Kindle Unlimited.

The Vicarage Bench Series (Books 1-7)
Angels with Attitude Series (Books 1-5)
Elvis Series (Books 1 & 2)
Vegas Series (Book 1-6)
Undercover FBI Series (Books 1-8)
Holiday Heartwarmers Series (Books 1-6)
Mob Tracker Series (Books 1-6)
Single Title Series (Books 1-3)
The Best in Romance Series (Books 1 & 2)

****

Many multiple-author Box Sets
Various other Single Titles

Chapter One

Cassidy Santino's life had become complicated, an understatement of huge proportions. Ever since her twin brother Raoul's murder at the hands of *Armas Jóvenes* members, guys in the same gang he'd joined months before, she'd changed from a naïvely shy librarian to a bartender at the sleazy nightclub where that same group hung out. She'd purposely gotten as close to all the lowlifes as possible so she could find her brother's killer.

Revenge had driven her. Money, hidden by Raoul, had funded her. And tenacity fueled the relentless need to make those responsible pay.

Riding her gleaming silver and black Kawasaki NinJarrmono O 250 to the gym where she worked out most days, she ruminated over the last time she'd been on a bike. Had it only been yesterday? God, it seemed unbelievable.

Arlene, the fighter she sparred with at Rusty's Gym, had driven up on her Harley just in time to save her life. If Cassi hadn't been able to leap on the back and get away from crazy Juan and his gun, who knows where she'd be today?

Considering that Arlene had rejected her the first time they'd met, having the girl help her surprised the hell out of Cassi. The incident that came to mind from that day was when they'd fought over Arlene's treatment of Rusty, the old guy who owned Rusty's Gym.

Arlene had been a bitch and Rusty had called her on it. Cassi hadn't intended to intervene. Wouldn't have if Arlene hadn't gotten in her face and if it hadn't turned physical.

By fighting back, using all the tricks she'd been taught over the years of sparring with her brother in their basement gym, she'd set Arlene on her ass. Remembering brought a satisfied smile. No one could disrespect Rusty, not in front of her. She'd lost all her family other than that grouchy old softie, so now he was hers to protect.

Funny thing, once Rusty saw Cassi's skills, he'd begged her to work with him to train Arlene. Turns out, the petulant fighter had huge potential and Rusty wanted to be Arlene's coach.

On her way there now, mind wandering to the recent happenings making her life crazy, she didn't notice the Hummer on her left until they honked and a waving hand motioned her to pull over.

Shit! Sergio Mandalas was not a person anyone could ignore, especially not her. He'd been the second person to help her escape from a killer yesterday.

Wishing the beauty of the morning and the enjoyment she'd experienced from her ride didn't have to be ruined, she swallowed another cuss word and dealt with Sergio.

Being that he was the leader of the *Los Soldados*, rival gang of the *Armas*, it wouldn't do at all to ignore him. In the past, he'd been her brother's friend. Because she'd done him favors, he'd transferred his loyalty to her.

She pulled to a stop, turned off the bike and swung both legs to the side so she could lean her butt on the seat. She removed her helmet and sat it on the handlebars, then fluffed out her hair. Next, she smoothed her jeans and lifted the strap of the black T-shirt that had the tendency to drop off her shoulder on one side.

He approached alone, leaving his bodyguards in the vehicle. She watched him scan the area before he stepped into the open.

"Hey, Sergio."

He cut to the chase. "You hung up on me yesterday."

Scrutinizing his manner to see if this had truly pissed him off or just mildly irritated him, she decided she really didn't care. "Yeah. So?"

Heat rose in his cold eyes, a warning. "So... I wanted to talk to you, Cass. You don't *ever* hang up on me, girl. You dis' me again, and we'll have words."

A serious, no bullshit warning, and it made her change her attitude. She decided only truth would get her out of this pickle, and so she shared.

"Detective McGuire had arrived, and I didn't want him to know we were talking. Sorry, Sergio, but you should know I wouldn't hang up on a friend if I didn't believe it was as much for his sake as mine. The less Trace McGuire knows about our association, the better. Right? If I'm wrong, tell me."

Sergio, face full of tattoos that flowed over his body and even onto his hands, the picture of a gang leader recognizable in any movie, scowled first and then relaxed, his face easing into a grin. "You two getting it on?"

She peeked at him from behind the curtain of her dark hair and let a smile answer him. "And if we are?"

"Damn, girl. You can do better than him. You want we should get together, you just give me a sign."

Cassi laughed. "My friend, you've way too much ego for me. We'd be butting heads every minute."

He winked and nodded. "And you've too much goodness for me. Under all that makeup and sass, Raoul Santino's little sister still exists."

Cassi began to feel nervous, a state she noticed that Sergio tended to create. No doubt it was because during all the time they talked, Sergio never stopped surveying his surroundings, overly cautious because his life depended on it. One of the men from the back of the Hummer, a bald-headed black giant had gotten out and now stood behind the car, his arms folded.

Cassi's nerves flared. Danger lurked, and she felt vulnerable. Being in the open beside this man was putting her life in jeopardy. She sensed his edginess. "You wanted to talk with me?"

"Yeah. You had Billy Duran at your place yesterday."

"Sure, he's an old friend of the family's." Stress jabbed her stomach hard enough to make her belligerent, and it showed in her tone.

Sergio leaned into her space, serious as hell. "You stay away from that bastard, Cass. He's not who you think he is. The man's poison. Drop him."

Cassi reached out and touched his hand. He gently gripped her fingers which gave her the strength to argue. "Sorry, Sergio. No can do. We grew up together. He's family. Billy lived with us while he studied for his law degree. I know he did drugs, lived on the streets. Hell, he was a bad boy. Now he's clean, I can't turn my back on him."

"Cass—"

"Don't ask me. Please, Sergio. He's a link to those old times when dad and Raoul were alive. Like a surrogate brother. I just can't."

"Fuck! You sure know how to make things tough for me, dude. What if I told you Raoul wouldn't like this relationship?"

"How would you know?"

"We talked. Before he joined the gang, we hung out. You know that. He'd be pissed if he knew the truth about the prick."

"Raoul did know about Billy's habit, his drugs and stealing money. But he also tried to help Billy get clean. He wouldn't have given up on him like you're asking me to do."

"Yeah, Cass. He would. Look, just promise me you'll be careful. Don't trust him. There's rumors, none I can prove, but when I get the proof, we'll talk again. Okay?"

She squeezed the fingers she still held before letting them go. "Okay."

From the corner of her eye, she noticed a car slowing down, a window opening, and the barrel of a gun inching forward.

RESOLUTION 7

Chapter Two

Unsuspecting, yet trusting Cassi when she dove from the stationary bike toward his body to take him down, Sergio went with her. Bullets pelting the side of the Hummer sounded like the ones hitting the beer cans that she and Raoul used to shoot when target practicing.

Only *this* noise scared the shit out of her. Death giggled maniacally and was the most frightening sound she'd ever heard. Except the giggler was the person behind the gun. Echoes of the horrific racket remained as the would-be assassin drove past.

Sergio hit the ground, twisted and dragged her with him to shelter behind the Hummer. His guard returned fire and they watched as the black SUV took the corner on two wheels and disappeared.

"Jesus! That was close." Sergio sat with his head lowered, his knees bent and hands hanging between. He still clenched the gun he'd withdrawn from the waist of his droopy jeans, only now it hung loose.

Trembling, her arm stinging from where it'd scraped along the gravel, she agreed. "You live dangerously, man. It must be horrible not being able to stand outside without having a target plastered on your forehead."

He looked at her, a sadness creeping over his expression. "I *should* be shot, putting you in danger. Sorry, Cass."

She surged to her feet and reached for his hand. "And I appreciate you risking your life to warn me. It matters, Sergio. It means a lot. I promise to be careful. But you need to promise me, too."

He stood. His gun had disappeared back inside his waistline and both hands were free to hold her cheeks gently. "I won't forget, babe. You and me, we're connected. I'll protect you if I can. But you gotta know your association with the *Armas* makes things very difficult."

"Except, I'm not one of them. I work at the Lipstick Club because I'm trying to find out who killed my brother. Once I know who the killer is, and we now suspect it's a female, then I promise, I'm finished."

"So that's what we gotta do, find out the name of the bitch who shot your brother. I'll keep on it." He stepped back. "Take care, Cass. I'll watch your back as you head off, then we'll follow to make sure you're safe."

"Thanks, Sergio. You're a good guy." She smiled with tenderness lurking.

He returned her look for a few seconds, and then his expression returned to his usual scowl that gave her a glimpse of the man everyone else feared. This stare held no mercy.

"Good guy?" The laugh he used made her skin crawl. "No, girlfriend. That's not me."

Trepidation from his warning made the nausea she'd tamped down increase. Controlling it so as not to embarrass herself, she swallowed repeatedly. Bent over so he wouldn't see her expression, she swiped at the dirt on her jeans, gave him one last wave and left.

***

Arriving at the gym, Cassi approached Rusty and saw him covering his concern with his normal grouchy attitude. His customary black tuke sat on his head askew, as if he'd pulled it off a number of times to scratch at the white mop underneath. "You're late."

"Yeah. Ran into an old friend, and we stopped to catch up."

Suddenly his eyes narrowed. He seized her arm and held it up. He wasn't rough but concern flashed in his astute blue gaze. "Did you take a spill on the bike?"

"No." She looked down and saw the scrape he was fussing over. After everything that had happened, the discomfort hadn't yet registered. But now that he'd pointed it out, the throbbing pain kicked in.

The hiss that followed called her on the bullshit.

"Truly, Rusty, I'm fine with the motorcycle."

"Then what happened? It's a fresh wound."

Shit! A lie would have been a lot better explanation than the truth. Now what was she to say? "I kinda fell."

"Fell? Uh huh."

"To the ground."

"Figured." At this point he crossed his arms and waited. She wasn't getting past him until she came up with a better explanation.

"The gravel did the damage."

"Kinda figured that too since there's still some embedded in the bloody skin."

"I tripped."

"Kid, you don't trip. You're a trained athlete who's faster on her feet than anyone I've ever seen. You're balanced and swift and trust me... you don't just fall. Quit playin' games, brat. I'm beginning to get worried."

Cassi could see the fear lurking, overriding his concern. If she let it change to anger, she'd really be in trouble. She had to tell him something. "Okay.

O-kay! You're hassling me. It's nothing. I'm fine, just a little misunderstanding. Don't you trust me?"

"Not even a little." Rusty lost the grim look and pure sincerity shone through. "Kid, you're hiding something, and I know it's not good. But you're all in one piece. I guess that's what's important. Just know this. If you need me, I'm here. There ain't nothing I wouldn't do for you."

Overridden with guilt, Cassi stepped into his space. Though uncomfortable with affection, Rusty let her lean her head on his shoulder. He even patted her hair.

"Don't get me wrong, Cassi Santino. I'd paddle your backside if I thought it would do any good. Should'a done a lot more of it when you was a little one and couldn't fight back. Now I gotta trust you know what you're doing. But it doesn't mean I gotta like it. And it sure as shit, doesn't mean I agree with you avenging Raoul. But I'm here if'n you need me."

Overcome with emotion, Cassi welled up and knew if he saw her tears, he'd be even more uncomfortable. Problem was, a sniff escaped before she knew it would, and he stiffened instantly.

Carefully moving away from her, he gave her a little shove in the direction of the change room. "Go get ready, then come to my office. I'll bandage it. I guess the session is a no go today."

"It's not that bad, Rusty. I'll be fine. Just bandage it and don't fuss."

"Put a bandage on what?" Neither Cassi nor Rusty heard or saw Arlene approach. Suddenly, she was just there. Her eyes zeroed in on the lacerations on Cass's arm. Her eyebrow rose.

Before she could ask, Cassi yielded. "I tripped"

Snorting her disbelief, she said, "Sure you did. And I'm a fucking Haitian princess. You gonna be able to work with me now you got that killer scratch?"

Cassi laughed. And Rusty looked from one to the other. He could see that something had changed between the two girls. Considering they'd battled in and out of the ring up till now, Cassi knew he'd be asking questions.

She was right.

By the time she'd changed into the gear she used in the ring, her shorts, athletic shoes and sports bra, he was waiting for her.

"You wanna tell me what happened between you two?" His keen eyes penetrated, waiting.

"What do you mean?" While changing, she'd made up her mind that during the inevitable interrogation to equivocate was acceptable but no lying. Not sure she could stick to the plan; she dodged the best she knew how.

His following sigh lasted for a long time and spoke more than words. His patience had evaporated.

"Okay. Don't blow a gasket, Rusty. You remember Juan Acedo?"

"Sure. The idiot who hung out with Raoul, another sleaze from the gang he joined. Looks like a monkey, and around you, he acted like a dopey, lovesick one."

"Yes. You pinned him exactly. Except he's no longer alive."

Rusty's attitude faded somewhat. "Can't say one way or the other whether that's good or not. Didn't know him well enough."

Sudden shock from all that had happened over the last few days hit her hard, and Cassi staggered against his cluttered desk.

"You okay, Cass? Come sit on the couch and tell me what's been going on. I need to know, kid." Truth rang in a voice filled with concern, and so she did as he said.

"Not sure how much you already know so I'll fill you in. After Raoul's murder, and because of what you'd told me, I'd been under the illusion that Juan couldn't have killed Raoul. In fact, I believed he'd been beaten up for refusing to be involved in Raoul's initiation."

"Hey, wait... I only repeated his excuse for not

coming to our boy's funeral. I had no way of proving if it was true."

"It wasn't. He lied. Turns out, from what I've been able to piece together, he was one of the three men behind the warehouse the night Raoul died. So far, we have the names of the others involved and strangely, all are deceased. But it's come to light that there was a fourth person there, a female. The police are looking for her but they have no leads."

"You think she's the shooter?"

"Could be. Juan swore on the life of his mother, he didn't pull the trigger."

"Yeah, yeah! But can you believe him?"

"No."

"What about the other two guys there?"

"Police can't place them behind the gun, their size says different. The lighting was poor but the shadows revealed enough. The person who pulled the trigger was shorter, smaller build."

"Therefore, it must be Juan. You've got your killer, Cassi. Put avenging Raoul's murder's behind you now."

She shook her head so hard, the band she wore to keep her hair back from her forehead slipped. She had to straighten it.

His eyes narrowed. "Why?"

"I can't. Not until I know the truth. Not until

the female has been caught and made to answer for her part in the killing." Cassi heard the grating vehemence in her voice and felt her resolve harden.

"Dammed, you're stupid-stubborn like your dad. Never could talk any sense into him either, or Raoul for that matter. You still didn't tell me why you and Arlene made up."

"Right, I was getting to that. It turns out that Juan helped his adoptive mother, Mary Devin, kill Kathleen McGuire, Detective McGuire's mom. Trace had hired Mary as a caregiver because his mom was in the last stages of bone cancer and needed special nursing."

"I remember you telling me something about that. I thought nurses were supposed to keep their patients alive not bump them off."

Cassi nodded. "They are, but Kathleen McGuire suffered terribly and it seemed that Mary couldn't stand to watch her agony. According to what Trace discovered about her previous nursing cases, he believes it's not the first time either.

"And... the other families were in the same predicament. None wanted to see their loved ones having to live through such horrible illnesses, so were mainly relieved when they passed on. No one ever thought to look into the circumstances. If Trace hadn't installed a video device in his mother's room, he'd never had discovered it, either."

"Holy sh- shinoly. Why didn't Trace arrest Juan? What the hell was he doing wandering the streets?"

"He did arrest him, but when they were transporting him to prison, someone high-jacked the transport vehicle and Juan escaped. He showed up out front with one of the guard's guns, intending to make me go away with him."

"Idiot must have known he'd need some kind of weapon to force you to do anything."

Cassi grinned. "Before he could get me into his van, Arlene pulled up on her cousin's Harley, drove between us, and I jumped on. In the end, we got away."

"Okay, now I get it. That's why things are better between you two."

"Yes. She could have ignored what she saw and let him take me. She didn't. I owe her."

The door swung open. Arlene pushed it wider. Her hands on her hips and a glower of pure meanness dressed her features.

Cassi and Rusty whirled her way. Both frozen.

Scraped back from her face, her auburn hair's framework emphasized her beauty more than usual. The stark look also highlighted her flashing eyes, cold with menace and glittering with what looked like shock.

She aimed her tirade at Cassi, her forefinger pointing. "I lost my mind for a short time and got involved, Cass. Don't go building anything into it. Truth is, I need your sparring abilities so I have a chance to win the upcoming fight against that bitch, Ariana Wilde. Otherwise, I'd have minded my own business."

Arlene slammed the door on her way out so hard, papers fell off the desk.

Chapter Three

"What the hell was that all about?" Rusty sounded furious.

Cassi had no idea that Arlene had been at the door, listening. What had she said to make the other girl turn from her earlier friendliness back to the chick with a huge chip on her shoulder?

Futility grew inside Cassi. She grimaced from the hurt Arlene's attitude created. What the hell would it take to get that prickly bitch to back off so they could become friends as well as sparring partners?

In the last few months, Cassi had spent a lot of time vexing over this situation. No matter how often she tried to get under Arlene's defenses and extend a hand of friendship, the other girl slapped it away with rude indifference.

Tired from the constant battle, Cassi stiffened

her shoulders and lifted her arm for Rusty to doctor. "Damned if I know, Rus. One minute she blows warm – never hot – and the next, icicles hang from her like barbs on a wire."

"Craziest freakin' female I've ever met. If she weren't so bloody talented, I'd kick her out the door and let it slam her backside on the way out."

Cass snorted, "Yeah. Sure you would. She's your star, Rus, and you love training her. It shows."

"It's you I'd love to train. Hell, kid, you've got more raw talent than anyone I've ever met." When he saw her glower he added, "Just sayin'. Thing is, she reminds me of some of the winners I've worked with. It's the way she moves, her instincts and most of all, her raw courage. That girl has such a will to win; for any trainer, it's pure gold. If I could take your skills and her determination to be the best, we'd shoot straight to the top, brat. And that's no lie."

Before Cassi could again tell him that would never happen, a rap sounded on the door. Rusty set aside his first aid kit, having finished cleaning and dressing Cassi's wound, and stood to open it.

"Hey, Detective McGuire. I didn't expect to see you here. Any trouble?"

"Nope. I just have a few questions for Cassidy. Won't keep her long."

Rusty moved to let Trace step inside and sent a

questioning look her way.

"It's okay, Rusty. Trace and I are together again. We're good."

Once the door closed behind her old childhood babysitter, she dove into Trace's hug. After her close call not an hour earlier with Sergio, her delight at seeing Trace made his arms a haven and his warm lips a need she couldn't get enough of.

"Baby, whoa, what's up? What's happened?"

Not wanting to tell him about the shooting earlier and get yet another lecture for her to stop her crusade in the underworld to find Raoul's killers, she just kissed him again. Tasting his mint-fragrant mouth, her tongue active and her hands framing his clean-shaven face and then sifting through his thick, dark hair, she lost herself in the joy of being where she felt loved.

Seeking, her lips found refuge in his ability to stir and delight every nerve in her body. She felt him ignite. Heat seared and their joint breathing became harsh with inflamed cravings.

"Stop, baby. I can't. We can't. Not here." He stepped away and held her face in both hands while he searched her features. "What happened?"

Shifty-eyed, knowing she looked guilty and having no skills to hide that from his all-seeing gaze, she fell back on the last situation that had her upset.

"It's Arlene. After she helped me yesterday, we kind of bonded, you know? I thought we'd gotten past all these crazy hostilities of hers. But just now, she slammed me again with her shitty behavior and it was the last straw. Seeing you, being held by you was the best medicine in the world. I'm fine now."

"No. You're not. You're wearing a fresh bandage. Why?"

Shit! Did the man miss nothing?

"Uhh...I cut myself shaving?"

"Not funny. Who hurt you?"

Okay – now she could tell the truth. "Some gravel."

"Seriously?"

"Yes. Even I can end up on the ground if I'm not careful."

Narrowed, his gaze scorched her defenses and aimed straight for her honor to be truthful. "You fell off your bike?"

Phew! No lying needed.

"No! What is it with you and Rusty? He accused me of the same thing. I did not fall off my bike. I'm getting better at controlling the machine. I've practiced a lot and it's becoming easier every time I go out. How did you even know I rode it to the gym today?"

"It's in the parking lot."

"Right. You'd notice that, wouldn't you?"

"Baby, it's my job. But I'm not here to talk about that. I've come with a request from Mary Devin. She wants to talk to you, if you'll come to the women's prison."

"Me? Why? I only met her the one time with you when we had dinner with your mom the night she died."

"She wouldn't tell me. Just says Juan talked about you a lot, and she needs to see you."

Cass collapsed on the couch and rubbed her shaky hands over her thighs. "Oh, God, Trace. I led Juan to believe we were friends while trying to trap him into telling me the truth about Raoul's death. He might have gotten the wrong idea and led her to believe there was something else going on. How can I face her?"

"You'll know what to say, sugar. The woman needs an ally. She's refusing counsel, says she only did what she felt was right to save her patients from further suffering."

"Killing them might seem a bit drastic to some of the jurors, don't you think?"

"Let's say she facilitated their imminent deaths, made it quicker and less painful than if they'd been left till their bodies couldn't withstand the agony any longer."

Cassi watched Trace's expression carefully. "You don't hate her for what she did to Kathleen?"

"Truthfully? I did when I first saw the video, her holding mom's hand, sobbing, while Juan used the pillow. But since then, I've come to see it as a blessing. Every day, Mom's suffering had been worse. That's what I hated. Not Mary for releasing her from her living hell."

"I'm not sure if I ever mentioned this, Trace, but I never understood why her doctors couldn't have upped her morphine to help her endure the pain?"

"Poor Mom had allergies to a lot of the medications, especially opioids like morphine that would bring on an anaphylactic shock. The treatment they were forced to fall back on was nowhere near as effective as the stronger pain relievers would have been."

"My God! How sad!"

"Nights were the worst. Sometimes, I caught her crying, and I felt so fucking useless." He stopped talking to swallow, his voice husky with emotion when he continued. "Because she'd been murdered, they did an autopsy and found a slightly higher level of her prescription drug. Enough to make her unconscious so she wouldn't have been aware of what was happening, but not enough to stir interest with the coroner. At the end, she looked very peaceful, like her body had finally eased over."

Cassi watched Trace's expression, and she had

to ask. "Do you want me to talk with Mary? I will if you say so."

He knelt in front of her, his hands enfolding her fidgeting fingers and his kiss calming her uncertainty.

"It's your decision, honey. She has no one else, only her previous patient's families who she's refusing to see. I'm amazed at how many are extending their condolences and want to help her now. Many remember how she made their family members happy in their last months, and how her ability to do so had been precious to them in their time of need. Hell, even I can sympathize. She brought Mom comfort, caring, friendship and in the end, peace."

"Okay, then. I'll go if you promise me one thing."

"Whatever you want, baby."

"Will you come with me?"

"You got it, Cassidy. Anytime you're ready, you let me know." He kissed her, a sweet meeting of their lips, his commitment to share a difficult undertaking.

He stood, urging her up with him. Wrapping her in his arms, he gathered her in and hugged long and hard, just like the famous hugs his mom used to share. Then with a final wink, he left the room, and she saw him wave at Rusty before heading down the stairs and out of sight.

Her gaze switched to Arlene now in the far corner, pounding the hell out of a punching bag. Cass had never seen her wearing that particular killer look before. Shivers raced over her body, and she had to brace herself before heading to where Rusty waited to wrap her hands and help with her gloves.

Chapter Four

Arlene knew shock affected a person, hell she'd felt it a time or two. Especially the night Raoul was murdered. But this time it was personal.

Standing outside Rusty's office, she hesitated when she heard what Cassi was saying. A smile pasted over her face, waiting to be shared with Cassi, deflated so quickly a painful needle jabbed in someone's ass couldn't have done as much damage.

The cops had found out that a female had been there the night Raoul had died. And they were looking for this girl.

Shit! Shit! SHIT!

Sure, they didn't know it was her, but they were looking for a female. It wouldn't be long before they pieced together the story. Only there was no one left to tell the truth.

She might have been the person whose finger had been on the trigger, but she'd had the gun aimed at Juan, trying to stop him from kicking the shit out of her friend's lover. She'd never intended to use it. Certainly not against the man she'd been there to save.

Leaning against the wall, praying her racing heart would slow before she lost her lunch or passed out from the lack of oxygen, she deep-breathed and forced her throat to relax.

The image of Faith Whitely emerged, known as Sunshine to most of the regulars. She felt the softening inside that always accompanied thoughts of the beautiful blonde who'd saved her from a vicious rape when she'd ended up in a place where she hadn't belonged.

This was back when they'd first moved their operations to Vegas. They'd just bought the Lipstick Club, the same place that Cassidy now worked as a bartender.

As a gang member back then, Arlene had worked mostly as a mule in the warehouse, did her duty and made herself scarce as often as possible.

Once she'd stopped using so many drugs and came back to the real world, the shine of belonging to a gang like the *Armas* had tarnished for her. By then, Juan had become more persistent that she belong only to him, and truthfully, sober, the guy didn't have half the attraction he'd had when she'd been constantly high.

After Mani had found her and began working with Dani Andino, the red-headed bitch of a mob boss, he'd made sure she'd backed off the junk even more. Sober, life had taken on a whole new meaning. Hers sucked, and she hated herself for being such a fool.

Hated what she'd done to her family, Mani's parents who'd taken her in as a baby and given her a home. And hated the losers she hung with, the soulless creeps who lived for one thing only... to get high, drunk, and laid.

Mani's insistence that she get clean brought her back from the damned. As he'd infiltrated the upper echelons of the mob, easy for him with the brain and skills he'd been born with, she finally benefited. When Dani had ousted their old boss and taken control, she'd put Mani as her second-in-command, and life began to look rosier.

Especially after the night Mani had shoved her into the back of the warehouse, the office space only he, Dani, and a few of the other more trusted members were allowed into and told her that he'd spoken to Dani and laid down his ultimatum.

He'd stay with her. But only if she cut Arlene loose. Dani refused at first, but she needed Mani who knew more about the business side than she ever would. So, she made the deal.

If Arlene waited a short while after they completed their move to Vegas, and then just vanished, she wouldn't send anyone to search for her. Normally, runaways wouldn't be tolerated. They'd suffer consequences meant to dissuade others who tried the disappearing act. Mani had saved her, and she fully intended to take the opportunity he'd provided.

She only had a few more days to fill in when she'd been sent to the clubhouse to deliver some papers to Rodrigo and had stumbled into the wrong area.

Next thing Arlene knew, some drunken Neanderthal slob had her planted against a wall with his tongue buried down her throat while his hands made free with the fastenings on her clothes.

Pushing against him was like trying to move a horny elephant with only one goal on his mind. It had taken Faith to force some sense into the ugly bastard.

Why she'd moved in to help, Arlene attributed to the tears she'd felt flowing down her cheeks, and the ineffectual screams and pleading she'd used to try to make him stop.

Their eyes had caught across the room. Arlene had seen the pity in the other girl. The next thing she knew, the blonde beauty had moved closer and started playing him, calling him sweet names and undoing her blouse, giving him a glimpse of her huge breasts.

"Hey, big guy. She doesn't work tonight. But I'm available. You wanna come to mama and let me take care of that massive bulge you have going on? She'd slid her hand to rest over the swelling in his pants, and he'd dropped Arlene so quickly, she'd fallen to the floor. As he followed Faith who'd taken his hand and was leading him to her room, he'd stumbled over her leg, which later swelled for a week.

Arlene had never suffered such fear and disgust before. And it was all aimed inward. How the hell could she be so pitifully ill-equipped, that a drunken prick could overcome her that quickly?

Fear had disintegrated her strength. Disgust had destroyed any intelligence she usually had going for her. And the ego she'd built since becoming a gang member had totally disappeared. Which just proved one thing; her bullshit arrogance had been nothing but a fucking sham built on drugs and influenced by others of the same ilk.

***

Next day, Arlene had begged Mani to give her Sunshine's home address. She'd visited, only to find her beaten and limping slightly. Her face and arms were colored with bruises, and the cut on her lip made smiling difficult. Though she managed a small grin when she saw the flowers Arlene had brought with her.

Arlene remembered the sick anguish that she hadn't been able to hide. "He hurt you. That bastard hit you."

"It's nothing." Childlike, Sunshine waved away her injuries like they were small in comparison to previous incidents.

A fissure cracked in Arlene's composure. How the hell could such a beauty be so cavalier about being brutally abused? Sadness flooded. Arlene had the biggest urge to hug the other girl close and swear she'd never let anyone hurt her again. Then Sunshine's words broke through her fog of horror, and she concentrated.

"Yellow roses symbolize friendship. Did you know that when you bought these?" Sunshine's eyes, cloudy from using, still revealed their delight in her gift.

"My aunt would get them every birthday from her friend, and she always acted pleased. So, I wanted to give you something for what you did for me last night. No one's ever saved me from my own stupidity like that before. I needed to let you know I appreciated your help."

Sunshine held out a hand that Arlene didn't feel

comfortable in holding but couldn't refuse the gesture either. Led inside a tiny apartment, she noticed a bed full of colorful pillows set up against the wall facing a huge window.

She saw the bachelor suite as the perfect hidey-hole, homey from the tender care appearing in the gleaming floors and faint smells of cleaning products. Across the room, a small wooden table and two chairs were placed under the lace curtains so one could see the strip in the distance. It would be a fabulous night view.

On the end of the bed, a huge tabby cat lay curled in a ball. It lifted its head to glare at Arlene, showing his dislike of being disturbed.

"Make yourself at home, Leni. That's what Mani calls you, right?"

"Yes, Leni's fine. I see you have a pet."

"Oh, him." Faith waved at the grumpy feline whose back was now arched. "He's the weirdest cat, belongs to the neighbor. Comes to the door and meows to be let in until I can't stand listening to him anymore. Lies at the end of the bed until Raoul shows up and then turns into the most lovey-dovey puss you can imagine. He barely puts up with me."

Sunshine bustled into the tiny kitchen, a small alcove off the main room. As soon as she disappeared, the cat leapt at Arlene, attacking, his claws coming within inches of raking her face. *Crazy, fucking thing!*

Before she could retaliate, he'd growled his fury and raced under the bed. Shaken, but not wanting to upset Faith, she swallowed her anger and shook off the desire to catch the monster and teach it a lesson.

She heard Faith rummaging around behind the thin wall. Suddenly, she began talking loud enough for Arlene to hear.

"I'm sorry you had such a fright last night. I could tell right off you'd just come in the wrong door, and the animal had misunderstood, thought you worked the room with us."

"He wouldn't listen to me, and then you led him away like a trained dog on a leash. Except from the look of your face, he must have turned vicious. God, I'm so sorry."

"Some of the men like to hurt us, but we have a button in our rooms by the bed that we can push. If it's necessary, one of our guys will come and help. Raoul got there before he did much damage and dragged the nut job out, kicking and screaming. Gave him a taste of his own medicine from what he told me later."

Arlene couldn't believe the matter-of-fact way that Faith accepted the treatment. "Thank God. Just imaging you with that greasy, bushy asshole made me sick all night. You looked half his size."

Sunshine laughed. "I might be scrawny but my knee still works really well. Raoul showed me some handy moves I can use if I get into a situation like that, and they've come in handy."

Arlene looked around at the comfy surroundings and couldn't stop the shock from sliding off her babbling tongue. "This is a really nice place, Sunshine."

The beautiful girl in her pale blue mini dress came from the other room, holding a milk carton she'd wrapped in silver foil where the roses now nestled safely in water.

She set them carefully in the middle of the table and then gently caressed one of the petals. "Like velvet." She turned to Arlene who'd sat on the bed, waiting for her answer.

"You can call me Faith if you like. I love this apartment. Raoul rented it for me. He stays with me a lot during the day when we're not working. We feel safe here."

"Tell me to shut up if you want to, but I have to ask. You're so beautiful. Why are you working at the Lipstick Club?"

"It beats the streets. Though Dani's as hard-assed as anyone I've ever known, she's fair with the money. Plus, the girls are protected. I didn't mind my job until Raoul came along. Now, we're trying to find a way that I can get out. Maybe it would have been a good thing if I'd have gotten more injured. Then I could stay home."

God. How horrible. Wanting to get injured so she wouldn't have to work as a prostitute.

It all seemed so senseless and utterly sad. It had then and it did now.

***

Suddenly a lull hit the gym. Arlene looked up to see Detective McGuire approaching, determination in every step the big, good-looking cop took. She slid away, moved over to where the exercise equipment hung, waiting for takers. She began smashing her gloved fist into the bag, taking out all her fury from earlier memories on the leather made exactly for that use.

Self-loathing, the culprit that had driven Arlene into Rusty's gym after she'd left the gang, had found a home in her psyche and drove her. That and her need for a place to hide during daylight hours kept her coming back. Learning the art of self-protection, well... that topped everything.

Who knew the unexpected love of boxing that filled her with such ambition would also be accompanied with healing. It was one of the stupider reasons she'd stayed in Vegas, taking the chance that someone in the gang might recognize her. Changing her appearance, dying her hair and using a fake last name had helped.

The truth – she could find a trainer anywhere in the country. The reason it had to be Vegas was because this is where her beloved uncle lived and depended on her to be there with him these last months of his life.

Though her Aunt Barbara blamed her for Mani's death, she also knew Arlene's presence was necessary to keep her husband happy for the time he had left. She'd admitted as much, even begged Arlene to come to him as often as she could.

For her aunt to have put aside her own muddled feelings against Arlene and ask her to visit, shocked her, yet it meant a lot. All her life, her aunt had looked after her niece's necessities. But stupid jealousy from having to share her son and husband's affections with her niece had destroyed any possible closeness.

Arlene knew Mani would have wanted her to be with his father and help alleviate his suffering. Since he'd been her best friend, as well as her cousin, she had no choice. And Uncle Phil had treated her like a cherished daughter. Now, it was payback time. Besides, she loved the old man more than anyone.

And if the truth were known, she blamed herself for them losing Mani. He'd only joined the gang to get her freedom. Vicious bullets that ripped through the walls of the Lipstick Club in an earlier raid had taken his life, and he'd been there because of her.

So leaving town wasn't an option. Yet staying was dangerous and stupid.

Chapter Five

Cassi dressed with care for work that night. She needed to cover her arm to stop questions. Thankfully, the pink blouse she wore as her Lipstick Club uniform hid the bandage.

She fixed her short hair making it glow with cleanliness and a soft shine. Then she grabbed the blue spray and covered the shaved side, highlighting the blatant difference in the length.

Once she added the earrings she'd become used to dangling over her shoulders, she fixed her makeup. Using the techniques taught to her by the hairdresser who'd cut off her hair after Raoul's funeral, she recognized her skill had improved. With eye shadow and liner, she'd accentuate the sapphire color, the size and even the slanted proportions.

She checked her reflection and saw where the longer side of her hair draped curtain-like to cover her eye. A trick she often used to hide her expression.

At one time, the mass of black waves had been waist length, though she'd usually worn it rolled up or tied back. She'd only left it long to please the macho males in her family, her brother and her father, José, who had some old-fashioned, crazy notion that long hair made a woman look more feminine.

Stepping back, she gave herself a once over and snorted with disbelief. Who would recognize her as the same girl from a few months ago who'd worked in a library, never swore and lived to please her family?

Naïve, shy, an honor-bound introvert, she'd been afraid of her own shadow. And lying had never been tolerated, by her conscience or her morals. *She'd been such a wuss!* Shame flooded and revived the sorrow that was always just a teardrop away.

God! Clenching her hands, she could still envision herself hiding behind that fucking fence, frozen, unable to move. Instead, she'd watched as the bullet had ripped through Raoul, her twin brother, and she had done nothing.

Well, the woman standing here now wasn't that same Cassidy from back then. She'd become strong, hardening the soft core that had formed her personality. Lying, cussing, hell, nothing shocked her anymore. This girl was a kick-ass bartender who wouldn't and didn't hesitate to take on men twice her size and put them in their place.

She leaned in closer, hands on the counter, and her face inches from the mirror. Staring into her slanted baby blues, she acknowledged with some pride that it had been through her persistence that they'd managed to find three of the men she watched kicking the shit out of her brother before one had put a bullet in his chest.

And though Trace had fought her all the way about putting herself in danger, it had been worth the risk. She didn't like working in the hell-hole club, nor did she fear the men; most were young drunken fools and drugged idiots who just wanted to feel like they belonged.

But there was one person who scared the hell outta her. One she couldn't ignore or hold off much longer. The leader of the *Armas Jóvenes*, Dani Andino, wanted her and not in any acceptable way she could live with. The lesbian boss of the club had put some moves on her already. It had sickened her at the way the leader had taken it for granted that she'd win.

Cassi knew that if it came to a physical battle, she'd already proven she could take the other woman. But the boss wielded a lot of power, and those trained monkeys who never left her unprotected would do whatever she told them to.

Should she leave the Lipstick Club like both Trace and Sam wanted, give up her quest? The anguish that filled her appeared in her eyes until grim determination took over.

No! Not until the last person they suspected – a woman – was caught and made to pay.

Therefore, Cassi had to stay on Dani's good side, no matter what it took. Her eyes filled with the intense anxiety she could no longer ignore, her stare all-seeing. She finally broke the spell and sagged, her face gripped in her hands.

There was one thing she'd never give the other woman who wanted her obedient and willing.

Her heart belonged to Trace McGuire.

But then, Dani didn't want her heart.

Chapter Six

That evening, before heading into work, Cassi drove to the hospital. She didn't see the Hummer until it pulled up behind her, blocking her way out. She stepped from her car and waited until the tattooed thug joined her.

"Hi, Sergio. We meet again. How's everything with you?"

"Ain't good, ain't bad, as my dad used to say."

"Can't really ask for more."

"Shit, girl, you can ask but it ain't likely anyone is listening." He chuckled. Then he lifted his hand, taking liberties with her hair, pushing the curtain back so he could see her full face.

Helping him, she tucked the strands behind her ear and faced him fully. "You've got something to tell me that I'm not going to like, right? You know the name of Raoul's killer?"

"Not that. But I do know who took those pot shots at us the other day on the street. They weren't after shooting my ass. Cass, this time the bitch was after you."

"What?" Stunned, and horrified, Cassi searched his expression and saw the intensity in his gaze and the honesty in his expression. Suddenly, it all made sense. "Maddie!"

As hard as it was for her to see the incident clearly, Cassi had to accept that when Maddie decided to attack her in the nightclub's ladies' room, she'd started the whole fiasco. Plus, the silly bitch must have known there'd be risks when shooting at Sergio Mandalas.

"Right. Seems she had it in for you, wanted revenge for her treatment from Dani. So rather than hurting Dani, she and some blonde bitch did the drive-by, thinking to get you. Problem is, my people are everywhere. We got the license number, and let's just say, I paid them a visit."

Heart dropping, his tone saying it all, she blanched. "You didn't."

"What? Kill them? I should have just for shooting at me, never mind putting your life in danger. But no—I knew you'd freak if I did. First, I made them see the error of their ways, and then I gave them away. Don't worry, honey. They won't be back."

"Back? My God, where did you send them?"

"Never you mind. They'll be too busy to even

remember your name from now on. Let's just say, they're at work, doing what they love – fucking people."

"God, Sergio, I'm sorry you had to get involved in my battles. Now I'm really glad you weren't hurt."

"Shit, Cass. I would have been killed if you hadn't moved so fast. Way I see it, I still owe you. Gotta go, babe. You take care. I'll be checking in from time to time and see that you're okay. You fine with that?"

"Of course. Thanks, Sergio." Without knowing she would, Cassi held out her hand and he took it, then he lifted it to his lips and gently kissed the palm before letting it go.

Tears suddenly choked her. This man, whose leadership skills and deep ingrained fairness along with his intelligence could have had such a different future if he'd been born with a silver spoon – as a citizen, a builder of men, a husband and a father. At least, she had the good luck to know him as a friend.

Cassi waved at the Hummer as it pulled away, leaving her standing alone. She spent a few seconds thinking about the two girls they'd discussed and then shrugged her shoulders. Nothing she could do for them now. They were responsible for their own stupid choices.

***

A little while later, shaking off the sadness caused by Sergio's words, she strolled down the hospital corridor until she came to the private room she'd arranged for Faith Whitely, Raoul's girlfriend.

Praying she'd see a difference in Faith's behavior, she stuck her hands in her tight, white jean pockets and stealthily peeked around the open door.

The huge vase of mixed flowers she'd had delivered brightened the room, but nothing could cheer up the blonde curled in a fetal position on the bed. Her long hair clung in oily strands around her shoulders and her pretty face wore only pain.

Cassi had visited earlier, only to find Faith withdrawn and uncooperative. She'd faced the wall and wouldn't listen when Cassi had tried to get through to her. One sentence had been repeated constantly through her sobbing moans. "Let me die. I just want to be with Raoul and my baby."

Guilt rode Cassi hard. After all, when she'd asked to talk with Sunshine, the nickname the younger girl used at the club as one of the upstairs hookers, she'd put her in danger.

Cassi had begged Sam, the other bartender, to arrange the meeting, which he had done a few nights ago. She'd decided to offer Faith a helping hand and enough cash to get away from Dani and break out of the rut of her profession.

Her ulterior motive, the hope that Faith might know who had been with Raoul the night he'd been killed, had aided in her decision. If Faith could identify the female they believed had witnessed the crime, or maybe, had been the enforcer, Cassi would have succeeded in her quest to get him justice.

But before they'd gotten into it, Maddie and her sidekick had interrupted, coming in and locking the door. Because of some skewed jealousy over Dani, some crazy far-fetched idea that Cassi wanted to steal her away from Maddie, her favorite at the time, the whacko had decided that Cass needed to learn a lesson.

When Faith had tried to intervene, Maddie had cut her with her knife and in the ensuing scuffle, Faith's head had come into contact with the sink and she'd passed out. Later, when the ambulance came to take her away, Cassi'd suffered the shame of the damned.

That wound had been meant for her and the following fight that Cassi eventually won didn't come close to making up for the damage Maddie's hatred had created.

At the hospital, not only did the doctor warn Faith about her drug habit, which had increased to the nasty shit after Raoul had been killed, he'd also flayed her soul with words no woman wants to hear. "You miscarried your baby."

Faith had been stunned. Not knowing she'd been pregnant, those words had ripped her wide open. Cassi believed her when Faith admitted the only person she'd been with who didn't use protection had been Raoul. The baby had been Raoul's.

And that had broken two hearts.

Cassi slowly approached the bed and settled in the visitor's chair. "Faith, please stop crying. You're making things worse. The nurse just told me that you've refused to eat again."

Faith sniffed, her hand clenched the soggy pile of tissues and her pain-filled eyes stayed shut, as if looking at Cassi was more than she could bear.

"You know what? I think we need to get you out of that bed and into a shower. Sweetheart, you'll feel a lot better. Come on, I'll help you."

"I don't want a shower. Just leave me alone."

"Faith, you can't go on like this. People care about you—"

Before Cassi could finish her sentence, a nurse came in carrying a vase stuffed with at least a dozen yellow roses. She whipped the card from where it had nestled in the blooms and handed it to Faith. "These just came for you, honey. They're so beautiful; I knew you'd want me to bring them in right away."

A spark of interest entered Faith's eyes and she reached for the little white envelope. Weakened, unable to sit easily, it dropped on the floor.

"I'll get it, Faith. Here, do you want me to open it for you?"

A nod gave her permission and Cassi quickly slit the top and pulled out the card. Only one word inside a huge heart appeared and it shook the foundations for Cassi.

She turned to Faith, handed her the note and said. "They're from Leni."

Questions churned in her head wanting answers but before she could speak, Faith's fleetingly pleased expression caught her interest. Faith held the card over her chest as if hugging it and more tears fell but this time they weren't accompanied by wretched moans and pleas.

These were tears of appreciation for another's kindness and for the second time in a short while, Cassi blessed Arlene's timing and thoughtfulness.

Chapter
Seven

"You're a bully!" Faith's voice sounded stronger.

Cassi grinned. "Maybe, but you feel better after the shower, don't you? Your nightgown and robe have been changed and your gorgeous hair is now clean and it smells lovely."

"Soon as they let me leave here, I'm cutting it all off." Mutiny appeared on Faith's face and her lips pouted.

"No! Why? It's so..." *Oh, God! Who was she to talk? Isn't that exactly what she did after Raoul was killed?*

"Okay, I'll take you to a girl I know."

Faith sat in the wheelchair where Cassi had forced her after the shower and glared at her fake stepsister. Since lying had been the only way Cassi could get past the nurses to visit, everyone had accepted their false relationship and it seemed that even Faith believed in Cassi's right to be with her.

"Raoul never described you this way. He said that you took care of the house you two shared and made chocolate cake and lasagna and had it waiting for him after his fights. And that you were sweet and caring, and had a huge moral compass where you never lied or swore. I was terrified to meet you."

"Yeah? Well, after they killed him, I changed. Made up my mind that he needed justice, and if no one else would get it for him, then I would. Once on that road, I had no choice but to become someone who could work at the Lipstick Club."

"Do you like it?" All-seeing and all-knowing, Faith's eyes dared her to lie.

"I hate every hellish minute I'm forced to be there. But I like working with Sam, the other bartender. He makes life bearable. Plus, being there has helped me discover the names of the three men who were involved in Raoul's murder."

"So, now, it's over."

"Not quite."

"One of them had to have shot him."

"Maybe not. I've recently found out that there was a female along that night. Until I know her name, and the part she played, I'll keep looking."

"Oh! No! Cassi, let it go. I'm begging you. This vengeance isn't something Raoul would have wanted." The faint light of interest that had shone in Faith's eyes dimmed, and she'd winced as if in pain.

Not happy for her to fade back into the mound of abject misery she'd found upon arrival, Cassi whipped the wheelchair around and headed for the door.

"Where are you taking me? I want to go back to bed."

"Nope. I need a coffee and you need some soup or whatever you'd like. Anything, as long as you eat." Cassi moved them out of the room and headed down the hallway.

Faith's chin dropped to her chest, spilling her now dry hair over her shoulder. She whipped it away, turning her head at the same time.

"Stop!"

Cassi pulled up and looked around. To the right were double doors and over the top, two words glowed red – Maternity Ward.

Cassi cleared the emotion from her throat and spoke softly. "No can do, Faith. It's a very bad idea."

"Can't I just go in and see the babies?"

Wheeling in the other direction, with a very faint wail from a tiny human echoing in the distance, Cassi headed for the elevators. "Why? It's torture. I won't let you do that to yourself."

"Oh, oh, Cassi, take me back to my room. I think I'm going to be sick."

Chapter Eight

After Cassi left her, Faith kept replaying Raoul's sister's words about how she hated every hellish minute working at the Lipstick Club. Understanding how that felt, her mind shied away from the endless soul-destroying nights she'd stuck it out. Only by closing off her true self and donning the prostitute's character of Sunshine had made it possible.

She remembered how everything had changed after she'd met Raoul. He'd saved her from yet another sadistic brute, one of many who thought that paying for a girl meant they had the right to treat her as less than human.

The first time Raoul worked as an upstairs bodyguard he'd become her friend, her defender, and life had transformed from slightly bearable to satisfying, exciting, and as they grew closer, to joyful.

Until the night she'd overheard Dani tell Juan and Miguel that it was time for Santino's initiation. From that moment on, things deteriorated. She'd stayed glued to the spot and heard Dani give the order she knew Raoul would decline.

Dani had become aware that in their youth, Raoul and Sergio Mandalas had been friends. That Raoul could get close to the rival gang leader and so Dani told them to give Raoul the order to kill her rival, her biggest threat to business on the streets and prove his loyalty to the *Armas*.

She'd heard Juan question Dani about what they were to do if Raoul refused to follow orders. And when Dani's harsh instructions were to teach him a lesson, Faith's blood had turned cold.

Running back to her room, she locked the door and had tried calling Raoul to warn him. Her hands had shaken so badly, she remembered dropping the phone and the gush of tears making it impossible to find it easily. Forced to crawl, her legs refusing to work, she'd scuttled around until her hands scooped it close.

It rang twice and cut to his voice mail. In a panic, she'd called the only other person she knew who would help her. Leni answered immediately.

"Faith, what's wrong? Why are you crying?"

"I need your help."

"I'm downstairs. I'll be right there."

Within a few seconds, Leni had shown up as Faith had known she would.

"Juan and Miguel are going to make Raoul kill Sergio Mandalas at his birthday celebration tonight. He won't do it. I know Raoul. He'll refuse. Dani told them to make him pay if he doesn't follow orders. I'm terrified what those animals will do to him."

"You should be. They're fucking maniacs!"

"We both know they'll never listen to me. I'm too weak to do any good. But maybe you can be there and make sure they don't go too far. Please, Leni, I'm begging you. If anything happens to Raoul, I'll die."

"Did they mention where this is going to happen?"

"Raoul's at the warehouse tonight. They'll go there to pick him up. Please, you have to leave now. And take this, just in case."

She'd passed over her small Glock that Raoul had given her weeks before when a particularly brutal bastard choked her to get his jollies. Raoul had been furious that she hadn't been able to get to her call button.

Fuming, he'd tried convincing her to give up her job and run away with him, a subject he'd been dedicated to for weeks. Again, she'd put him off, knowing Dani wouldn't let him go easily.

Regret burst in her mind, but it was too late for it to do any good. One thing for certain, if Raoul escaped tonight, she'd run to the ends of the earth with him just so he'd be safe.

After Leni left, Faith had spent the next two hours in a state of mind-shattering panic. When her friend had returned stunned and broken-hearted, she'd explained what had happened. How she'd aimed the gun at Juan and ordered them to stop kicking Raoul.

Except Juan had wrenched at her hand, wrapping his fingers over hers, and before she even knew what was happening, he'd switched her aim to Raoul. Then he'd forced her finger to pull the trigger. She'd ended up as an accomplice in murdering the guy she'd come to save.

Traumatized, sickened and scared, Leni had been wretched about what had happened. At the time, neither girl thought about the murder weapon. All that broke their hearts was Raoul's death.

From that moment, the light inside Faith had been extinguished. And that's when living became a cruelty beyond bearing. When the only reason she'd move from her bed and go to work was to get the mind-numbing drugs they provided.

Leni had tried to stop her from self-destructing

but nothing mattered anymore. Recriminations ate away at every vestige of her healing until all she wanted was oblivion through drugs and pain.

When she thought things couldn't get any worse, God had punished her selfishness by taking away the one thing she'd have lived for—her baby. Death teased and it appeared to be the answer to every question her mind continually tricked her into asking. How could she survive without Raoul?

But there was one stream of affection that lingered inside her tormented heart, one small flicker of light that still had meaning.

Leni.

Her true friend, who'd come when she'd called and tried to help, only to be entangled in a murder she didn't commit.

And now, Raoul's sister intended to find that woman and make her pay. When would this madness stop? She couldn't lie to Cassi and take the blame because Leni's fingerprints were on the gun. And as Juan had mockingly warned her friend the day after the killing, he'd worn gloves so his weren't. And... he had the murder weapon to hold over her.

Therefore, if he decided to turn her in, the cops would charge her for the murder, or at the very least, as an accessory to the crime. And Leni didn't deserve that label.

Hell, if anyone was guilty, Faith knew where the blame lay.

***

Unable to stand the destructive insanity inside her mind for one more second, Faith allowed two words to sneak in, "Maternity Ward." There were babies there. Tiny little human beings like the one she might have had if she hadn't taken those devastating drugs.

Somehow, her being pushed against the sink in the fight with Maddie didn't register as the reason for the miscarriage. She knew whose fault it was that she'd lost Raoul's child. And the responsibility lay directly on her shoulders. Anguish filled her and ugly guilt followed.

Considering she'd only begun using the really strong stuff after she lost Raoul, the baby might have had a decent chance to be healthy. If she'd only been aware of the pregnancy, the knowledge would have stopped her from taking the mind-destroying shit.

And if she'd known while Raoul had still been alive, she'd have listened to Raoul and Leni and would have gone into hiding, gotten away from the life she'd hated but had always accepted as her punishment for being such a loser.

A sob escaped and then another. God knows, she'd have loved being a mommy, having a chance to do better than her single mom had done for her. Though, she knew it wasn't her mom's fault for being schizophrenic and making terrible choices. The sickness had taken over in her thirties and had left her unstable, unable to function properly.

In fact, they hadn't even been aware that she suffered from the disorder until it had been too late. Too many boyfriends who'd liked bedding both mommy and daughter. Too many parties where she'd brought Faith along not able to distinguish that her fourteen-year-old daughter wasn't an equal but her child to protect.

Faith had learned early on that if she went with her mom, she could protect her, keep the men happy. Then most times, they'd walk away with enough money so her mom could get her liquid medication that came in a vodka bottle.

Grinding grief tore through her. Some memories should be kept locked away. A feeling of suffocation took hold. Throwing the covers aside, she began to stumble around the room. As remorse drove her to keep moving, from one wall to the other, the steel trap of her emotions loosened.

As if a silver chord of energetic force tugged, compelling her toward the place where Cassi had fled from earlier, Faith slumped into her wheelchair and wheeled herself to the door. In no time, she arrived where two lighted words glowed in red.

Pushing through the swing doors, she wheeled herself to a wall of windows and there she watched as four, tiny, pink-hatted darlings slept with little clenched fists close to their serene faces.

Tears clogged her throat while sorrow dug its talons deep into her sorrow-filled heart. *How beautiful!*

A thin wail caught her attention. Over to the other side, one baby lay awake, crying heartbrokenly. He wore a diminutive blue cap and his small body writhed, engrossed in his tormented screams.

Faith looked around to see if any nurses were close by. Where was everyone?

Her heart went straight to the tiny being whose distress made her ache. Without hesitating, not even caring if she broke rules, she pushed into the area and stopped next to the hospital crib. There she reached for the tightly clenched fist jammed into his mouth and crooned soft words of love. "Shush, baby. Faith's here, honey. You're not alone anymore. Shush now, that's the good boy."

Screams fading to sniffles, the baby's crying lessened as if he knew the person nearby cared about him. Eyes searching blindly, he turned to her presence, his head movements jerky and weak.

She crooned and all the while gently patted his

body, touching him carefully, letting him know he wasn't alone. She was there. If she'd have had the nerve to pick him up and cradle him, she would have. Scared, she decided it would truly be breaking the rules, and she didn't want to get into trouble. But, oh God, she wanted to hold the little darling so badly.

She checked the chart on the end of his crib, not moving it but she was able to read the name tag which said he was Boy – Corella.

He was a beautiful baby, not as wrinkled as most, his smooth golden skin looked healthy and in a strange way, his large blue eyes appeared to focus. Dark hair with the tendency to fluff out from his head in a comical but loveable way had her reaching to smooth it down for it only to fuzz out again.

Faith was so absorbed in the child; she didn't hear the nurse approach.

"Honey, thanks for settling him. He's been very upset, poor baby." A nurse bustled into the area, her face wreathed in smiles. "It's been hellish here these last few days. We have a staff shortage due to that horrible flu that's been going around."

Faith stared into the stressed face of a middle-aged, slightly overweight woman whose kind eyes dismissed her earlier worries. "I couldn't bear to hear him crying."

"I know what you mean. He wrenches at my heart, too, poor lonely little tyke." Her voice gentled as she questioned Faith. "Do you have children of your own? We moms can't help but be drawn to a baby's distressed cry."

Faith shook her head, not chancing words in case she broke down.

"No matter, you seem to have a way with him. In the few minutes I get free, I've tried to soothe him but nothing helps."

The nurse rambled on, not waiting for Faith's answer. "Oh, he's starting again. Look, I have to deliver these girls for their feeding. Would you like to give him his bottle?"

Curiosity overrode her craving to hold him. "Why can't you deliver him to his mother so she can feed him like the others?"

"Because the silly girl ran out on him just hours after she delivered. Her boyfriend looked all day yesterday to bring her back, but as of earlier this afternoon, he'd had no luck. Poor guy is beside himself. Doesn't know what he's going to do on his own with a baby."

The nurse handed a bottle to Faith and then picked up the little guy and settled him in Faith's arms. Hurrying away with two carts, one in front and one pulled behind, she disappeared, leaving Faith's heart aching for her new little friend.

Chapter Nine

Arlene had been happy when Faith called to thank her for the flowers. She'd offered to come and get her keys and then fetch whatever she needed from the club and her apartment.

Though Faith's voice sounded as if she didn't really care one way or the other, she did agree that it would be helpful to have her tablet and her toothbrush and stuff.

When Arlene showed up at the hospital looking forward to seeing for herself that her friend was okay, a harried nurse stopped her.

"Her stepsister came by earlier and talked her into using the wheelchair. She took her for a walk. Maybe she's decided to go again on her own. You could check the cafeteria. I'm sorry, I can't tell you more. We're short of staff tonight, and I just don't have time to search her down."

"No, no I don't want to be a bother. I'll wait in her room if it's okay."

"Sure. Sorry I can't be more help." The lit board behind her grabbed the nurse's attention. She hurried to answer the summons.

Arlene had gone into Faith's room and saw her handbag lying open on her night table with keys protruding. She reached over and lifted them closer, deciding that they must be the one's she needed to get into Faith's place. She could go over now, and by the time she returned, Faith might be back.

Once she arrived, she unlocked the door and before she could stop it, the crazy neighbor's cat dodged between her legs and scooted to the bed.

"No. Get out. Go on. You can't stay here."

She swung her hand in his direction and in a flash of pure spite, the rotten devil attacked, his claws ripping the skin and leaving her furious. "You mean son of a bitch." She grabbed one of the pillows so as not to hurt him but to make him mind, and she whapped him good. He growled, hissed and understanding she meant business, he fled out the door. She slammed it shut behind him in case he decided to try returning.

Sucking the blood from the raw wound, she wrapped it in a tissue and put pressure to stop the bleeding. Then she went into the bathroom and gathered up the personal belongings she hoped would come in handy to someone in a hospital.

She found the plugged-in tablet on the table and dumped everything into a cute carry bag that hung in the tiny kitchen. Before leaving, she stopped to look around. The yellow roses were now a collection of petals Faith had dried and kept in a pretty bowl. Seeing them tugged at Arlene's heart.

She slowly approached the bedside table and leaned down to stare at the large framed picture of Faith wrapped in Raoul's arms, both with wide smiles lighting up their faces.

A sob broke and then another. It was some time before she left to return to the hospital.

Chapter Ten

Later, working at the club, Cassi's mind shifted back to Faith who she'd left huddled in a ball under her covers. The poor girl had barely made it in time to the sink where she'd lost the puny amount of food they'd managed to force into her.

"Earth to Cass! You wanna give me a hand here? Hell, just because we pay you, I can understand that might not be sufficient motivation to do your job. So how about this? Your poor partner could use some help."

Cassi heard the sarcastic note from the man who always made her feel better about having to be in the place. Though his words were harsh, the twinkle in his eyes belied their message. Sam had managed to become a good friend over the many episodes they'd had to deal with when working with a bunch of dysfunctional losers who ran off at the mouth. People who thought they could have whatever they wanted and reacted like childish idiots when they found out they couldn't.

She sent a smile his way and shook her hair back so he could see her full expression of regret. "Sorry. I was still at the hospital with Faith."

"Poor, kid. How's she doing?"

"I'll tell you later." An influx of people streamed through the door, mostly males. Many wore the *Armas* tattoo, proudly showing off their gang affiliation.

They worked through the busy mob until the waitresses carried full trays to serve at the tables and the customers at the counter were satisfied.

Rodrigo, the manager of the club, approached the far end of the bar and with a jerk of his head, motioned Sam to his side. Their discussion lasted a few moments, and then Sam returned to work alongside her. Rodrigo headed behind the bar and disappeared in the storage and small office area.

Stunned as to why he would even bother to go in there, Cassi's eyes questioned her partner who shrugged and looked away. Cassi'd worked with Sam long enough to know something was up but she had no idea what it could be.

Suddenly, Sam's shoulders stiffened and his body shifted from lazy norm to acute attention. Even the aura around him heightened, sending off strange vibes. Muted disgust blazed as Pete Bradford sauntered over and slammed his hands on the railing.

His straggly unwashed-hair, studded leather vest and wiry beard might have come off as a typical gang uniform in a comedy movie but there was nothing funny about the sneer on his face or the cold hatred in his eyes.

Heartless, the man whose body wore tattoos on every surface except his eyelids, gave one the creeps. Cassi had met him on the night Trace had come into the joint to arrest Juan Acedo for the murder of Kathleen, Trace's mother.

At that time, Sam had told her Pete had arrived from L.A. and was to take Mani's place as second-in-command to Dani. God help them, this scary dude could never treat the others with the same respect Mani had managed. The men had loved him, would do anything for him.

Already, Cassi sensed the dislike seeping from the guys nearby. Fear and distrust for their new commander permeated causing a muting of the brash talk and drunken laughter from seconds earlier.

Pete pointed at Cassi. "You! Gimme a Bud Light."

The regulars nearby watched for her reaction. They knew she didn't put up with that kind of rudeness. Everyone stopped to listen.

She edged closer to the buffoon and questioned

him. "You talking to me? If so, my name is Cass. And *gimme* doesn't work in this joint. A *please* will get you any drink you want, though."

As if she'd kicked a killer unused to the treatment, silence began to build until it radiated throughout the area around her. The background din faded and Sam's groan came through loud and clear. His *"Cass, don't"* warning emerged louder than the whispered cuss words that followed.

Staring into beady black eyes filled with challenging menace and a strange glee that discomforted her more than his other obvious reactions, she waited.

Pete's lips curled. His eyebrows rose, and he reached for the weapon he never went anywhere without. The gun appeared and slowly lifted to point in her direction.

"You wanna rethink that, little lady?"

Cassi sensed Sam edge toward her. She also noticed the guys at the bar had put down their drinks and were drawing away. Hell, it was becoming like a gunfight in an old western saloon.

"You need that gun to make me?" Cassi tossed her hair and let him see her challenge.

"Honey, you don't know who you're foolin' with here. And I usually don't give warnings."

In a crazy move she'd perfected from her martial arts training, Cassi somersaulted over the counter and landed, standing in front of the asshole who, not expecting this move, stepped back. Before she knew it, a bunch of the regulars had formed a semi-circle around her, saying nothing, but their presence alone told a story.

Mess with her. You mess with all of us.

Pete growled like a cornered dog who had to use brains rather than intimidation, and his were lacking. Before he could lash out, Sam had slammed a cold, opened can of beer on the counter and slid it close to him.

"Hey, man. Loosen up. Cass's my partner, and we don't like anyone giving her a hard time. Check it with Dani. She'll tell you the same."

Appearing from inside the crowd, Dani herself stepped up. She wore her favorite uniform, tight ripped jeans with high heels that added to her height. Her wine-red hair was short but spiked fashionable so it looked like something she'd seen in the pages of Cosmopolitan.

To cover her pebbly skin, the woman had applied layers of makeup which hid her age effectively, but looked as if she'd just stepped off a Broadway stage. And the filmy, white, off the shoulder blouse showcased her store-bought boobs, allowing a great deal of them to be on display.

Obviously overhearing Sam's words, she

repeated them. "What'll I tell him, Sam?"

Dani's appearance seemed to shock Sam. She must have arrived while the scene at the bar had revved up, and his attention had been diverted with Cassi.

"Hey, boss. All I said was that Cass deserves respect. She works with me and shouldn't have to take any shit from these guys."

"Who's messin' with her?" Her glance caught Pete, his gun now hanging loosely by his side but his pissy attitude still plastered over his face.

"She gave me lip cuz I asked for a beer. Ain't that her fucking job, serving your customers drinks?" He stepped closer to Dani, and Cassi saw her eyes widen before she switched her glare back in Cass's direction. It stunned her to see that the boss had a healthy fear of this animal.

The expression Dani wore didn't bode well for her, and she knew it instantly. *She'd overstepped the bounds. God, would she never learn?*

Dani pointed to the frosty can and then to Pete. "This the drink you wanted?" She handed it to him, forcing him to put his gun away before he could take it from her.

Then in a move no one expected, she swung around and backhanded Cass across the face, her power such that Cass flew against the bar. Before she could retaliate, Sam had Cass's arms, holding her back from making a big mistake.

Sam broke the electric silence. "She's sorry, boss. Got some bad news about Sunshine that put her in a piss-poor mood. Won't happen again."

Dani shook her head, looking regretful enough to calm troubled waters. "Shit, Cass, I can't let you get away with mistreating my boys. You gotta reel it in, girl."

Pointing to her favorite table, she turned to grin at Pete. "We need to talk. Join me there. Drinks on the house. Come on, guys, loosen up. We're all friends again." She waited until Pete left, and she edged over to Cassi.

"I'm good, Sam. Let me go." Cassi looked his way so he could gauge her sincerity.

He studied her, and seeing the swelling, his eyes filled with rage.

"It's okay, Sam. I deserved it. Thanks for stopping me."

Though her cheek stung, she didn't raise her hand to soothe it. She hung her head so her hair would cover the red. Ignoring the other woman, she took a few steps to return behind the counter. She didn't want Dani to see the anger she'd had to swallow.

But Dani's quietly spoken words close to her ear stopped her. "Cassi, I had to make a point. If it hada been anyone else, I'da let you hurt the son of a bitch. But I need Pete. Especially now."

Cassi nodded. She didn't make eye contact, instead she shrugged. "Okay. I was outta line, anyway. But you keep that bastard away from me, Dani. He's a soulless prick and scares me silly."

"Well, you coulda fooled me, sugar. You sure as hell didn't look scared. You looked like you wanted to tear him to pieces. If he does the job I have for him to do, maybe one day I'll let you." Her snicker followed her to the table and left Cassi behind with a burning question.

What the hell did Dani want Pete to do?

Chapter Eleven

For Cassi, the rest of the night crawled by. Many of the men left extra tips and made crude gestures of sympathy that she knew meant they cared about her just a little.

Some of them were the same ones she'd helped the night of the shooting weeks before when the members of *Los Soldados* arrived with guns blazing, a retribution for another shooting done by the *Armas*.

On and on it went, constant war wounds inflicted in retaliation. The drugs, prostitution, and crimes never stopped. They just shifted when premises got too hot or adapted when people like Mani died.

Remembering her earlier suspicion about Rodrigo disappearing into their storage area, Cassi waited until a calm moment and shifted over to

Sam so she could question her immediate boss who knew about most things that went on in the club.

Ponytailed and braided, his silvery-gray hair hung down his back so it stayed out of his way while working. His lithe body, strong and fast as any she'd seen at the gym, attracted a lot of female attention. His experienced hands worked the taps and rinsed the glasses automatically while his steely-eyed glance never missed a thing.

"Sam, where did Rodrigo go?"

He looked at her and his eyes narrowed. "Haven't you gotten into enough trouble for one night without asking questions you don't need to know the answers for?"

He was still fuming about her earlier run-in with Pete. She could tell and it made her feel bad. "You're mad. I'm sorry. I was acting like a bitch and shouldn't have pushed him. But Sam, he's a shit. I just didn't know how much of a shit until he pulled the gun."

Sam slouched back against the counter and crossed his arms. "Why are you still working here, Cass? You've got what you came for. All of the men who were at the killing the night Raoul died have been punished."

"You're the second person who's said that to me today and I'll tell you what I told them. There's still one person who was there and the police have no idea about who she was. Once I find her, I'll gladly leave this world behind, trust me."

Sam stiffened and he now seemed totally immersed in her words. "A female was there? You're sure. You thinkin' it was Dani?"

"I can't imagine who else it could be. I've heard she gave the order for Raoul to kill her rival, Sergio Mandalas, the guy she hates more than germs. Makes sense she might have wanted a front-row seat if he'd agreed."

"Hell, girl. Nothing makes sense in this whole shit-show. I know she was here earlier that night. And I seen her leave after they say Raoul was shot. Can't say I know her whereabouts in-between those times." Sam pondered, his next words spoken as if he were talking to himself rather than to her. "But you could be right that she showed up. She's pulled the trigger before."

Suddenly keen, Cassi stiffened, hoping Sam didn't notice her response to his words. "Have you heard anything?"

Still unaware of her reaction, he mumbled, "All I know is when she did come back later, she had blood on her and Juan ended up in the hospital. I overheard the guys talking about how pissed she was at him for not obeying orders."

"Do you know what the orders were?"

"Haven't a clue."

"So maybe what he swore was true. That he didn't kill Raoul and it sure as hell wasn't his gun."

As if he'd come out of a trance, Sam studied her face and his closed down. "None of our business, sugar. If Dani is the culprit, then you gotta leave it the hell alone. She's way out of your league."

"You're lecturing me."

"Fuckin' right, I am. I never knew anyone more deadly or colder than that bitch when she's on a mission. Story is, she charmed the original leader of this gang back in Los Angeles to let her in and then pulled a double-cross. Left him a broken-down, sorry-assed joke of who he'd been when they'd met."

"Well, she can't do that to me because I'm not into her and I never will be."

"Hell, cupcake, you, she'll just shoot."

"Maybe. Only way to find out is to get closer and see if I can come up with any evidence or..."

"Or what?"

"Get to Rodrigo and see what he knows. Why did he disappear downstairs?"

"Christ, Cass. Haven't you figured it out yet? They have hidey-holes all over this joint. Not only do they sell drugs, they need a place to store them, too. And to count the cash they rake in. So, when I tell you to keep away from there, I mean it. The guards have been given the order to shoot to kill anyone who shows up without Dani, Rodrigo, and now Pete."

Thoughts ricocheted in Cassi's head about how she might use this information to get to Dani. Only nothing came to mind. She went back to minding the bar and lost herself in her imaginings of ways she could trap her boss. She was so deeply immersed; she didn't see Dani get close enough to slap the counter in front of her.

"Cass, I want to see you upstairs. Sam, get one of the waitresses to pitch in to help you." Dani strutted past. She smiled evilly, and using her finger like a hook, she aimed it at Cass.

Sam stiffened. "Don't go, Cass. Leave the place now. She's in one of her moods. I can tell. And Maddy's no longer here."

Cassi headed for the counter that opened and turned back in his direction. "Hell, Sam. What can she do to me if I say no?"

"That bitch has never understood the word no. Just walk away, sugar. I'll cover for you."

"Can't do that, Sam. Don't worry. I can take care of myself." Brave words rung in her ears but the shaking inside belied them as did the panicky mess her guts were in.

The second she turned her back, Sam's phone appeared.

Chapter
Twelve

Trace hadn't been able to settle for days. After finding out what Juan Acedo had done to his mother, he'd vacillated between relief that her agonizing suffering had been ended and furious that the person who'd so cavalierly carried out the act had escaped imprisonment by dying from a heart attack.

It would have appeased some of his crippling frustration to see Juan on trial and watch him squirm when he got the death sentence.

On the other hand, Juan's accomplice, his adopted mother, Mary Devin, was being held for trial and he still didn't quite know how he felt about her future. Accepting that she must never again be free to carry out her mercy killings, he didn't believe she should end up in a high-security prison in solitary, either. Maybe a hospital for the mentally insane would be her proper punishment.

Paperwork piled in front of him, evidence he had a lot of other cases that needed his attention. He also had a prick of a boss who'd been riding his ass about closing those files.

He stood and grinned as his creaky chair erupted with its usual complaints. One day he had to get some oil and fix that bastard.

His phone rang. He jumbled piles of papers into a mess while rummaging for the screeching cell. Only one person used that dial tone. His calls were infrequent but usually foreshadowed trouble.

"Hey, Sam. What's up?"

"Dani's taken Cass upstairs. I got a bad feeling. Maybe you need to create a diversion."

Trace's heart dropped to the floor and lay there writhing like a snake with a knife spiking it to one spot. "You thinking a raid?"

"A lot of fire power in the premises tonight. Be interesting to see who's carrying legally. Just don't take too long."

"On my way."

Trace looked around and saw his partner had stayed to work late, too. "Hey, Diane, you wanna get a swat team organized and have them meet us at the Lipstick Club? I just got an anonymous complaint of illegal firearms."

Her eyes drilled his and caught the unspoken

message. "On it." Diane's organizational skills were unbeatable. Trace relied on her to follow orders in her usual skilled way. In a short time, she gave him the nod, grabbed her own weapon from the drawer and was ready to go.

As they headed their police issue in the direction of the club, Trace fought to keep his cool. Terrified of what Cassidy might be going through, he applied more pressure to the gas and took the next corner a bit too fast. He looked over at the woman who rode beside him every day. Her serious expression caught his attention.

She'd done something different to her hair, clipped up the straw-colored softness but strands had come loose and hung past her shoulder. Her arm lay against the window and her fingers played a tune on the leather.

"What's on your mind, Diane?"

"Have you heard about Billy Duran?"

"You mean the junkie, Billy, who used to be my snitch. Yeah. It looks like he's off the streets and has a new lease on life."

"He's back lawyering, hired on with Sampson and Little."

"If I remember correctly, he'd built quite a name for himself before he hit the skids. Cassi thinks he might be persuaded to take on Mary Devin's case."

Diane swivelled her shocked glance his way.

"You'd do that? Let her support the woman responsible for your mother's death?"

"She was also responsible for Mom having the best care in her last few weeks. Mom was happy being in her own home. Mary made it possible. I talked to her, and dammit, Diane, she didn't make excuses. But she did make clear that she'd done it *for* Mom not *to* her."

"And you believed her."

"Yeah. I guess, I did."

"You're a good man, Trace. You make me think there's hope for humanity yet."

He turned her way and grinned. "Your old man driving you around the bend again? Is that what's keeping you at the office so late?"

Trace had met Diane's husband, a bank accountant. He'd thought him nice enough but boring as hell. Diane had picked up on his assumptions and later explained. Sure the man had very little vision of what truly went on in the world around him. But she found it relaxing to be with a guy wrapped up in his own job, their garden and making her happy. Policing never came up in their conversation and that was exactly the way she liked it.

"Nah. He's cool. But our esteemed chief gave me the evil eye yesterday when I left. I figured I'd soothe the savage beast. Stick around tonight and keep busy. We're almost at the club. How do you want to play this?"

"Sam, the bartender, said that Dani's taken Cassi upstairs."

"Why?"

"Sam's thinking the worst."

"Shit! That's why you're driving like a lunatic."

"He's not happy about the situation. I'm thinkin' if we make everyone nervous, it'll get Dani involved and stop whatever the hell is going on. We might get lucky. If we find a few assholes toting with no licence, we can make some arrests."

"Okay. Sounds like fun."

Chapter Thirteen

Cassi followed Dani up the stairs. When she headed for her office, Cassi breathed a sigh of relief. She knew there were other kinds of rooms that were in use and had no idea what she'd have done if Dani had opened the door to one of those.

"Sit." Dani pointed to the same hot seat Cassi had sat in once before.

Then she pulled a bottle of alcohol from the drawer of a filing cabinet and snatched two short glasses the club used for shooters. She poured two shots and pushed one in front of Cassi.

Considering she stuck to beer and very little of that, Cassi hesitated to take the drink. Until she saw the look on Dani's face. She decided it would be the lesser of two evils to consume the alcohol rather than to piss off the boss even more.

After she'd followed Dani's actions and downed

the drink, acid-like flames ripped her insides. It was all she could do not to cough and spoil her image. Man did it burn!

Hoping her eyes weren't crossed; she shook her head when Dani used the bottle to point at her glass. Frustrated with anger, she silently groaned as the other woman ignored her and filled it anyway. She needed to distract Dani. No way could she drink that shot and still walk.

"Why am I here, boss? If it's because I pissed off Pete earlier, I already told you I regretted that."

"And I told you I hated having to discipline you. But I never got the chance to make up for it."

Cassi rose unsteady. "No need, Dani. I understand."

"Sit down." Words that were silken, but nonetheless a command, made Cassi drop back in her seat. Just as well because she felt dizzy from moving so quickly. Shit, one drink of whatever the poison was, and a shit-faced streetwalker had more control on her body.

Dani crouched down in front of Cassi, effectively blocking her escape. Both Dani's hands covered Cassi's that were now sliding up and down her thighs. "I heard Sam say you were upset about Sunshine. You wanna tell me about it?"

Covering her sigh of relief with a small sound of agreement, Cassi lightened up, her unease diminishing. "You know Faith stuck up for me with Maddy or tried to. It was Maddy who pushed me against her, and resulted in Faith smashing her head against the sink."

"Don't feel guilty. Shit happens. I've banned Maddy from coming around here. Both security and the bouncers have their orders to keep her out."

Cassi nodded and didn't mention the rumors about Dani having taught Maddy a lesson for her part in Faith's being injured. She really didn't want to know. Nor did she mention the drive-by incident or Sergio's name.

"The doctors are keeping her in the hospital because of her injuries but also because she's dangerously depressed. I'm warning you now. If I have my way, she won't be back here to work." Cassi knew she was provoking an unpredictable psychopath but it had to be said.

Dani, on eye level, didn't pretend. The woman knew when she was being baited.

Cassi watched for Dani's reaction to her challenge and didn't have long to wait.

"What do you care if she works here or not?" Dani moved in a bit closer, aggressive, and yet Cassi knew she questioned her because there was curiosity too. She could see it.

"In case you weren't aware, Faith and my

brother, Raoul, had a relationship. In fact, Faith lost his baby when she took that abuse from Maddy and that's what pushed her over the edge. She's suicidal now."

"And you figure she's better off not working?"

"Not here. If she comes back, she'll be dead of an overdose in a matter of days, if not sooner." Cassi didn't try to soften her words. If there was a chance to get Faith out of Dani's clutches, she needed to push hard. Plus, the booze was giving her tongue license to flap.

Dani's eyes narrowed. Her study of Cassi's face had started to bewitch her and Cassi felt tendrils of the other's sexy concentration beginning to weave a spell. She had to keep the conversation going before Dani decided to make a move. As it was, her fingers had started caressing the backs of Cassi's hands. Discomfort tickled her temptation to push Dani out of the way so she could get the hell out of there.

"What makes you think I give a shit? She's one of my best girls. I don't let go lightly, sugar. You should know that about me."

Anger sizzled. "You don't own her, for fuck's sake. What matters is her wellbeing, right?" Cassi's eyes linked to Dani's. She hated her weakness but knew Dani had seen her plea.

Dani's narrowing gaze preceded her question.

"You want me to let her go?"

Not sure if she was being played or not, Cassi still nodded.

"Fine. She's all yours. Tell her stay the hell away from here and from me."

A breath of relief escaped in a small sound. As interest flared in Dani's enlarged pupils that gleamed like ebony, Cassi quickly responded. "Thank you."

Sarcasm flashed in Dani's grinning response. "You're welcome"

Feeling childish, Cassi changed the subject. "You've already replaced them?"

"Replaced who?" Still crouched in front of her, Dani's hand pushed Cassi's hair over her ear, ending her habit of hiding behind the curtain of black as she tended to do in times of stress.

"The upstairs girls." Cassi's voice came out even huskier than usual. An overwhelming urge to clear her throat had to be tapped down. If she didn't get away from the Parana soon, she'd panic.

Sweat dampened her back and she hoped her eyes didn't reveal her anxiety. The booze played havoc in her stomach. Churning, it reminding her why she shouldn't drink strong alcohol.

"Sure. There's always more bitches who need a job in a safe place rather than the streets. But there ain't a lot of bartenders like you who can deal with my men and keep them in line. I admire you for that, Cass. You once saved my life, and I don't forget." Dani started to close in, her breath smelling of whiskey and her emotion-filled eyes daring Cassi to stop her.

Cassi turned her face so that Dani's lips grazed her cheek. They began to move to her throat. No way could Cassi pretend this was an innocent thank you kiss from a friend.

A strange flutter started low in Cassi's groin, the beginning of sexual interest that made her clench the muscles and panic.

"Don't." Her voice throbbed, pleading. How could she sit there and let Dani go any further? And yet, leaving the Lipstick Club would stop any chance of her finding out the truth about Raoul's murder. Terribly torn, she faced a pivotal moment.

Dani hesitated, her hands surrounding Cassi's face to hold her in place. "No."

Cassi stiffened. Her lunge for freedom already started.

Suddenly an alarm rang from under Dani's desk and they both froze. Dani wrenched away from Cassi and stood. "What the fuck's happening now?"

Chapter Fourteen

Trace pulled into the parking lot just moments before the full swat team arrived. They quickly secured the premises by making the outside guards stand down and then the bouncers.

He and Diane were the first to enter the bar area. He could see at a glance that the place rocked, most tables were full with a long lineup formed at the counter.

His eyes darted to where Sam frantically worked the taps, pouring beer into glasses from a loaded tray while one of the skimpily-clad female servers helped him get the orders filled.

Sam purposely glanced upstairs in answer to Trace's unspoken question. A frisson of fear danced over his composure and detective or not, a man dedicated to preserving the law and protecting the citizens, a killing rage invaded and overruled his senses. If that bitch has hurt Cassi, he'd be up on a murder charge—sure as shit.

Sam turned down the music and the quiet became eerie. "What can we do for you, Detective?"

Trace answered. His voice was cold and his eyes hard. "We've received a complaint that there're unlawful activities happening here at the Lipstick Club, including illegal weapons." On purpose, he raised his tone so everyone in the room would hear his words. "We'll need everyone to have your weapons and permits ready for my officers to inspect. Any trouble and we'll issue felony charges instead of fines if you don't have the necessary paperwork. Just step over to the other side of the room and we'll get this handled as expediently as possible."

Pete moved in close to Trace, as intimidating as hell. "You got to be fucking kidding. Who'd call in bogus bullshit like that?"

"We have concerned citizens visiting this city, and if they don't feel safe amongst the locals, it's their right to call the department and lodge a complaint. What's your name, sir?"

"It's Mr. None-of-your-fucking-business."

"Well, Mr. None-of-your-fucking-business, how about you let me see your permit for the gun you have stuck in your pants behind you?"

"My permit's from California."

"Funny thing is, Nevada doesn't recognize California permits. You need to get a Nevada license. Until then, we'll confiscate your gun and you can redeem it as soon as you show your proper paperwork."

"Ain't gonna happen, cop."

Before Trace could follow through on forcing the issue, Dani's voice rang out. "What's going on here?"

He looked over to see her rushing down the stairs, Cassi close behind. A well of gratitude saturated his fears and his knees weakened. Cassi looked fine. Or so he thought until he saw her stumble on the stairs.

***

Dani raced down the stairs, but Cassi was forced to follow more slowly. Unsteadily, she maneuvered the stairs. The room spun making her remember an experience she'd once had when a bunch of her high school friends had shared what they called a Magic Mushroom, and she'd had a nibble.

Totally disoriented, she wished she could just drop where she was. Everything was woozy; her mind, encased in fog, wasn't connecting. She forced herself closer to the action so she could pay attention. When she got there, Trace faced-off with her old foe, Pete.

Happy to see the tall detective and sickened by the memory of what she'd faced only moments earlier, she wanted to go to her man, wrap her arms around him and let him take care of her. Since he was a bit busy at the moment, the best she could do was back him up.

She scanned the room to get her bearings and saw a dozen or so swat characters circulating amongst the tables. They were issuing orders for everyone to expose their concealed weapons and permits.

One could chew the tension and Trace's grin ignored the underlying anger of the crowd. He looked to be thoroughly enjoying himself, especially once he'd spied Cassi unharmed. His brief wink gave her the strength to shake off her own fogginess and join the group by the bar.

Meanwhile, Dani had made her way to Pete's side and yanked on his arm to hold him back. Then she planted herself in front of Trace, her manner disrespectful, her eyes flashing hate. "This is the second time this week you've paid us a visit, McGuire. It's becoming tiresome."

"Hell, it's no fun for me either, Miss Andino. If I had my way, I'd close this seedy shit-hole down and run you the hell out of town. Unfortunately, there're laws that protect parasites like you."

Silence rang after Trace's diatribe. Cassi

stiffened and moved even closer, standing between Pete and the other two. She sensed Diane coming up to them and saw her step next to Trace.

"You got no call hassling us. We run a legitimate business—"

"Sure you do. What about the working girls upstairs?"

"They soothe the animals, give lap dances, serve drinks, nothing goes on that's against the law."

"Hey, we both know prostitution is illegal in Las Vegas unless you're a licensed brothel. And... we both know you don't have a license. Therefore, there's criminal activity on these premises."

"Show me your proof." Nothing fazed the red-head.

Pete pushed in, his attitude one of pure aggression. "You're just hassling us for nothin' cop, cause you ain't got no proof. These bogus firearm's charges are a bunch of bullshit, you ask me."

Trace grinned. "You heard anyone asking you, Mr. None-of-your-fucking-business? Back off."

Unwilling to step down, cornered like a rat, Pete pushed past the hand that Dani held up to stop him and rushed Trace. But he didn't reach his target. Cassi, seeing the concealed knife he'd palmed, let loose one of her high-flying kicks and caught him in the side of his head.

Instead of going down, he fell against a bunch of

the guys who instinctively pushed him back into the fray. Using the momentum, he again lunged toward Trace.

Unbalanced by her kick, her normal abilities hampered from the liquor, she couldn't move with the speed of a cat which would have been normal. Instead, Diane intervened and grabbed his wrist.

Animal-like, roaring with fury, Pete's brute strength overpowered her attempt to stop his attack. He used the knife and sliced her arm from the top of the shoulder to the elbow, blood following in the blade's path.

Trace, swatting Dani out of his path like one would swat an annoying pest, reached Pete in time to stop his rampage against both girls. His bellowing backhand had the other man dropping to his knees.

Cassi, aware that Pete carried a gun and was prone to using it when things got tough, held her breath. Fear sliced through her earlier fog and left her alert and itching to step in.

But it was Trace's fight, and she knew better. Sam's hold on her arm helped sway her decision, too. From the side, she watched, heart trapped like a terrified wild bird in a tiny cage, and she held her breath.

Trace, sensing the other's movement meant he was pulling out a gun, reached for his own. But before Pete actually got his weapon free, Dani stepped over and slapped him so hard, his face spun to the side. Then her hand dragged on his beard as she yarded on it to get his attention. "Fuckwit, you aren't here to get into trouble with the law. You gotta stop now or I wash my hands of you and your shitty temper."

Cassi watched the man swallow hard, his fist shaking before he lowered it and pushed at Dani to let him up. "Yeah, boss. I got it."

Cassi rushed over to Diane at the same time as Sam who'd fetched a clean towel first. With the idea of using it to stop the blood and add pressure to the wound, he knelt beside her. "We have to stop the bleeding, Diane. Let me help you."

"Son of a bitch pulled a knife."

"Yeah. I know"

"He was after Trace."

"I saw it. You stopped him." Cassi saw the shock in Diane's eyes and heard it from her stilted words.

"He cut me."

"Uh huh. It's pretty deep. We need to get you to the hospital."

Sam spoke. "I called for the ambulance. It'll be here in a few minutes."

Thankful for her partner's swift reaction, Cassi gave him a small nod of thanks.

Once Sam had the towel wrapped around

Diane's arm as tightly as he could, he used another to tie it over the first. Diane groaned from the pain, but she didn't flinch or pull away. Cassi's admiration for Trace's partner soared and it was all she could do not to hug her silly for protecting Trace.

"Diane?" Trace rushed over to check on her, his voice full of concern, his trembling hand smoothing the wispy hair from her cheek.

Cassi, wanting to ease his worry, spoke. "Sam's called the ambulance. She's bleeding heavily, Trace. We put on a makeshift bandage, but they'll take care of her."

Meanwhile, Diane's head lolled to the side. Her faint had him cussing, his fear for his partner throbbing in the tension-filled space.

In the background, two officers had Pete in custody and were hauling him outside. The angry tirade from the unhappy idiot caught their attention.

Dani had stepped toward the fracas and could be heard telling Pete they'd have him back in no time and to shut the fuck up.

Trace moved so fast, Cassi wouldn't have believed a big guy like him had that kind of speed. White-lipped with fury, his nostrils flaring and his eyes slit, he blocked Dani's escape. Raising his finger an inch from her face, he wagged it back and forth as if words were too much for him at that moment.

Something in Dani's expression must have loosened his control. Because the harsh words that spewed out tightened the muscles in Cassi's stomach and fear made her ill. She'd never before heard that darkness in his voice or seen the anger of a man at the end of his endurance.

"I'm warning you right now, Dani Andino. You might want to think of moving your operation back to where you came from. You make one wrong move, take one step out of place, and I'll get the search warrants I need, and I'll be back. And next time, I'll be laying charges against you and your losers and closing this slum-joint down."

Chapter Fifteen

Cassi couldn't believe how quickly the place cleared once the law enforcement folks had taken away the offenders who didn't have proper documentation. Many of the grumbling *Armas* members disappeared to party upstairs. A pall hung over the place and the few people left behind kept their voices low and soon even the drink orders fizzled out.

This gave her plenty of time to think about what had taken place earlier. Like the unexpected stunt Trace had pulled.

Before leaving, he'd swept her into his arms in full view of everyone, imprinting such an intense kiss on her mouth that she still tingled.

At first, she'd pushed against him, instinct kicking in, but his hard, searching lips had overcome her resistance.

"Later, darlin'. Just wait till I get you alone."

Hearing his husky promise made her inevitable response more intense. She'd floated for the rest of her shift, tingling with passion and experiencing a damp yearning for what promised to be an eventful night with her lover.

Dani'd disappeared upstairs moments before Trace cleared out to follow the ambulance with Diane to the hospital. Disgust imprinted on her heavily made up face, she'd bolted, fury evident in her cussing.

Moments earlier, she'd listened to Trace's warning with an evil smirk and cold, empty eyes. Slouching in a sarcastic stance, she'd kept her mouth shut.

Cassi'd noticed that Rodrigo had returned to the bar area in the middle of their clash. She'd seen the silent message and responding nod they'd communicated and instinctively knew what it meant. They must have an alarm hooked up downstairs, too. So when it rang in Dani's office, it would ring there at the same time.

That would have given them ample warning to clear away any evidence of drugs or other unlawful activities. The SUVs parked behind the building were always available to haul away any product and the cash they stashed below.

It also answered the question of why Dani had

stepped in to stop Pete from shooting Trace. For certain, she didn't give a good goddamn about the detective, quite the opposite. But until she'd gotten the signal from Rodrigo that they'd taken care of business below, she couldn't take any chances for things to escalate.

If there'd been a killing on the premises, the cops would have been all over the place, no warrants necessary. So, she'd given her guys the time they needed to sweep the joint.

Even though Cassi hadn't yet ventured to the area below, Sam's description had been enough for her to imagine what it must look like. And if all worked according to the plan niggling at the back of her mind, one day soon she'd see it for herself.

The day she took Dani down.

The day she'd finally get her revenge for Raoul.

Chapter Sixteen

Trace left the Lipstick Club and followed Diane's ambulance to the hospital. While driving, his satisfaction from laying his claim on Cassi prompted the grin he couldn't lose.

Cassi hadn't seen Dani at the top of the stairs watching him, but he had. Kissing Cassi, laying down his possession for everyone to see, had been too big a temptation for him to resist. He'd caught Dani's eye after Cassi had floated out of his arms, her passion plainly exposed. His warning had been plain to any adversary with brains. *This woman belongs to me.*

Of course, Dani Andino didn't play by any rules but her own. If she wanted something, she mostly took it and fuck the consequences. He just prayed that between his verbal warning and her seeing with her own eyes that Cassi cared for him, she'd back off.

An incoming call ruined his daydreams. "Yeah, McGuire here."

"Hey, asshole. You sure know how to make an appearance. I thought you'd just send in a couple of the boys to make some noise, enough to get that bitch out of her office and free Cassi. I sure as hell didn't expect the whole fucking cavalry to wreak havoc."

"You're welcome, Sam."

"Why am I supposed to be thankful? You're busting the case I've been working for months. My bosses are laying the groundwork, wanting to move in on a lot of these neighborhood gangs. We just need more of their drug sources and the name of the bigshot from L.A. who's in charge."

"I thought you told me Dani got rid of him and took over."

"She did take over. But the *Armas* group is small fry, man. We're after bigger fish. It's the main supplier who has strings throughout the country, he's our target. I'm just trying to get close enough to secure any information I can to that pipeline."

"So how did I mess that up?"

"You arrested the one person who's the liaison between L.A. and Las Vegas."

"Fuck!"

"Yep."

"Pete, the prick."

"That's him."

"You want me to drop the assault charges."

"Can you?"

"Yeah. It'll make me sick to my stomach, but I can make it happen. I just can't breathe when I think of Cassi mixed in with scum like him and Andino. God help me, it was all I could do not to punch that sick broad right in her smirking face. Good thing my sweet mom taught me that lesson way back when I was still getting nighttime stories."

"What lesson?"

"There's no acceptable reason to ever hit a female, not when a guy has a mouth and a brain to back it up."

"Shit, man. Your mom never met Dani Andino. I kinda think she might have added an addendum to that rule."

Chuckling, Trace agreed. "Ya think?"

"Gotta say, dude, your control is impressive. For a few seconds, I thought I'd have to jump in."

"So, what's the procedure now?"

"We play along, keep things low-key, and hope I get a break."

"As long as we can restrain Cassi and keep her from messing things up again, I guess I can give you more time."

"Good. But that means no more romance shit, Romeo. Up until now, Dani had no idea you and Cass were an item. I saw the boss's face when you laid down that stupid challenge. She was pissed. When that chick grinds her teeth, look out."

"As long as she takes the hint, I don't care if she gnaws the inside of her mouth raw. Cassi's never going to be hers. She's taken."

"What if all you've done is provoke the crazy bitch?"

"What are you getting at?"

"She's less aggressive with Cass than anyone else around here, and I doubt it's because she's hot for her body. She's got her pick of girls she can use for that, know what I'm saying here?"

"Shit."

The silence at the other end of the line had the nerves in Trace's body jump to high alert. "What?"

"Nothing."

"Bullshit. Spit it out or I'll come back there."

"You won't like it but it needs to be said. Cassi made the decision to obey Dani when she barked out the order to follow her upstairs. We both know, she could have made some excuse or even just said no."

The dial tone told Trace that Sam had hung up. Left alone with his thoughts, he agonized all the way to the hospital.

She *could* have said no.

Chapter Seventeen

Cassi's heart dumped when she pulled up to her house and didn't see Trace's vehicle where he normally parked. After he'd left, anticipations from that kiss had her counting the minutes, imagining what would happen when she got home. Now, disappointment drove spikes into her plans for the night.

Once inside, she decided to heat up a bit of her leftover lasagna and have a small snack. Hoping he'd eventually show up, she chose enough for two and placed it in a baking dish in a low oven. Then she wondered how Diane fared in the hospital and prayed the slash on her arm didn't need more than stitches and a bandage.

After the ruckus at work, when things had calmed, she'd followed up with a phone call and got the usual yada yada hospitals tended to share.

"We've made the patient comfortable, and she's as good as can be expected." Knowing Trace would be able to give her an update; she'd backed off to wait and get the lowdown from him.

Deciding to grab a quick shower and change into her pj's, she followed her nightly routine, cleaning off the makeup, removing the earrings and brushing her teeth. One cheek still wore the imprint of Dani's hand and the other felt seared with the impression of Dani's mouth. It seemed vital to remove all traces before seeing Trace.

Again, for the millionth time that night, she blessed his perfect timing for arriving at the club. Alone with her conscience, she asked herself what she would have done if he hadn't shown up?

Naivety didn't cut it anymore. Over the last while, she'd become aware of the underworld and had grown up. Whether she wanted it to happen or not, the lifestyle she now lived had forced her eyes open.

Therefore, being honest, she knew exactly what Dani had in mind. Nausea made her shiver at the thought that she'd let that psycho get so close.

Sure, she'd promised herself that she would do anything it took to find out about Raoul's murder, even playing along with the gang's boss. But would she have allowed things to continue in the direction they were headed tonight?

Dammit, she still couldn't truthfully answer that question. When it came right down to it, would she have pushed Dani away? A sick kind of knowledge had to be accepted if she was at all honest. She really had no idea for certain. And the thought made her wince with shame from her lack of morals and self-pride. Just how far was she willing to go for revenge?

Shaking off the depression from her torturous self-doubts, she soaped her chest and reached for the special cream to help remove the transitional tattoos she'd applied there and on her arm. Thanks to her hairdresser, she'd been having fun with these packaged images. She scrubbed off all signs, then she washed every part of her body.

Her recent thoughts had left her feeling unclean. Even though soap and water couldn't scrub away one's lack of morals or convictions, she did feel better.

Soon, dressed in her off-the-shoulder soft blue pajama top that hugged her ample breasts and then draped in such a way that made them seem larger, she added the blue and gray silk shorts to match. Having lost her appetite, she turned off the oven and snagged a bottle of beer instead.

Rather than choosing her lonely bed, she wrapped her fuzzy white throw over her and curled up on the sofa in the living room. Two sips of beer, a few seconds with her eyes closed, and she drifted off, only to have Dani invade her nightmare.

She was on her couch sleeping and the red-head suddenly appeared. Her approach took forever as she drifted closer. Until, with a suddenness that startled her, she was right there, bending over Cass, intentions obvious, seduction imminent.

Her breath warmed Cassi's skin while whispered words made her nerves leap. She heard them more than once with echoes ringing over and over in her befuddled mind. They sounded more like threats than the beguiling pleas of a person trying to seduce.

"You're mine. I'll never let you go. Mine. You're mine."

She felt Dani's caressing fingers sliding up and down her arms in a way that showed ownership. Her voice held a menacing tone that filtered through words that should have been passionate and gentle like the hands she now placed on Cassi's throat and then her chest.

Shaking with panic, Cassi's mind screamed the same question over and over, "What are you going to do?"

Then the boss made her move, her lips descending, intentions clear. In seconds, she'd be placing her smirking red mouth against Cassi's.

"No. I can't. No!"

"Ow! Stop that, Cassi. Holy hell, girl, it's me."

"Oh my God, Trace. I'm so sorry." Cassi found herself scrunched into the corner of the couch, her cover clutched in her hands, a barrier to hide behind. "I thought it was Dani. She was here, and I couldn't let her touch me." Tears spurted and her whole body began shaking so hard that even after he'd scooped her into his arms and sat rocking her like a baby, she still couldn't stop her reactions to the horror of her dream.

At least, now she had her answer to the question that had plagued her earlier. No way in hell would she let that bitch come near her again.

Chapter Eighteen

"Come on, honey. I'm here now. Stop crying before you get me started. And I'm a freaking mess when I blubber. Snot everywhere, hiccups, wailing, I'm warning you it's a regular gong show."

Giggles replaced the sobs and Cassi let go of the last of the life-like dream. Hugging Trace so hard, he grunted in pain, she blessed the fact that her nightmare hadn't been real at all. In the weird way that things happen sometimes, she seized on the experience as her answer.

"Baby, you gotta loosen that grip a little. That's if you want me alive so I can make you feel better." He pretended to cough and she backed off.

His teasing eyes were shining, the sapphire highlights mesmerising. She'd seen them black with fury earlier and had shivered in reaction at the time. The man could devastate a weaker person with one glaring look of pure disgust. Though Dani hadn't appeared to be affected, Cassi had seen the small step she'd taken to widen the gap between her and the rage Trace hadn't tried to hide.

"I was worried when you weren't waiting for me. I missed you."

"I'm here now, darlin'. And I'm yours until the morning." He slid his hands over her hair to push the soft mass behind her ears. The scent of her shampoo wafted around her, his favorite, and she grinned when he moved close to sniff the strands and inhaled happily.

"I love that smell."

"I know. I used it on purpose."

"Thank you." He kissed her nose, his hands delving into the silky blackness again.

"Anytime." She smiled her approval.

His searching gaze wandered over her features, his look soft with affection. "You're so different here at home compared to what you appear to be at work."

"What do you mean, different?"

"Right now, you seem ordinary—"

"Excuse me?"

His eyes widened at her tone and he gave her head a gentle shake, his hands still on both sides. "You know what I mean. You're not all made up like the girl who works in a strip joint. Instead, you could be mistaken for a teenager." Then he glanced at her chest, swallowed and grinned. "A very well-endowed teenager, thank you, Lord."

His hands wandered to where his eyes had been and he began to stroke the sides of her breasts over the top of her shirt, then he cupped them. They swelled to his touch and her nipples hardened with delight.

While he played, caressing and lifting, his thumbs stroking the points, she mewed in appreciation. "I love it when you touch me."

"Baby, trust me, I'm happy to oblige, anytime."

Moisture poured from between her legs and bathed the tingles that suddenly formed. Her body clenched, the muscles working in tandem to every move of his hands, readying her for the coming invasion.

Not wanting to be a silent partner in the proceedings, she leaned in to kiss him where the open top buttons of his shirt left bare skin. Lips greedy to taste worked their way up the column of his throat and under his chin.

Her fingers filtered through his longish hair, the strands thick and surprisingly soft. This close, she picked up on Trace's scent. Audacious, manly, it made one think of the beach in the heat of the sun. For her, it worked like an aphrodisiac. Once she caught a whiff, urges took hold and her blood heated.

While her fingers undid the buttons on his shirt and then helped remove it, she whispered, "Are you hungry? I have some lasagna ready."

"Yeah, I'm starving." His lips had left a trail on her throat and were now aiming for her chest.

She pulled away and stared at him, shock on her face she couldn't hide. "Really."

"Yep, really. But food won't satisfy this hunger, honey. I need you to do that small service."

Laughing at his playfulness, she admitted, "You had me fooled for a minute."

His lips took hers in a kiss that could power a turbine. "Any more doubts?"

"Not even a little. Come here." Her stroking hands found the nubs on his chest that she knew he loved to have kissed. Her tongue lathed them and her teeth scraped in a teasing way that turned him vocal.

The groan he released proved she did know what he liked. Not to be outdone, he lifted her shirt off and did the same to her.

Straddling him, her arms wrapped around his head while his mouth drove her crazy, she listened to his low growls of pleasure and drifted into a vortex of passionate response.

When his warm, gentle hands explored her

thighs past the edges of her shorts and gripped her ass cheeks, she hummed with him.

"I love your hands on me."

"I'm glad, since I intend to have them on your body for quite some time." He opened the button on her shorts and pulled down the zipper to loosen them.

He continued sucking her breasts while his fingers traveled to the hems and forced their way inside her, sliding in and out of the damp passage.

"You're wet. I love it when you're wet."

"I get that way just seeing you. It's crazy."

"Hell, if what I do to you is crazy, then what you do to me is downright insane. Baby, I want you every minute, even when I'm away from you. While we're together, I'm so hot for you, I can't get enough." His husky tones made sweet love to her with words that delighted.

That's all it took for her to lose control. His touches were the tinder to set the fire raging inside her, but those magic words, they were the sparks that ignited the blast.

Undulating, aching, her need to have him buried deep became paramount. She rolled over to one side and divested herself of the shorts. Taking the hint, he pulled the rest of his clothes off in seconds and had her back on his lap, her legs on either side, his body deeply imbedded in hers.

Groaning with delight, she leaned back so she could watch his expression. He seemed to be in pain, his features tight while his hands clutched her bottom, trying to coax her to move.

"I love watching you make love to me. You're so intense." She whispered the words, slowing her movements. Wriggling slightly from side to side, she tightened her muscles and watched the battle he fought to let her play before he lost control.

"God, Cassi, I'm glad you're having fun but I'm not going to last much longer, baby. I need you now."

"Not yet. I like this part too much to stop."

"Lordy, I've created a monster. You were such a sweet little virgin when we first met. Now you're a tease who can drive a man crazy. Where did I go wrong?"

His words made her chuckle. "You taught me how much fun sex is. I love having you inside me, wanting me. It's kind of powerful." She watched him and saw the acceptance her words had created. He understood. She could see it mixed in with the craving he couldn't hide, the desire that had turned his blue eyes smoking hot.

Continuing her slow drive-him-crazy moves, rubbing her nipples against his muscled chest and then briefly driving the full weight of her breasts against him to further tantalize, she felt all-powerful and her hunger grew stronger.

"I never taught you to torture me." He caught her mouth in a kiss so scorching that she forgot all about her earlier playfulness. Boneless, already weak from passion she'd initiated, she thrilled at his sudden wildness.

When he flipped them over so they were lying on the couch, she went willingly. From soft and playful to hard and rough, their lovemaking reached new heights. Drenched, clinging, Cassi loved every second he drove into her. And when they reached their ultimate pleasure, they both glistened with sweat and glowed with delight.

Chapter Nineteen

On his arrival, when he'd first let himself in with his key, Trace's intentions had been to talk with Cassi about Diane and other things on his mind. He'd follow up their conversation with sweet sex and show her just how much she meant to him. That had been his plan.

But once he'd seen her in the throes of a nightmare, writhing in anguish, dread painted over her face and then disgust, he couldn't have changed the way the evening had flowed. He wouldn't have wanted to.

She'd needed him to be supportive and not condemning. He'd sensed that and had backed off, let her take control and now he thanked the good Lord above for his not blowing it.

She'd seemed conflicted when he'd seen her at the bar earlier. She hadn't looked at him with her usual openness, her normal soft side-looks that melted every bone in his body and turned him to mush.

Instead, he'd sensed a withdrawal. It had forced him to take the action he had, kiss the hell out of her to remind her that she was nuts over him. No way could he have left her there in that dive without reinforcing his possession both to her and that bitch who'd watched them and then sneered with intense hate before whipping around and disappearing.

Sam might have disagreed with his move, but he could no more have stopped himself than cut off his own arm. He couldn't stand it if his Cassi withdrew from him in any way.

And he didn't trust Dani not to take what she wanted, even if Cassi had no intentions of playing along. After what he'd seen tonight, when she'd fought her way out of the nightmare, she'd seemed relieved about something he knew they'd never talk about. A private conflict she'd been caught up in.

If her screaming the word *no* and fighting him meant she'd do the same if it had been Dani, then he could breathe easy, at least, from her end.

Of course, Dani's intentions were altogether different. He'd have to warn Cassi that she needed to take even more precautions after tonight. She couldn't play fast and loose with a sicko and not reap some kind of consequence.

While Cassi sauntered around the kitchen getting their lasagna ready to serve, once again clad in her sexier-than-hell pj's, he watched her every move with the low-flame of his hunger still pulsating.

This small bundle of pure fighting energy could turn him into a simpering dolt as proved by his earlier behavior. She'd delighted him in her playfulness, and he'd held off as long as he could stand it before taking over.

"Trace, I've asked you twice and you're lost in your own world. What did the emergency doctors say about Diane?"

"Sorry, sugar. Still back on the couch with you." He winked and loved her satisfied grin. "She's in a lot worse shape than we thought. The prick cut through the muscle and tendon so they had to operate. Not sure how long she'll be in recovery but I know she won't be back on the job anytime soon."

"She'll hate that."

"I know. Plus, the boss'll be livid because we're short-staffed as it is. Bloody hell, Cassi, she's the best partner I've ever had. I'm sick to my stomach about what happened to her because of me."

Cassi moved to lay his plate on the table in front

of him. She wrapped her arms around his shoulders and leaned her head against his. "Trace, you mustn't feel guilty. You'd have done the same for her. She saw Pete move, stepped in, and saved her partner. It's what you people do."

"I know, but it doesn't make it okay." He hugged her waist and squeezed. "I talked to her husband before I left the emergency ward. The poor man had tears streaming down his face, and you know what he said to me?"

"What?"

"He said that now maybe he could sleep at night."

"Poor guy. It must be terrible for him to know his wife is in danger every day."

Trace moved Cassi to stand in front of him. And while her hand reached to smooth back his hair, he leveled his own shot. "I know exactly how the poor sucker feels, Cassi. Every day you're in that joint, my guts are clenched so tight, it's hard to breathe. Please tell me you'll give up this crazy vendetta you're on and go back to living safely. Give me back my sanity."

She looked at him, her eyes soft with understanding. She kissed his mouth, hers tasting of sweetness and love. Then she pointed at his plate and he got his answer.

"Eat before it gets cold."

Chapter Twenty

Next morning, Cassi finished her workout in the basement gym and decided to forgo her run. Soon Trace would be fetching her for her promised visit to the woman's prison to see Mary Devin. Since she still needed to shower and get dressed, time was running out.

From the moment they'd woken up in each other's arms, and experienced the quick intense love-making they both enjoyed, she'd been anxious for him to leave.

Worried he'd bring up his fears for her safety again, she wasn't sure if she could continue to hide her own concerns about the club. At least, with that barbarian Pete in jail, the scary shit would ease up a little. The thought gave her a sense of relief.

Without his threating presence, things would settle down, and she could start working her nebulous plan. If she could get enough evidence of what went on downstairs to blackmail Rodrigo, she hoped to force him to admit that Dani had been there the night Raoul had died. If she had this proof to take to Trace, surely he'd reopen the investigation, and they could get some answers.

Working at the joint night after night, watching the main characters, Cassi had soon realized there was no love lost between Rodrigo and Dani. She'd seen his disgust many times at the boss's behavior with the gang members, her callous treatment and mean disposition.

And if he had no respect for Dani, from the way he acted, he positively detested Pete. If Cassi could get him in a compromising position where jail time was imminent, and with his previous records of money laundering and extortion hanging over him, maybe he'd turn on them. Come clean about Dani's involvement with Raoul's death. It might just work. Fact was – she had nothing else to try.

With the case solved, she could go back to being a person she liked, a woman who'd taken pride in the fact that she never lied. With the skills and knowledge she'd gained over these last months, she'd not be the exact replica of the old Cassi. Some experiences couldn't be erased.

In retrospect, she'd be stronger and smarter, and the awareness she'd gained would help her live more fully. Never again would mousy Cassidy Santino be allowed to exist—the virgin girl who'd idolized her family to the detriment of her soul.

***

Trace arrived, and her revolving gloomy thoughts faded. The man oozed sexy-lover vibes. His business suit paired with the white shirt and blue tie that matched his dazzling azure eyes had her blood simmering.

His uncut mass of waves, longish but in no way unattractive, had her hands itching to grab hold. He approached, leaned in and gave her a warm kiss. "You ready, sweetheart?"

"Yes. Just need to get my phone. Does Mary know we're coming?"

"She does. As I told you before, she's wanted to talk with you ever since her arrest. After you agreed to the meeting, I could see her relief. It was the one time she's showed any emotion. During the arrest and being booked, she was completely closed and wouldn't say a word."

"Has she ever told you why she wanted to see me?"

"No. But I could tell it was important to her."

While Cassi locked the door and followed him to his SUV, she decided to drop the curiosity, knowing she'd get her answers soon.

Minutes later, riding beside him, Cassi got the

impression he had some bad news. "What's wrong, Trace? Is Diane worse?"

"No. Other than she's furious that she let the scumbag hurt her. With time to heal and therapy, she'll be fine. Guess I'm still smarting at the blast from Hank Lester, my chief, and the fact that he's forcing this new dude on me rather than letting me chose a partner from the ranks. Who knows what kind of a cop I'll end up having to partner. It's frustration that's making me ornery. Sorry, baby. I hoped you wouldn't notice."

"I don't mind, Trace. I'm here to listen to you as much as you do for me. We're passengers on the same streetcar, right?"

He glanced at her with a one-sided grin. "Right."

She put her hand out so he could take hold. Then she squeezed his fingers. "I'm sorry you're unhappy. And I'm sorry that Diane got hurt." Deciding to change the subject, she added, "But I'll admit I'm not sorry that Pete won't be around anymore. That degenerate scares me silly." She felt Trace's scowl burn her skin. She turned to face him.

"About that, Cassi. We had to free him. His lawyer worked a deal, and he walked."

Shock tore through her fine mood. "How could that happen? He used a knife and cut a cop."

"And he swore it was in self-defence. That you

kicked him, and when Diane attacked, he was defending himself."

"That's bogus bullshit, Trace. You know it."

"I know, baby. But the guys with the power said to drop the charges. He's free. So now maybe you'll agree you need to stay away from him and that place."

Dark despair dropped over her earlier good mood. It took everything she had to shrug it off and hide her distress. "Okay, I won't go near him. If he comes into the bar, Sam can handle his orders. I promise. Will that help?"

His voice ringing with exasperation, he exploded, "Crissakes, Cassidy, nothing will help until you're finished with that blasted joint." He swung through the gates of the prison, flashed his I.D. and parked in the lot. Then he turned, and using her hand, he tugged her closer so he could kiss her.

"I need you, baby. You mean the difference between a happy future and me praying to die. You gotta understand. I can't stand you taking crazy chances."

While his caring flooded her heart, his words echoed in her head. She felt the same way he did so she knew how difficult it was for him that she put herself in danger.

"Don't worry, love. It'll be over soon, I just know

something will break." *Hell, she'd make sure.*

He shook his head and bit off whatever he'd intended to say. Instead, he got out of the car and slammed the door a might harder than necessary.

Shaking off her unease, she focused on the landscape in the front window. The blistering sun beat down like it did every day and the distant sand hills and desert scrub of chaparral and cacti blotted the empty landscape. How dismal for the inmates forced to live out here.

Trace opened her door and waited for her to step out. Then he took her hand in his, and they walked into the huge, overpowering building that housed such misery and so many wasted lives.

***

"Hi, Mary. Trace said you wanted to talk with me." Cassi approached the woman who stood in front of the window in the small meeting room and thought how sad it was to see her clad in orange prison garb.

What a waste of talent and knowledge. Trace had shared his opinion with her – that it was only because of Mary's nursing skills and warm-heartedness that Kathleen had endured her final days with any amount of comfort.

Before this woman had arrived to nurse his mom, Kathleen had not only suffered from her cancer, but from the earlier fools they'd had looking after her. The minute Mary had taken over her care, her existence had improved to such an extent that Trace had relaxed, knowing she was as happy and comfortable as he'd seen her in a long time.

Who could have imagined this benign woman would be the instrument of his mom's death? The person who organized for her adopted son, Juan Acedo, to murder the sick woman while she watched. It was inconceivable.

"Thank you for coming. I would have understood if you'd refused." Mary's soft voice wavered, her words sounding forced.

"It was Trace's request. I couldn't say no, could I? He told me how you made Kathleen's last days as pain free and peaceful as possible. From the minute he knew she'd passed, Trace felt a sense of relief that her wretched existence was over. In a crazy way, you made that happen."

Mary stood with her back to the window and was silhouetted in the light. Her expression might have been shadowed but the agony in her voice rang with truth. Words poured out as if the dam holding them had shattered, and her soul needed to purge.

"I made Juan kill her. I made him kill them all. My poor boy told me about an accident he'd survived when he was a child, and what had happened with his mother; how she'd begged him to stop her suffering while they were trapped in their crashed car hour after hour. And that he'd used his jacket and ended her life. I knew his guilt had driven him over the edge of being completely sane, that killing had come to mean so little that he had no conscience."

Listening to the hysteria, Cassi had goose bumps spreading over both her arms and back. Insanity had sounded in Mary's confession, and it gave her pause. Then she heard the soft moan and knew it was remorse that drove the poor mother to her mad confession.

"Juan loved you, Mary. He bragged to me about the way you took care of sick people."

Cassi's words lessened Mary's distress, and she nodded. "We had many wonderful times together. Mostly, he was a good son, caring and thoughtful. Until he joined the gang—then he changed. It was around that time I started doing private nursing. I didn't see as much of him, and I think he was lonely. He became addicted to finding a girlfriend. It drove him to doing stupid things."

"You mean, like stalking and snooping?"

"Yes. He told me he couldn't stop, couldn't help it, he wanted someone to care for him so badly, he behaved inappropriately. When he confessed to having broken into your house, I scolded him."

"You knew?"

"Oh, not to begin with. He admitted he cared about you on the night I called him to end Kathleen's suffering. When he first arrived, he refused to help me. Said he couldn't this time because he knew if you found out, you'd hate him."

"How did you get him to change his mind?"

"I begged. Cried, used the tools I knew would work. Because he loved me, he stopped her pain."

Cassi thought back to the night he'd come to her, broke into her house. How she'd woken up to find him in her living room. And how he'd appeared tormented; his expression full of hate when he'd mentioned his mom.

She'd never admit her beliefs to Mary because he hadn't actually confessed his feelings; it was instinct that convinced her she was right. That he'd come to detest his mother for what she made him do to show his love.

"I'm sorry, Mary. It must be horrible for you to lose Juan."

Tears glistened and were visible. When she walked closer and Cassi saw her face in the light for the first time, she caught her breath. Mary looked years older, ravaged. As if every waking minute, and no doubt her sleeping moments, too, she lived in a nightmare.

With her soft heart taking over, Cassi reached

to help the older woman into a chair. She'd lost weight. And her beautiful hair, that had once been stylish with soft waves, was now short, frizzy and lifeless. It stuck out all over her head in a way that would horrify most caring women.

Compassion overwhelming her, Cassi sat next to Mary at the table and took her hand, wanting to give some warmth to the sad soul.

"Mary, do you have a lawyer for your court case, someone to help you get through these next months?" An idea had been simmering at the back of Cassi's mind ever since she'd heard about Mary's arrest. It intensified when Trace had mentioned about Mary refusing help.

"No. It doesn't matter. I don't deserve to live." Her bloodshot eyes finally connected to Cassi's. The depth of despair that Cassi saw made her pity surface and added weight to her decision. She gave Mary's hand a sharp tug before she spoke.

"Stop that. You're feeling sorry for yourself. It doesn't become you. When you helped those patients escape their lives of pain and horrific misery, who you were doing it for—yourself?"

"Of course not." Mary's shocked denial rang with truth.

"For money then?" Cassi kept at her, forcing her voice to be harsh. She had Mary's full attention.

Disgust appeared. Her head shook back and

forth, like a child who knew she had to respond but had no words.

"Good! You didn't help them for any other purpose but to stop their torture. You used Juan because you knew he could do as you asked. That he didn't have a conscience like a normal person. I'm not saying what you did was right. I'm certainly not saying it was lawful. What I am saying is that you did it for acceptable though unconventional reasons."

Mary's groan of sorrow erupted. Her shoulders began to shake. She dropped her face into her hands and wept with an abandonment that for her seemed out of place and yet strangely appropriate.

She rocked back and forth, her hands clutched in front of her mouth like a person would do if they were praying and yet trying to hold in their torment at the same time.

Cassi heard her whispered pleas, "I'm sorry, son, so sorry. I'm the monster, not you. Please, forgive me."

Cassi waited patiently, all the time rubbing Mary's shoulder and patting her back. Once the deluge lightened, she spoke. "You're not a monster, Mary. Never, ever believe that what you made happen was the work of a monster. Some think of you as an angel."

Voice harsh and cracking, Mary answered. "I

know. The angel of death. Just like the papers named me. How ridiculous!"

"Well, I have a friend who's just dragged himself out from the pits of hell. I think you two would make a good team. He's a first-class lawyer, Mary. He'll get you justice."

"Oh, child, nothing makes sense anymore. I don't care what happens now."

Cassi read the truth in Mary's voice and knew she had to convince her not to give up. She said the words she knew might help persuade the old woman to agree. "If you don't care for yourself, then do it for me."

Mary searched Cassi's face and must have seen the pleading. "Juan cared about you, Cassi. And Trace loves you. If you insist, I'll do whatever you say."

Chapter
Twenty-one

Faith couldn't stay away from the nursery or her tiny friend wrapped in blue. She'd spent a lot of the previous evening helping feed and settle him, singing low and cuddling to quiet the little mite.

Lying awake that night, her thoughts had concentrated on the neglected baby boy whose mother had abandoned him and whose father had disappeared, likely to search for his missing girlfriend. For the first time since Raoul died, he hadn't haunted her dreams. And the pain of remembering didn't consume her through the long dark hours.

This morning, eagerness had acted as her internal clock. Anxious for the nurses to do their morning routine and the doctor to do his rounds, her aim to get to the nursery had her silently railing at their slowness.

The doctor seemed impressed with her astounding recovery from the day before. The brightness in her expression had him questioning her closely.

Watchful, his keen eyes drilling into her conscience, Faith lost all color when he began to talk of releasing her from the hospital that day so she could out-patient to a nearby clinic for depression. The shakes appeared to take over and her chin wobbled to make speaking almost impossible.

Once he saw her reaction, he backed off. Then he admitted that maybe one more day was in order, rushing her wasn't the answer.

Relieved beyond reason, Faith bobbed her head and agreed, tears gushing as the result of her thankfulness to have one more day with the baby boy who needed her.

Heading to where her little pal waited, she heard him crying as soon as she approached. She imagined he was calling for her. His wails tore at her heart. Twisting the wheels on her chair as fast as she could, ignoring the pain from the wound on her arm, she skidded close to his bassinet.

A different nurse worked the morning shift and wasn't as accommodating as the middle-aged lady from the day before. Her name badge indicated Susan Mayne.

She stood in Faith's path. "Excuse me, miss, are you the baby's mother?"

"No. I'm a patient." Thankful, they hadn't put her on the psycho ward because of her depression, she added. "I'm down the hall a ways on this floor. Yesterday, Nurse Layton let me help her with this baby. She was very busy, and he seemed to settle for me."

"I see. He's been fretting for some time now. I attempted to feed him a while ago, but he refuses to take his milk. His father arrived and spent an hour. He tried, also, but this stubborn fellow would only take a few mouthfuls before he began crying, and hasn't let up. Poor man had to go to work. I could see it was tearing his heart out to leave his son."

Faith edged around the woman and began patting the baby, her hand gently rubbing his stomach as she answered. "He seemed to like me yesterday, became quiet and let me feed him. I've come to offer my help again today."

As soon as he heard Faith's voice, the baby's screaming quieted. The fuzzy hair glued to his scalp was damp and sweaty. His features, contorted from crying, began to soften and ease. Now, he was making sounds like he was coaxing her to pay attention.

Nurse Mayne stepped closer and gently lifted his

hand. "Look, he's searching for you. Say something again."

Faith crooned the loving words she'd used the day before, and the baby turned toward her, waving his hands like a mini conductor in front of an orchestra.

Once she saw that Faith had a way with the poor babe, Nurse Mayne seemed pleased and backed down from the stance she'd adopted at the beginning. "This is unbelievable. The strangest thing I've seen in a long time. It's like he knows you're there and wants to get your attention."

"I know. May I?" Faith gestured to pick him up, and the nurse didn't hesitate to nod her consent.

"Aww, he's happy. Look, it sounds like he's scolding because he had to wait for you to come to him. That's the cutest thing I've seen in a long time. I'll get his bottle and if you don't mind looking after him for a while, I'd be grateful."

"It's my pleasure. Trust me; there isn't anything I'd rather do." Faith didn't want to gush or make the nurse uneasy, but if the woman had handed her a bowl full of diamonds, it wouldn't have given her near as much joy.

For the rest of the morning, Faith held the now quiet baby, rocking him gently, watching him sleep, and the world faded. Happiness filled her, there was no room for hate or sorrow.

In her thoughts, she shared her pleasure with Raoul, begging for his forgiveness in losing his child. While absorbed in her memories, the baby's eyes opened. He stared at her as if he could actual see her features, his big eyes seeming to pass on a message. A tide of contentment swept over her as if Raoul had pulled mystical strings to grant her what she requested, and the dreadful agony in her heart eased.

***

Steven Corella, an assistant hotel manager for one of the larger Vegas casinos on the strip had taken his lunch hour to come to the hospital and see his son.

The day before, he'd finally tracked down his girlfriend, Natalie, and was stunned at her behavior when he'd tried to convince her to return and take care of their baby. At least help him until he could figure out how he could do so himself. He still reeled at her words.

"I don't want no baby. I never signed up to be a mommy when we met. It wasn't part of the deal. But it happened, and I gave you nine stinking months of my life to give the kid a decent start."

Sickened, Steven finally faced the truth. In his heart, he'd hoped she'd see the baby, and a miracle would happen to change her mind. What a fool! "Who're you trying to kid, Nat? You did it for the money."

"Whatever. I'm sure as hell not gonna wreck his chances for a good life now, trying to handle the day to day shit. You wanted him. You got him. Don't come back and bother me again. Just get your lawyer to send me the check and whatever papers I need to sign and he's all yours."

Steven had rushed to get away. He couldn't stand another minute in the presence of the obnoxious person he'd never really known. True, she'd been a bitch throughout the pregnancy, but he'd put it down to her whacked-out hormones.

When they'd first met, the gorgeous dancer had lit up his world, made him feel like he'd inherited a kingdom with her holding his hand and them facing the world together.

He'd never had a lot of self-confidence. Being the youngest son in a family of three boys, he'd always been picked on and bullied for his sensitivity. To survive, he'd learned to hide the tenderness and to adopt the mask of a man who had it all and knew everything.

It worked enough to get him to where he was today, in a job with huge responsibilities, one that demanded a lot more than an eight hour shift every day. The excitement had drawn Natalie into his world but it hadn't taken long before she'd discovered the sham he couldn't maintain in his softer moments. She'd begun to lose her respect for him. When she freaked out about the pregnancy, threatening to have an abortion, he'd made her a deal.

If she stopped drinking, ate properly, and gave his baby a chance to be healthy, he'd pay her twenty thousand dollars after the birth. And she'd agreed. She'd kept to the bargain, because in the hotel where he worked, they lived in a small suite, and he'd had her watched.

The day they made the deal, he remembered assuming his working persona of a man not to be trifled with. He'd warned her, his voice harsh, his finger in her face and his eyes boring holes into her soul. "Don't screw with me, bitch. I find out you've been a bad girl, and you won't get a penny."

Thankfully, she'd behaved. And though they'd given up all pretense of being a couple in love, she'd kept her side of the bargain, and because of it, his son was a strong, healthy boy. One who was now being cuddled in the arms of a golden-haired stranger, a beautiful girl he'd never met.

"Nurse, who's that woman holding my son?" Steven stood in Nurse Mayne's path, demanding answers. "She looks like a patient."

"She is, Mr. Corella. But she has a huge heart and your baby has taken to her. When she's around, he's an angel. When she isn't, the poor mite cries his heart out."

Not willing to pretend he misunderstood, he admitted, "Like he did this morning the whole time I was with him."

"Yes, he isn't happy with us nurses, either. They have a strange bond those two, and he settles as soon as he hears her voice. I've seen it before but it's usually with the mother. We think it's the recognition of their voices but who knows for sure. Miss Whitely has mesmerized your son, and he's happy with her, that's all I know."

"Has she been in an accident? Can she walk?"

"Yes, she walked with him earlier. But I can't really say much more."

"I understand, thank you, nurse." Steven strode into the windowed room and approached the wheelchair where his son lay happily gurgling in the arms of an angel.

"My son seems to be smitten. But he's a bit young for you, don't you think?"

***

Faith didn't hear any footsteps. All she heard was a male voice, teasing and pleasant.

"Oh, I'm sorry. The nurse let me hold him. He's happier, and I had nothing to do anyway. I-I hope you don't mind." Faith looked up into the eyes of a stranger. A Latino male who had wonderful dark eyes and a pleasing face where the tanned skin never lightened and the dark hair, cut to stand up on the top and short at the sides, made one think of a well-groomed businessman. His light gray suit, white shirt, and blue tie added to the image as did his manicured fingers, gold ring, and the matching bracelet that dangled slightly.

Instantly, she shrunk inside, knowing that he saw a hospital-gowned female with a bandaged arm, a bruised face and hair that straggled over her shoulders. She'd never felt so inadequate. The disadvantage made her stumble over her words, and she hated the lack of control.

"No, I don't mind at all. Nurse Mayne says he likes you. That he's bonded with you is what she actually told me, and it seems to be true."

They both glanced at the happy baby, spread over her knee, his fist working hard to find his mouth. He'd been staring at her for a few seconds until his focusing mechanism failed. Then he'd twist his head slightly and find her again.

"I keep calling him, baby. Have you named him yet?" Faith couldn't ask about the baby's mother but she was curious as hell. Rather than snoop, she hoped he'd share when he answered her question.

"No. My girlfriend never stipulated a name, said it was up to me. I haven't thought of anything I like. Every time I come up with something, either my brothers make fun or the crew at the hotel knock it down. Why, do you have any ideas?"

"I used to know a very nice man called Raoul. It's a strong name for a strong person. But that's just my opinion."

"No, I like it. We never came up with that one. Let me think about it. What's your name? I'm Steven Corella."

"Pleased to meet you, I'm Faith Whitely."

"How long will you be in hospital, Faith? That's a lovely name by the way. Tell you the truth, it's like a sign for me. I've kinda lost faith in a lot of things lately, especially in women. So, it's nice to meet a good faith person."

Blushing, Faith tried to hide the warmth in her face by lifting the baby closer to her. Without any conscious intentions, she kissed his soft cheeks, nuzzled his face and nestled him onto her shoulder. When she thought the baby's father wouldn't notice her discomfort, she chanced a glance and found him watchful, his keen gaze never leaving her. Regretting the necessity of having to do so, she handed the baby over to him. "You'll want to have a cuddle. I can come back later."

"You didn't answer me."

"Excuse me," Faith had started to leave the room and stopped her wheelchair to face him again.

"When do you leave the hospital?"

Saddened by the unpleasant future she faced,

Faith said, "Tomorrow, I guess." Her depressed tone rang clear and embarrassment flooded. This man didn't deserve her discourtesy. "I'm sorry, I've recently lost everything that ever mattered to me and the thought of going back to my old life makes me cringe."

With the now fussing baby held over his shoulder, Steven seemed focused on her words. He knelt in front of her chair and leveled her with a look that meant business. "I need to ask you a question, and I need you to be honest. My son's fallen for you. Since his mother has given up all ties to him, he's my total responsibility now. And I can't do it alone and work. The hospital administration has informed me they expect him to be taken home tomorrow, the next day at the latest. Therefore, if you can provide me with at least a couple character references, I won't demand job experience. And if you're willing, I'd like to offer you a job as his nanny."

Stunned, a glow beginning deep inside that had her heart lifting from despair to hope, she nodded, scared to speak in case she broke down.

"First, I need to know, did you try to commit suicide?"

"What! No. Why would you ask me that?" She knew shock had appeared on her face; it rampaged throughout her body and made her clench her hands.

"Because when you looked at me, sadness was the first adjective that came to mind. Your eyes overflow with the emotion and there's a bandage around your arm to your wrist."

Relived that his reply made sense, and she could alleviate his worry, she confided, "My boyfriend was killed a short while ago. Then one of my co-workers attacked me, and I was injured. Yesterday, the doctor told me I miscarried because of the injuries, and I wasn't aware of being pregnant. As of this moment, I'm out of work and alone. So, yes, you're right. I am unhappy. But I'm not suicidal, that you can depend on."

Steven finally passed the cranky baby back to her, and seemed relieved when she reached for him. "Then I'm begging for your help. Will you look after Raoul for me, Faith Whitely?"

Lightness descended over her spirit as if a loving force shared her delight. "You're going to call him Raoul?"

"I am. I like the name." His soft brown eyes found hers. His searching gaze never wavered. "Faith, I need to know before I go back to work, will you be his nanny?"

"Yes. Please. I can think of nothing I would like better. But you should know one thing about me before this goes any further. You might change your mind when you hear what I have to say."

Suddenly, leaping off a mountain to jagged rocks below seemed less intimidating to her than admitting the truth about her past. Clammy, her hands gripped the baby's blanket at the same time as the pounding in her temple got serious. This moment was more painful than any she'd experienced in the last few days. Breathing hurt as she tried forcing words past a blockage of pure humiliation.

Sensing her distress, Steven added, "It's all right. You can tell me."

"I have no references to be a nanny." She spit the words out and shame at her deceit made her sick inside.

Seemingly relieved, Steven smiled. "Truthfully, I really don't care about that. You have a kind heart and it's connected to his. I'll take those as qualifications any day."

She squeezed the baby closer, the smell from the powder she'd used after his bath soothing her guilt.

I'll be the best nanny anyone ever hired.

Chapter
Twenty-two

Later that same afternoon, Cassi visited Billy to get him on board with her plan to help Mary seek justice. The thought of leaving the poor woman to rot the rest of her years in the women's penitentiary, surrounded by hardened criminals, just seemed like piling another sin on top of a mountain of them.

She accepted the system couldn't free the old nurse, and so they shouldn't. But there were options, separate institutions that would work in her case. Places where people suffered from mental disabilities, treatment facilities where she could be sent rather than being locked up in a jail that had little or no services for people like her who posed little or no threat to society.

The office Cassi arrived at was a smaller building with the front window overlooking the sidewalk and outdated gold printing on the glass, *Sampson and Little,* like one might have seen fifty years ago.

She entered to find a receptionist who looked as old-fashioned as the building. Her glasses were midway down her nose and her bouffant blonde curls had so much lacquer, she used the end of her pen to scratch at an itch.

Cassi watched and waited until the secretary looked up to acknowledged her. After she suffered the once-over that made her glad she had worn her librarian clothes and not those she used at the club, she smiled.

"Yes, can I help you?"

Slightly intimidated, Cassi said, "If possible, I'd like to speak with Mr. Duran?"

"Do you have an appointment? He's very busy."

"No. I don't. But he's an old friend. If he's here, I'm sure he'll see me for a few minutes. Just tell him it's Cassi Santino."

Sighing, a long-suffering kind of sound that suggested she was doing a favor and one should be grateful, the woman picked up the phone and hit three numbers. She barely had Cassi's name out of her mouth before the far door flung wide and Billy rushed out, his arms ready to gather her in close. "You finally decided to visit me. I texted you the address last week."

Allowing the embrace, Cassi nodded. "I'm sorry.

Life has been kind of crazy for me. Do you have a few minutes that we can talk?"

"Sure. For you, sweetheart, I always have time." Billy glanced back at the woman paying close attention and added. "Gladys, Cassi is my girl and can come and go as she pleases. Just so you know."

Before Cassi could correct the false impression, he wrapped his arm around her waist and ushered her into his office.

It was a big room, with the large desk in a corner surrounded on both sides with windows. There was a wall of cabinets where many of the drawers had been left open and files spread everywhere. The table at the end of the room also sported stacks of papers and documents, which added to the concept that a lot of work was being done on these premises.

It made her happy to see Billy in his element and that lightened her irritation at the way he'd presented her earlier.

Before she could speak, a young woman, arms loaded with manuals approached the open door between the two offices. "Billy, I found that case you mentioned, Baxter versus Main, the proof you'll need for the hearing later today. It completely backs up your claim... Oh, sorry. I didn't know you had a client. I'll come back later."

"Wait, Maria, come and meet my best girl, Cassi

Santino. Cassi, this is Maria Delgado, an up-and-coming star of the courts. She's smart and works like a Trojan."

This time Cassi didn't let his reference to their being involved slide. She reached out her hand to shake and while doing so, she said, "Billy's like a brother to me. We've known each other for years. I'm pleased to meet you, Maria."

The other girl had laid down her manuals on the open file drawer and held Cassi's hand in a firm grip. Her expressive brown eyes were welcoming and the surprising match to her medium-length hair added to her good looks as did her curvaceous body and chic blue outfit.

"How nice to meet you, Miss Santino."

"Cassi, please. Your office building is rather quaint, but very well restored. Are there many people working here?"

"Thanks, we love this old place. Right now, there's the boss, Richard Little. Mr. Sampson has semi-retired and still takes on special cases periodically, myself and Billy. We're a small group but we keep busy. I'll leave you two and get back to my desk." She turned to Billy and added, "Just ring through when you're finished with Cassi, and I'll show you what I found."

Leaving behind a whiff of expensive flowery perfume, Maria closed the door behind her. Cassi turned back to Billy who leaned against his desk with his arms crossed, watching her. A smile lit his gray eyes and his teeth gleamed, she assumed implants had been purchased on a payment scheme. His auburn hair, worn slicked back with product to give it an added shine, had been cut. What made her the happiest was his healthy vivaciousness.

Looking so much like the old Billy, her earlier fondness revived, filling her with satisfaction. Pleasure surged that she hadn't expected to feel. Not surprising, this man made her remember good times, her youth and the contentment of those days when everything had been safe and normal.

"You look wonderful, Billy. I'm so glad." She forced away the remembered warnings from Sergio and decided that she had to give this man a break. He'd been through so much.

"Thanks to you and your help. By the way, I'll have some money for you soon. To pay you back for investing in me."

"Hold it, Billy. It was never about the money. I wanted you to have a chance. And it was your grit and determination that got you through the worst. By the time you came to me, to a good extent, you'd beaten the drugs."

Cassi held the back of a chair she stood behind, the chrome trim feeling cold to her touch. "There is one thing you could do for me, though. I know of a woman who needs your expertise. And she needs it right away. I'm not sure how much you charge your clients, but if this person can't pay for your services, I'll cover the costs."

Billy perked up. "Who are you talking about?"

"Mary Devin—"

"The Angel of Death case? That's the one you want me to handle?" Glee shone from eyes suddenly piercing and filled with interest. His body's relaxed stance shifted immediately to that of someone paying full attention. "I'd heard that she refused to hire council and the court appointed her with some young newbie."

"She did and they did. But I went to see her earlier, and she's changed her mind."

"Hold it. How are you related to this case?"

"It's a long story, and you're busy."

"I'll make the time, tell me."

"I've told you about Detective McGuire, right? He's a friend of mine. When his mother was dying from cancer, he hired Mary as her caretaker."

"He's the detective who arrested her. Wait, he also arrested her son as the actual killer." Recognizing Cassi's surprise, he added, "Cassi it's on TV and in all the papers. Don't you watch the news?"

She shook her head. "Life's been too hectic."

"Mary Devin's been charged with multiple homicides. What makes her case fascinating is that many of the families whose loved ones she *took care of*, and I'm not being facetious," he grinned, "are demanding she be released. They say she eased the last days of her patients and helped them escape from their worlds full of pain. It's the craziest case I've heard of in a long time."

"There're two sides to every story, Billy. Part of her defense is she stood by as her son carried out the crimes; therefore, she never actually murdered anyone herself. But it's because of her son that the woman's filled with remorse. She'll never forgive herself for the damage done to him. For this alone, she believes she should pay and up until now, has refused to hire any legal counsel."

"And what do you believe?"

"I agree. She should be held responsible for breaking the law and using Juan. But I also want justice for Mary. So she can be allowed to serve her sentence in a more acceptable facility than where she is now at the prison. She's not crazy, but her actions can be misconstrued to look that way. If she's sentenced to life in a hospital setting, where she receives therapy and kindness, it would be much more fitting than for her to be treated like a hardened killer."

"Eloquently put, my girl. You should have been

the lawyer in the family." Billy rubbed his hands together, and she sensed his brain filtering through words before he spoke.

"A lot of the lawyers in the city would give their first born to get this case, Cassi. You know that, right?"

Shocked at his words, she shook her head. "No, I didn't."

"They're like a pack of jackals, trying to get to the woman. In fact, more law firms have offered pro bono and their best legal brains just for the publicity."

"Seriously?"

"Every so often, a case comes along that ignites the public so they form armies on both sides of an issue. Those trials always bring with them a huge amount of media coverage. The Devin situation has ignited the public and the media. If you want me to take the case, hell, I'd be delighted. Just so you know, there are others more reputable than me salivating to be chosen."

"She won't hire any of those firms. But she'll let me bring you in if you want to help her."

Billy sprang forward and shoved the chair aside to get to Cassi. His arms scooped her up and he swung her around. "Are you kidding me? You tell that little lady that I'm her guy."

"I've already told her to expect you later today.

The preliminary hearing is soon and you need to get to work."

"Pretty sure of old Billy, weren't you, honey?"

"Let's just say, I believe in you." Cassi grinned when his face lit up.

"Flattery like that will have me genuflecting, beautiful. I'll do my best, Cassi. I promise."

Pretending a fierceness that surprisingly turned out to be true, made her voice ring with honest emotion. "You're best doesn't interest me, Billy. I need you to win."

Her intensity brought a stunned surprise to his expression before he hid it with his usual cheeky grin. She had no way of knowing what he was thinking, but one thing was for sure, he wasn't used to her new arrogance.

Tough.

She knew he was fond of her. Now she wanted his respect.

Chapter Twenty-thre e

Cassi hurried to get to her afternoon training session with Arlene. She'd called Rusty earlier and changed their time for an hour later because of her busy morning at the prison and the subsequent visit with Billy.

Driving to the gym, she thought about her discussion with the lawyer and remembered his situation a few months ago. Living as a crackhead in the Vegas gutters, a mess of humanity on a downward spiral, Billy had hit bottom.

According to him, Raoul's death was the motivation he'd needed to overcome his addiction. Shortly after the worst day of her life, he'd arrived on her doorstep, seemingly to help her, only to have her turn the tables. With Raoul's money, and

Rusty providing a driver to deliver him, she'd paid for Billy's rehab treatment in a center in California that had a good reputation. In a few months, they'd performed a miracle.

Today, it had done her heart good to see the old version of Billy, and his excitement to work with Mary. Lately, her indecisiveness about her old friend upset her a lot.

She remembered the days when her father, José, would be at the gym. And she'd cook dinner with Raoul's help. Sometimes, Billy would arrive unexpectedly to join them. Those had been fun times and full of happy memories.

Billy had always been a showman and could make people laugh. Those skills had helped him in the courtroom. In the early days, after he'd passed the bar and started working cases, she'd gone to a few of his courtroom sessions. She'd been fascinated at the intrigue that underlined the cases he'd won.

Some of the litigators were skillful in drawing out the real truth during cross-examination, but it enthralled her to see how they could manipulate the answers by the way they worded a question. When clever, they could stress a witness's weaknesses and even put the focus on if they were lying or not.

She remembered one particular case where Billy

had used a cell phone message to prove the guilt of a husband who'd shot his wife. The coroner had been able to pinpoint the time of her death to within a half an hour.

The husband had maintained to have left the office at a specific time and was starting the drive home when she'd been killed which provided his alibi.

On the witness stand, Billy had asked the man if he ever phoned while driving. The self-righteous, convincing denial on the accused's face was the first crack in the case.

Billy had led the husband to describe where he'd been when he'd made the call. He'd sworn on oath that he'd made the call from his office, which happened to be an hour's drive from his house.

When asked why he'd used his cell phone while there and not the phone in his office, he'd bragged that he often did. Especially when talking to his wife, because he could press the home number without having to dial it. It had bothered him terribly when he'd lost that phone shortly after her death.

Once Billy led him to speak about his work as an accountant, he'd boasted about his office on the twenty-sixth floor of a downtown building. After being asked if the traffic noises bothered him, he shook his head and added, "Of course not, it's a new building. We don't hear anything from the street." Billy had verified that point with other witnesses also.

Then Billy presented the transcript of the phone call to the court, the one from her husband that had gone to their answering machine. He'd told his wife he was leaving the office and would be home in an hour.

When they finally played the actual message that convicted the idiot, not only did they have records of when the actual call had been made giving them the time, but after taking possession of the old-fashioned answering machine, very distinctly one could hear traffic noises recorded in the call. The proof of his lie had broken the husband's resistance, and his case fell apart. He'd obviously been driving while making the call, which meant, he'd gotten home earlier and would have had sufficient time to kill his wife.

Billy won the case. Over something as simple as that.

Cassi remembered thinking at the time, how she wished she could be strong enough to stand up in front of a roomful of people and bring justice to those deserving.

Pulling her mind away from those memories, Cassi drove into the gym's parking lot and parked her car. Unnoticed, she strode through the exercise area. On the way to the locker room, she stopped to watch Arlene skipping rope only to notice her rhythm was off today.

Cassi hesitated. Something didn't seem right. On a normal day, Arlene's skill had the rope flipping so fast, one had trouble keeping up with her footwork.

Sweat poured off the fighter and her panting breath gave Cassi reason for concern. She headed to Rusty's office rather than the change room and found him in a meeting with an obnoxious ranter. His loud bluster filtered through the closed door and caught her attention. She knocked and entered the small room, then waited for Rusty to acknowledge her.

"Hey, kiddo. Did you want to see me?" Rusty's tuke sat awry on his head, his white mass of hair stuck out from the sides which added to his appearance of an infuriated man. His blue eyes were always bright but not often with fury.

"Is there a problem, Rus?"

"Nothing I can't handle. I've wrestled with swindlers all my life, this bozo's no different."

The bozo's booming laugh had him shaking his head in disgust. The heavyset arguer sneered and added. "You wanna play – you pay." He held both hands up in front of him as if saying, not my rules and laughed again when Rusty snorted his derision.

The dude's attention zeroed in on her and his searching gaze didn't miss much. "You a fighter, sugar?"

"Nope."

"Should be, you got the body." His leer said it all. When he saw Rusty begin to rise and sensed his aggression, he added. "I mean the muscles."

Rusty's second snort brought attention back his way. The hustler reiterated his stance. "You sweeten the deal, old man, or the fight's off. Your girl is up and coming, but she hasn't hit the big time yet. This fight with Ariana is going to be her step to the big fight tickets. But that's gonna cost you. You know how the game works, so don't play innocent."

"Yeah, yeah. You'll get your money. And when Arlene wins, you'll be whining at my door wanting to promote her. Then we'll see who gets to set the deal."

Bozo's laughter could be heard for a few seconds after he left and the sour look on Rusty's face had Cassi's heart wrenching for her friend. "They taking you to the cleaners, Rus?"

"Nothing I didn't expect. That girl's gotta have her chance, I just wish it wasn't gonna cost me so much. So, what's up? You looked worried when you first stepped into the office."

"Have you watched Arlene practice today?"

"Sure. I worked her hard earlier. She did good. Why?"

Aha! No wonder she was drooping when Cassi saw her. "No reason, just wondered how you feel about her chances."

"Whaddaya mean? She's in top condition and is as good as she's ever been. This fight is her ticket, you know that."

"Yours, too, right?"

Rusty's sly grin produced an answering one. "That's the way the game's played, brat. She's my fighter. If she does good by me, we both benefit. You're gonna be there on Saturday, right? We need you in our corner. As much as she'd hate me to say this, Arlene fights better when you're around."

"Sam gave me a few extra hours off so I'll be there. My free night is tonight, and I tried to switch but he said no. He likes me working the weekends."

"Good. Now go change and teach her to keep her chin guarded on that three-two punch routine she likes so much. Wear full gear, chest and groin protectors, and a mouthpiece too. From now on, I want she should get used to fight gear in practice."

Chapter
Twenty-four

Trace's heart lifted as soon as he heard Cassi's voice on the other end of the line. He asked, "Where are you, darlin'?"

"I'm headed to the hospital to check up on Faith. It's my night off, as you know, and I wanted to visit her before we meet at the house. What are you up to?"

"Oh, just protecting the citizens of this godforsaken hellhole of a city. Putting my life on the line every minute while doing a job they don't pay me near enough to be doing."

Trace heard Cassi's laughter, and he loved the sound. "You think I'm joking?"

"No, love. I've no doubt you're serious. What or who bit your bottom today?"

"I just met my new partner, Michael Kowalski. The guy's a putz."

"Trace! He can't be that bad."

"Yeah, well he shaves his head, wears face hair, and thinks he's a stand-up. Never stops with the joking. I'm having a hard time dealing with the guy. You know what he told me earlier?"

"No, what?"

Trace heard the smile in her voice, so he carried on with the teasing note even though it covered up a serious annoyance. "He says as how I should lighten up. Me! Says I'm too serious and it's a heart attack that's waiting for me down the road if I don't take it easy. Wants me to sign up for hot yoga classes, for crissakes."

She snorted and then giggled. "And what did you tell him?"

"To do something to himself that's too rude to repeat." Trace knew the droll tone he used had her giggling. Damned if he didn't love the sound so much, he kept up the banter. "Being that he's new in town, he wants I should introduce him to some girls."

Still giggling, she played along. "And what did you tell him?"

"To do something to himself that's physically impossible." They both cracked up at this point. Trace didn't want to hang up – ever. Unfortunately, you don't always get what you want in life. When the subject of their discussion stuck his head around the doorway, he knew his fun had ended. "Gotta go, baby. I'll see you later."

After he put the phone down, he watched Michael Kowalski fold into his visitor chair, the big guy slouching, his leg over one knee in the way men always relaxed. His well-groomed red beard and mustache had a lot of gray which might have aged him if his twinkling, vivid green eyes and smooth skin didn't tell the truth. He was late-thirties and carried himself like a man one didn't trifle with. "I've been studying our case load and wanted to question you about something that's bugging me."

Trace kept a straight face, hiding his disgruntled reaction to this man who irritated the hell outta him. Seeing him at Diane's desk with his feet on her open drawer this morning, making free with her things just didn't sit well.

Yet the guy appeared knowledgeable. Hank Lester, the chief, had high expectations. Therefore, Trace knew that Michael's record must be stellar or he wouldn't be on the team. Still...

"You like staring at me, pard? Should I comb my beard?"

Trace couldn't help himself. "You sure as hell can't comb your hair."

Michael grinned. "Funny thing is, even if I grew it, I couldn't comb it. I took after my old man, and he's bald. Guess I'm lucky the styles today work in my favor. Now you – sitting there with a mop of shaggy hair that's in need of a cut and you have no idea how I envy you. Oh well, we can't have both hair and brains so I guess I got the better deal."

"Fuck you."

Laughing, his eyes full of glee, Michael quipped, "You sure are easy, man. Really, let me take you to the hot-yoga studio I recently found. They'll help with your chronic bad mood disorder."

"What's the case you wanted to ask me about?" Trace ignored the other's remarks on purpose, wanting to get his questions answered so he could work on his own stack of files that never seemed to lessen.

Michael sat forward and held his hands between his open knees. "The Santino killing – why is it still open? You've got all three of the men that were at the crime scene, and though you can't pinpoint one as the killer, it's a done deal."

"Not really. I could have sworn the person who appeared at the last minute before Santino got shot was smaller built. All the men involved were big guys. Then my girl Cassidy, Santino's sister, who as you know was at the warehouse that night heard from a reliable source that there was a female suspect, and she could very well be the shooter. Which kinda proves my theory, too."

"Except you haven't filled out that part of the details in the files."

"Hey, asshole, look at my desk. Does it appear as if I'm caught up here?"

"Sure is a mess. What you need is time-management training."

"Fuck you." Trace didn't see the humor in Michael's comment though the annoying poser was wearing a gleeful smirk.

"So, you've surmised there's a female involved. What has forensics come up with?"

"Nothing. We also never located the murder weapon."

"Have you any suspects in mind?"

"The main person of interest is well protected; she's the mob boss for the *Armas Jóvenes.*"

"That's the same gang Santino was running with."

"Yeah. But without any real evidence placing her there that night, she'll walk faster than I can get a coffee."

"So, what's the next move?"

"I'm collaborating with an undercover FBI agent that's close to them. His case depends on her running her business while he collects the evidence he needs to put the whole bloody trafficking chain in the city away for good. Figure it's smart to give him lots of leeway. In the meantime, keep your eyes open and bring whatever you hear to me."

"You got it, partner. Now, about you getting your girl to hook me up..."

"Fuck off."

"Man, it's good you have multiple uses for your favorite word. As long as you don't team it with 'up,' I'll be happy." Seeing Trace's middle finger point at him and then the doorway, he laughed and left.

Trace's thoughts flipped to Cassi and the fight coming up that Saturday. Maybe he should take Michael with him and hook him up with Arlene. She was just bitchy enough to make Michael sweat. The thought of seeing his partner fall for the boxing beauty uplifted Trace to such an extent that he turned back to his computer wearing a nasty grin.

Chapter
Twenty-five

Cassi geared herself up for the impending visit to Faith not knowing what to expect. Setting aside her own happiness took some effort; nonetheless, she tried putting herself in Faith's place, and her heart ached for the other's miserable situation.

Therefore, when she entered the room and found the patient missing, fear crowded her throat. Thinking of the worst scenario, she lowered the basket of fruit she'd brought as a temptation to get Faith to eat and headed for the nurses' station at the curve in the hallway that separated two wings.

"Excuse me, ma'am. Can you tell me where Faith Whitely is?"

"Oh, sure. She's been helping out in the maternity ward. Ever since that darn flu hit with a vengeance, we've been really short of staff. We're convinced the full moon must have caused a moon-induced baby boom. Can't believe how many mothers delivered these last few days, many who still had weeks before their due dates."

Cassi grinned at this kind of remark coming from a highly educated RN, but had no intentions of playing devil's advocate. As a librarian who'd done a lot of reading, there were unexplained mysteries in the world she'd spent hours researching with an open mind and no definitive answers.

"Is it a good idea for her to be amongst the babies? I mean, she found out recently that she'd had a miscarriage. I'm concerned for her."

The nurse leaned closer to Cassi as if she had a secret that had to stay between the two of them. "When she arrived, I thought – there is a lost unhappy soul with no hope. Since yesterday, it's like she's morphed into a whole new persona. I can't explain it, but you'll see for yourself. She's coming now."

Cassi thanked the nurse and turned to watch Faith walking slowly toward her. She appeared steady enough, though she hesitated as soon as she spied who stood beside the nurse. The smile that lit her face had Cassi believing in miracles.

Rushing forward to hug and then help her to her room, Cassi swelled with gratitude at the unexpected change in her friend. "You're walking.

And you're smiling. What happened?"

"You won't believe the wonderful luck I've had since I saw you last. Remember yesterday when we passed the maternity ward?"

Cassi had no idea where this story was going. Showing interest, she plunked herself down on the end of the bed and watched the other girl's expressive face. "Sure."

"I know you refused to take me in there to protect me, but after you left, something drew me to go back. When I got there, I found a tiny baby who wouldn't behave for anyone. He cried so hard it broke my heart. I approached and after I talked with him, he quieted almost at once. When the nurse who was run off her feet saw me with the baby, that we had a connection, she let me help her with him."

"Oh, Faith. Where was his mother?"

"She'd taken off, left the hospital, her boyfriend, her baby... everything. I found out from the baby's father, Steven Corella, she wasn't coming back."

"Oh, no, the poor guy. What's he going to do with a brand-new baby? Hope he has family who'll help him."

"Not in Vegas, he doesn't. He's an assistant floor manager at the Mirage Casino and works weird shifts. And he mostly stays at the hotel. Of course, they won't let him take a baby there."

"What will he do? Is he planning to give the baby to a foster family?"

"No. Instead, he's hired a nanny."

Cassi knew instantly who the nanny in question was, and she felt a huge weight lift off her shoulders. What a perfect solution! Faith would be away from the Lipstick Club and doing something that obviously made her happy.

"Will you care for the baby at your place?"

"No, I offered but Steve has an apartment he arranged for his girlfriend. Since she's out of the picture now, he wants me and the baby to move in there."

"And this works for you?"

"Sure. Where I'm at now is filled with memories of Raoul and how happy we were together. It's best for me to leave all that behind."

"You're right. It's a lot healthier, too, Faith. You know that, right?"

"Of course, except I'll be taking one huge part of Raoul with me."

Not understanding where this was going but sensing it was a good thing and in no way bad, she asked, "How's that?"

"Steve didn't have a name picked out for the baby. When I suggested that Raoul was a strong name for a boy, he jumped on it."

"So he's calling the baby Raoul?"

"Yes, and I'm thrilled. I know Raoul would have been delighted."

Cassi grinned and nodded. "Oh, yes. He'd have loved having a baby named after him." Suddenly, Cassi's cautious nature awoke and kicked in. "Hold it! What do you know about this dude, Faith? Are you sure you can trust him?"

Tears appeared and dimmed the mask of happiness that Faith had worn from the moment they met in the hallway. She clenched her hands, the knuckles appearing white. Lifting the fists to push on her chest, as if to hold something inside from seeping out, she let Cassi read the anguish in her expressive eyes. "He's a gentle man. You should see him with the baby. It's not me facing a trust issue, Cass. It's him. I never told him what I did for a living."

"Oh, Faith..."

"I know, right?" Faith turned beseeching eyes her way. "I need a favor. He wants some character references. I know Leni will give me one, and I was hoping you'd write a letter for me." She sat waiting, questioning, scared.

Again, a reference to Leni. Cassi couldn't help but wonder how these two girls became such friends that Leni would send flowers to the hospital and be relied on to write a character reference. The girl she knew, or thought she did, wouldn't be the type.

"Cassi?"

"Of course, Faith, I'd be delighted."

Chapter
Twenty-six

After Cassi returned home from her visit with Faith, she bustled around in housemaid mode hoping to impress Trace with her wifely skills.

She had steaks ready to barbecue, a salad that looked like something one might find in a five-star restaurant and the all the trimmings one could want with that kind of a meal. She'd fried the mushrooms and onions with garlic, the incredible smells making her mouth water. Now, all she had to do was zip them into the microwave for a few minutes at mealtime, and they'd be ready.

Even the Merlot she'd bought had been suggested by Google as being the best with red meat and sold for a reasonable price.

All the time she worked, she thought about Faith and her dilemma. It was easy to feel sympathy for the poor girl. Cassi knew what lying did to one's soul and wouldn't wish that stress on anyone. When Faith first told her she hadn't admitted to being a hooker to baby Raoul's father, Cassi's first instincts were that she'd made the wrong decision.

After they discussed it at length, she had to support Faith's reasoning. Once he saw her with the baby and how much she cared for him, then the time for truth-revealing would be safer. He'd accept it better, knowing that prostituting wasn't who she was, but just a job she'd done.

A faint shiver of uneasiness wrestled with common sense, and she felt overwhelmed. An impulse to go for a bike ride and blow out the cobwebs, clear her mind of problems she couldn't change, seized and wouldn't let up.

Checking the clock and finding hours had passed meant she wouldn't have time before Trace arrived, and her eagerness dwindled. Damn! It was just the pick-me-up she needed to put things into perspective and stop her from brooding.

***

"Best meal I've tasted in a long time, baby. You're spoiling me."

"Right, you cooked the meat. All I did was toss the salad, pour the wine and bake the potatoes."

"Yeah! And them suckers were the best damn potatoes I ever tasted. And that salad!"

She hid her grin behind her curtain of hair and

her husky voice lowered theatrically. "Your pathetic compliments won't get you into my bedroom, so you can stop laying it on so thick."

"Okay, so what will get me into your bed?" Trace's playful mood was dangerous. His quirky grin highlighted the dimple that almost never appeared. It made her hand reach to stroke it. When the sultry stare turned hot with passion, she leaned over and kissed him, tasting the wine that still flavored his lips.

"A bike ride in the desert, a blanket under the stars and a cold beer. It's what Raoul and I would do sometimes to enjoy the nights and the coolness after the sun went down."

"Seriously? You'd like that."

"More than anything. You can ride, can't you?" She waited with her heart in her throat.

"Sure. Used to own my own Harley when I first started at the police academy but Mom hated all bikes. She'd seen a few horrendous accidents in her time as a street cop. So, to calm her worries, I sold it. Plus, I needed the money for living expenses."

Exhilaration spiked Cassi's delight so high, she all but bounced over to drag him from behind the table. "Let's go now. I'll change into my leathers, you can use Raoul's old jacket. I'm sure it will fit."

"Really?"

"I can't think of anything I'd rather do."

"Oh, darlin', I can. But if going for a ride puts those stars in your eyes, then let's go. Bring that blanket. I have a good idea what we can do while we stargaze."

***

Elation flooded Cassi as she rode her Kawasaki alongside Trace who'd been happy to use Raoul's Harley. She'd never had the experience of riding beside another person. Having this first time with Trace meant the world.

They shared a grin that soon turned into a full laugh as they bombed along the empty highway side by side. Her heart crooned with joy and she decided that life couldn't get much sweeter.

The roar of the engines gave her huge satisfaction as did the cool wind in her face and the pungent smell of the desert air. Intense happiness swelled and sudden tears blurred her vision. Raoul would have approved.

Years ago, Raoul had found a perfect hideaway for such trips as these and Cassi yelled at Trace to follow her lead. He nodded his agreement. Releasing the throttle to go slower and then downshifting, she took the next turn and headed to where the cliffs overlooked the city. From that point, one could see a magic show from the Vegas strip in the distance.

They dismounted, parking their machines on

the hardened sandy ground next to each other. Trace hung his helmet on the handlebar and came to get her.

The usual jumble of glowing colors made the sky appear like the northern lights had tripled their display. They dazzled her every time she came here. Her breath caught and she sucked in the moment. Once they'd arrived at the secret spot one could only reach on foot or by bike, it was no different tonight. Better, because she was with Trace.

"How did you know this was here, baby? It's freakin' amazing!"

"I know. Raoul found the place, and he showed me. We used to come here a lot, called it our spot. Many a night, we'd sit at the edge over there and argue about making extreme choices. And how one needed to understand there were consequences, especially after he joined the *Armas*. Come, I don't want to be sad. I'll get the blanket and show you the best part."

She took his hand and led him to the prettiest little wedge of land near the edge of the cliff, hidden on both sides by Nevada sagebrush. Here, she fixed their blanket and took off her jacket. Using it as a pillow, she lay back and smiled an invitation.

***

Trace had always thought Cassi beautiful, but

tonight she glowed. Her inviting gaze twisted his heart into a malleable mess in his chest, thumping so hard, he had to sink to his knees or fall.

He'd never loved her more or been so fucking glad she was his woman, his mate—his to love. He knelt and towered over her, needing to look down into her lovable features, to imprint this memory and immortalize the moment he'd never forget.

With the brilliance of hovering stars offering plenty of light for him to see her loving expression, he memorized her features. The almost full moon added its two cents making the night sky a lover's paradise.

She reached up and twined her arms around his back, never taking her eyes from his, telling him without words that this moment was perfect.

He kissed her gently, tasting her mouth, her neck and then back to where he couldn't get enough of her soft lips. Wanting this to be a special time, needing to do something to make a perfect memory, he pulled back and stared into her eyes. She smiled, first with her blue dazzlers glowing with promises and soon her lips produced the favorite cheeky grin she saved for him.

He scanned the rest of her face seeing dark eyebrows that arched perfectly over her large slanted eyes. Her delicate cheekbones added to her beauty and gave her appearance a kind of model-like guise that captured male attention and made other women envious.

The fact that she didn't seem to know how damn alluring she was turned him on even more. Gently, he smoothed his finger over her lips and caught his breath when she nipped the end, her teasing a huge turn-on.

"What?"

Still looking his fill, he had to concentrate so he could answer. "What, what?"

That broke her up and she grinned. "You're staring."

"No, I'm memorizing."

"Am I that easy to forget?"

"Good God, no! Just the opposite. It's the moment I'm memorizing. Hell, baby, you're already so imbedded in my brain that your face is the last thing I see at night. And your image is waiting for me as soon as I regain consciousness.

"You're why I never hug the pillow anymore, trying to put off getting my ass outta bed. The sooner I get work over with, the sooner I get home to you. I swear, darlin', you're like those stars up there. You've sweetened my life in the same way they light up the night sky."

"Oh, Trace. You're charming me and I love it. That's the most beautiful thing any woman's ever heard from her man. I swear I feel the same—fortunate to love you and have you in my world. Come here and let me show you."

From that moment on, stirred by the need to express his love, Trace committed to making it a special night for them both to store away. He'd had some experience with women, probably as much as most unmarried men his age. Some of his girlfriends had been kind enough to show him what made them zing and the things women liked for a man to do to them.

Every trick he'd ever learned, he applied tonight. Every kiss and stroke he placed on her body held adoration. There wasn't an inch of her he didn't explore with his hands, his lips, and his tongue. His devotion to her needs worked in his favor as well. She sensed his unique efforts to make this night memorable, and she reciprocated in kind.

Her whole body trembled from his expert manipulation, her voice rang with whispered love words while her legs wrapped around him and squeezed his body tight and close. He never wanted their lovemaking to end. And it didn't for a long time.

Ecstatic, filling her, joined together, he reached for the stars blazing above and carried her along with him.

Chapter Twenty-seven

After a brief snooze, the cool breeze woke Cassi. Although she'd snuggled close to Trace, held in his protective arms, thirst drove her to fidget him awake.

He opened his eyes and smiled at her. "We must have fallen asleep."

"Probably all that strenuous activity tired us out."

He grinned. "My favorite kind of activity."

"Strenuous?"

"Oh, yeah! That works for me. If I could get–ahh–strenuous with you every night for the rest of my life, I'd die happy."

Hearing those words made shivers of apprehension start attacking. "Don't talk about dying. Let's go and get a coffee at a nice place I know close by."

"Another of Raoul's hideaways?"

"Yep. Usually, we'd end up there after a few hours of stargazing. The fresh air seems to bring on hunger attacks and this place serves the best coffee and apple pie."

"Is it a bar?"

"Well, there's a bar but it also has a restaurant. Come on, just follow me."

Within a few minutes of speeding along the highway, she turned her bike into a well-lit parking area. The casino-like building blazed with so many lit signs in the windows that one had to take a few seconds to appreciate the colors and variety. The joint was quaintly old-fashioned but inviting.

They met at the path, hooked hands, and headed to the front entrance. Stepping inside, they could see that the late hour had cleaned out most people other than the regulars who never slept and a few stragglers.

One of the booths was packed with a group of women who added to the noise level so that the place wasn't totally silent. The smell of beer permeated the air and reminded her of the Lipstick Club. Thankfully, cigarette stink didn't mess with the air quality here.

Trace and Cassi ignored everyone as they made

their way to the booth that Raoul favored and had become their spot in the place.

Cassi slipped out of her jacket. "I meant to tell you that Billy called me earlier and said that the preliminary hearing went well for Mary. The judge seemed to be sympathetic to her mercy – shall we say – executions. Billy thought it's because he had a cousin who died a decade ago from Huntington's disease.'"

"Yeah? Now, that's a horrible death. I wonder how Billy found out about that?"

"He's very resourceful. And he has a fabulous partner working with him at his office, a young lawyer named Maria Delgado. From what he's let drop, she's in the background doing all the menial tasks while he's hyping it in front of the media."

Trace took both her hands in his, gently soothing them with his casual caresses. "I've seen him interviewed on all the news channels over the last day and a half. He's working the system, building support for Mary every way he can. From the size of the crowds he's been gathering, the public sympathies certainly seem to be going her way."

Cassi nodded. "I know. He has a kind of magnetism that draws in the masses. I watched him, too, and I was full of compassion by the time he'd finished."

Trace stiffened. "He's got that personality that can hook you and reel you in all right. But he's a faker and a liar. I know from when he lived on the street. Can't trust a man like that."

Cassi started to pull away and felt Trace cling, refusing to let her loose. "Trace, you wanted me to help Mary and that's what I did. Billy is a good lawyer. And as long as he stays sober, he'll help her."

Trace's face cleared and the subtle fierceness disappeared. "Sorry, you're right. I can't stand to think of that woman rotting away in a jail cell with hardened criminals. So, I guess if he can make a deal with the prosecution, get her a suspended sentence or even a lifetime in a minimum-security facility, I'd be satisfied."

Relaxing, Cassi added, "He says it helps that she wasn't the actual killer. They're making Juan out to be the bad guy here and it makes me a bit sad."

"Sad? Why? He killed those people in cold blood."

"Well, that's one way of looking at it. The other is that he was re-enacting his mother's death by helping put those folks out of their misery. I guess it just got easier for him. In the end, taking another's life didn't register."

"Baby, just so you keep your head on straight here, that's called cold-blooded murder."

"You're right. I've got to stop feeling that I let him down somehow. He was a sick man who received justice in the end."

"See. Now, you've got it." He leaned over to give her a soft kiss, and she melted immediately.

"I have to go to the little girls' room for a few minutes. Can you order me coffee and a big piece of apple pie with vanilla ice cream? I seem to be famished for some reason. Guess I used up a lot of energy tonight." Her grin caught his and they shared their private jest in a loving smile.

Cassi made quick work of her time away, freshening her appearance. The glow deep in her eyes made her heart speed up and memories of earlier in the evening surfaced. Feeling special, fortunate, and oh so loved, she left the room and began to make her way to where Trace sat waiting.

"Slumming tonight, Cassi Santino?"

Cassi stopped and looked to where the voice came from. She watched as a girl approached, befuddled as to where she'd seen the female before. Suddenly, it hit her. "Hi, Ariana. How's things?"

"Not bad. And you?"

"Good." Cassi didn't want to get into a conversation with this chick, who looked like she'd drank more than one should when they have a big fight coming up shortly. The other girl had a stubborn glint in her eye, and her stance could be mistaken as one used if a fight was imminent.

Cassi tried moving past with a nod and a short good-by phrase. "Take care."

"Hey, you don't get to walk away from me." Ariana clutched Cassi's arm and tried to swing her around.

Big mistake.

Acting purely from instinct and just a tad of pissiness, Cassi pivoted. Taking the other girl with her, she flipped her over and made sure the landing was eased more than she might have if she'd really wanted to injure. Rather than holding her there, she backed away.

Ariana was on her feet in a split second, her body reacting like that of an acrobat in top condition. Three of the other girls left the booth and formed a semi-circle around the two now squared off.

Cassi couldn't believe what was happening. "Hey, back off, Ariana. I came in here for a coffee and pie. I'm not here to mess with you. So just keep your hands to yourself and we're good." She lifted both hers as if to show everyone her sincerity.

Before she could step to the side, Ariana got up close and personal. "No one puts me on the ground and gets to walk away. Since you're too chicken to meet me in the ring, how about I teach you a lesson here and now?"

"Seriously? You're kidding, right? Why the hell do you have it in for me? I'm not the fighter. You're up against Arlene on Saturday. All I do is train her. You want to win a fight to show the world how great you are, try winning that one."

"Oh, I'll win the fight. But it's not her who I want in the ring. You're the show-off, the bitch with the skills. I saw it clear when I was at Rusty's. I want you." Her finger came out to poke at Cassi's chest and met with Cassi's retaliatory reaction that came just short of another toss on her ass.

She stopped in time, her martial art move blocking the other's hand and effectively imprisoning it so Ariana couldn't shift without breaking a bone. Cassi stared her in the eye and saw the flare of angry resentment the other couldn't hide. "Once and for all, get it into your stubborn head. I'm not the fighter you need to worry about."

Ariana pushed away from Cassi, who'd loosened the hold enough so she could break free. "Oh, baby, you have no idea. Your girl is good but she doesn't nearly measure up. It's you I wanna beat so bad, I can taste it. We'll get it on one day. I'll make it happen."

Trace stepped into the circle, his badge plainly showing on the waist band of his jeans. His attitude stern, his blue eyes cold and his words were inarguable. "Time to call it a night, ladies."

The grumbling girls in the semi-circle began to disband, moving to their table to collect their belongings.

Ariana glanced at him and then back to Cassi. She leaned in and spoke. "Anytime, sweetheart. You and me. Anytime." She gave Cassi a last push, swiveled away to grab her belongings and then followed the other women from the place, slamming the door behind her. Trace stopped Cassi from reacting to the shove by hugging her waist and pulling her close to him. "Calm down, baby."

Just then, the waitress scurried over. "Dick had his phone ready to call the cops until he saw your badge, Officer. Thank you for breaking up the misunderstanding and sending those nutty gals away. They were getting pretty boisterous. Glad they're gone."

"You're welcome, ma'am." Trace guided Cassi to her seat and sat across from her. She appreciated him holding her hand, his expression filled with kindness.

The waitress hurried over with their tray. "By the way, the pie and coffee are on the house, folks. Enjoy."

Cassi took a deep breath to calm her racing heart. The surging adrenalin needed a few minutes to cool and so did she. Finally, she looked up to see Trace's eyes on her, watchful, waiting... tender.

"Why in the world does that girl have it in for me? I've never done anything to her."

"She mentioned that she saw you fight, right?"

"So?"

"Oh, baby. When you fight, it's like magic. Arlene's good. But you're perfection. No wonder that bitch wants you in the ring. She'll never feel like the winner until she takes down the best."

Chapter Twenty-eigh t

"Arlene, can you come over tonight?"

"Of course, Barbara. What's wrong?"

"Your uncle is asking for you. He's failing, Leni. I think we're losing him."

"I'll be right there."

Twenty minutes later, Arlene sat across from her aunt as they each held hands with the sleeping man on the bed between them, the man they both loved.

"He looks frailer, Barbara. Is he eating?"

"Not a lot. He took some food from you the other day, and I think it's the last real meal he's been able to keep down. I've been making him smoothies, he likes those. His favorite is blueberry with banana, the one you told him to try." The last word was choked out and Barbara's eyes filled.

Without conscious intentions, Arlene reached across to pat her aunt's hand that grasped her husband's. Once she realized she'd touched Barbara willingly, she pulled back.

Barbara sensed her withdrawal and her gaze studied Arlene so deeply that she felt uncomfortable.

"What's wrong, Leni? You don't look good either. Are you coming down with something?"

"No. Just a lot on my mind. I have a title bout this Saturday that I've been training hard for. I guess it's wearing me out a little."

"Are you sure that's all it is? I don't like how pale you are. And flushed. Do you have a temperature?"

"Don't fuss. I'm fine." Arlene didn't intend to speak so sharply but the words burst out before she knew her attitude would stink. As soon as she saw her aunt's distress, Arlene felt terrible, like a person with no class... like a bitch.

"I'm sorry, Barbara. I'm just so damned worried about Uncle Phil, I spoke out of turn."

The man they were discussing opened his eyes. "Don't know why you're fussing so, Babs. If Leni says she fine, then she's fine. And me – I'm feeling a lot stronger than I look. In fact, if you want to share a bit of ice cream, I'm up for it. I'll have chocolate with some of that whipped cream stuff."

"Uncle Phil, you sneaky old reprobate, you've been awake and eavesdropping, haven't you?"

His cheeky grin wavered slightly but the twinkle in his rheumy eyes looked the same as it always had. The wink he shared had love bursting inside her chest. How was she ever going to survive in a world without him?

As soon as the older woman left the room to get their ice cream, he reached for her hands and held them in a surprisingly tight grip. "Promise me you'll look after your aunt when I'm gone, child. We've done a lot of sharing lately. She has no one else. And she's terrified to be alone. Promise me."

Stunned by his vehemence, sad that she hesitated before giving him the assurance he so desperately needed, she made up for it with her words. "If she wants me around, I'll be here. I promise, Uncle Phil."

"Oh, child. You have no idea how much she regrets not being kinder when you were growing up. You must let her make up for it. She needs you now."

"Don't you worry, Uncle Philly." Arlene purposely used her old pet name that she'd called him as a little girl. She knew he'd get a kick out of her remembering, and he did if his chuckle was any indication. "I'll stick around like mold on a damp wall." She giggled when he grinned. "Honestly, I'll do whatever I can."

"In case I forget, when you clean out the garage, there's a box left there by your mother years ago. I-I don't want Barbara to throw it out before you've had a chance to see her things. I-I've never looked myself but it's obvious she isn't co-coming back, and so it now belongs to you."

Arlene could see he was getting tired. "Shush, darling, don't upset yourself. I'll take care of it."

He rested his head back on the pillow, and his sigh became a cough that he struggled to overcome. "That's all one can expect. I-I love you, Leni. You've always been my little girl and I couldn't be prouder of you."

Tears filled her eyes. She choked on the words that came too late. He'd drifted off before he heard her whispers of devotion.

"He's failing, Leni." Arlene hadn't heard her aunt come into the room until she spoke.

"He's been so good to me. I'll be lost without him, Auntie." Tears blurred her aunt's reaction to Arlene calling her by her old title. But the arms that surrounded her were strong and gentle, and they mattered so much.

"We'll get through this together, child. He'd want that." Suddenly her aunt pulled back and lifted her hand to Arlene's forehead.

"You're burning up, Leni. What in the world is

wrong with you?"

Chapter Twenty-nine

Cassi had just finished her morning workout in the basement gym and was heading out for a run when the phone rang.

"Cassi? You got a minute. We need to talk."

"Rusty, hi. What's up?" Cassi heard the worry in her old friend's voice and reacted to it immediately.

"It's Arlene. She's in the hospital."

"Excuse me? Did you say she's in the hospital?"

"That's what I said. Seems she has an infection in her hand, it's swollen almost twice the size. The stupid little idiot didn't see fit to mention it was sore. Figured she'd hit the bag too hard the other day. Doc says it's probably from the gash she has by her thumb."

"You were there?"

"Yeah. Her aunt called. She was worried because she couldn't leave her husband; looks like the old man is dying. She wanted someone to be with Arlene. I went and spent an hour, hovering around until she kicked me out. What a grouch! She's furious that she can't take the title bout on Saturday. Says after she won, it would have kicked her into the big time."

Cassi smiled. Arlene's devotion to winning would take her a long way. "I'm sorry, Rusty. Is there anything I can do?" Suddenly, Cassi remembered the visit Rusty had gotten from the dopey fight producer who'd squeezed a lot of money out of her old friend to make the fight happen. He'd pulled strings for Arlene to get the title match but it had cost Rus bigtime, money he couldn't afford.

"Actually, kiddo, there is something. First, could you go and see Arlene so she gets off my case and then drop by here. We need to talk."

"Oh-kay." Foreboding struck, making Cassi's stomach queasy. "I'll see you soon."

***

Cassi held her hands under the antibacterial dispenser and added the face mask they insisted she wear. Then she opened the door to the private hospital room and tiptoed close to where it appeared Arlene was sleeping.

She looked like hell, no other way to describe the pasty, mottled skin or the feverish trembling, even with a mound of white blankets covering her to her neck.

Sliding the functional beige visitor's chair closer, Cassi sat and waited for the other girl to open her eyes. She let her mind return to the previous night and her glorious encounter under the stars with Trace.

That man was everything she ever wanted in a life partner. He made her feel like a princess, his princess, and she loved him more than she ever thought possible.

Picturing him in the jeans and leather jacket he'd worn while riding down the highway next to her on Raoul's Harley produced a welling of emotion that journeyed from her chest to her stomach and settled with a blast in her groin. Palpitations began to tease and had to be stopped. She crossed her legs, tightened her muscles and enjoyed her body's playful reminder of the sensations it could produce when aroused.

Together they made magic. Thinking about him, she couldn't wait till after her shift to get back home so they could reproduce the hot sweet love they'd managed the night before.

A groan jolted her from her fantasies. She watched as Arlene's eyelids lifted and then zeroed in on her visitor.

"You came?"

"Of course. Rusty called and said you asked for me. I had to pretend we were stepsisters so they'd let me in, but I'm here now. What happened to your hand, Arlene?"

Arlene's expression soured. "I got bit by a fucking cat. The doctor's sure that's where the infection originated. I was visiting a friend's place, and her neighbor's crazy-as-shit cat took an instant dislike to me."

"It did? Imagine that?"

Arlene grinned slightly, and then sobered.

"Is there anything you need, Arlene? I'm happy to get you whatever you want."

"Good! Because there's one huge thing you can do for me. Only you." Arlene struggled to sit up. Weak, in pain, she fell back. "You have to take my fight on Saturday."

"What?" Shocked to her core, Cassi leaned forward, and that's when she noticed Arlene's swollen, discolored hand. It had to hurt like a bitch. She felt sympathy welling up and a soft feeling of commitment seeped in before she closed it off.

"Rusty didn't tell you?" Eyes watering, drug induced, her face looked blotchy, and she appeared so sickly that Cassi's worry ramped up to where she choked back sudden, unexpected tears.

Shocked at her emotion, not realizing over the

last months she'd become so attached to Arlene, she took her healthy hand and squeezed.

"You don't know what you're saying. You're the fighter, not me. They can re-schedule the fight once you heal. I'll help you train again."

"No. You don't understand. Ariana's making a stink. Says if we don't produce you in the ring, she'll not only win by default, but she'll make it impossible for me to ever get a title bout again. She's got a lot of pull, Cass. You know she does."

"Maybe, but even she can't force the boxing commission to blackball you."

"She can if her uncle's on the committee."

"Aww, fuck."

"My sentiments exactly."

***

While driving to the gym, Cassi's mind flipped from one scenario to another, trying to find her way out of the rotten predicament prodding her conscience.

Lordy, I'm screwed.

As soon as she opened the door to his office and saw her old friend's face, she knew things were worse than she'd imagined. On the way over, she'd known that Rusty would never try and force her into doing something she didn't want to do. That was a given.

Instead, he did the opposite.

"Whatever Arlene said, you clean that crap outta your head, little girl. She's got no business trying to guilt you into fighting a match you never signed up for in the first place."

"She'll be blackballed. That's what she said. Is it true? Can they do it?"

"I don't know, brat. Ariana's uncle is a con artist and a crook. He's done a lot of illegal shenanigans in this business and gotten away with breaking the rules a number of times. Doesn't mean she can't go somewheres else and fight again."

"Oh, Rusty. Why would she do that when you're the best trainer in the state?"

"There's others, kid. Never doubt it. I don't want you forced into doing something against your principles. I've always known you hated the whole competition scene. So, let it go."

Rusty rolled up the posters he'd taken from the walls, a stack of them, and threw them into the trash. "You win some, you lose some. It's the way the game's played."

"Wait, what about the money you paid for Arlene to get this title bout? Will they refund it to you?" Even as the words left her mouth, she realized how stupidly naive they were. "Of course, they won't."

"It's not your problem, kiddo. Drop it. I just didn't want her making you feel responsible. It ain't right."

A knock at the door warned that they were going to be interrupted and sure enough, the same half-bald, too fat, promoter entered before Rusty even had a chance to ask who it was or go to the door and check.

"Hey, Rusty. Figured I better come in person and find out if the fight is still on or if your stand-in's a chicken. Ariana said she might refuse. Remember, if she says no, the clause you signed says you pay double the entrance money for a no-show."

Cassi swiveled in time to see Rusty blanch. Suddenly, he grabbed his black tuke off his head and slammed it onto the desk. His gnarled fingers shoved into his mop of thick white hair, standing it on end. His one clear blue eye blazed while his blind, milky-white one stared at nothing. "Christ on a stick, man. You couldn't wait until we were alone to start hassling me for the money? Freakin' asshole."

The overweight, sloppy dope headed toward Rusty who stood and shoved himself away from his desk. Though a foot shorter and thirty pounds lighter, the old fighter's hands formed fists and he growled. "Just keep a-coming, you prick. Why I'll lay you flatter than a pancake. Come on, you pussy."

Before the other could take Rusty up on his

invitation, Cassi stepped in front of him and her eyes dared him to move. Maybe it was the rage on her features, or the loose stance she'd taken of a person used to using her body in a fight, or maybe he just grew a brain.

He backed off with a parting shot. "You'll pay every cent old man. Or I'll get the authorities to close this joint down."

Cassi pushed at the creep's chest to get him out of her space. "That's not necessary. You tell Ariana for me, I'll meet her on Saturday. And tell her she'll be sorry she ever started this bullshit."

"No! Cassi," Rusty groaned his disapproval and reiterated loudly. "No!"

"Oh, yes, Rusty." Her eyes never left the pale-faced prick whose nasty smile slid from his face like a raw egg in a cold frying pan. "The fight's on."

Chapter
Thirty

That night, Cassi headed to work while trickles of apprehension played havoc in her belly. Earlier, being forced to step up on Rusty's behalf, she hadn't hesitated. Now, dread rode her something terrible.

Hell, she wasn't afraid to box. After all, only the first punch hurt. What bothered her was her reliance on the martial arts and how her mind automatically switched into using those other fighting techniques.

During their sparring, she controlled her urges with Arlene because they were training and Rusty watched their workouts like a hawk for any funny business. It took concentration, but because Arlene hardly ever stepped out of line, she managed.

Remembering back to those times when Arlene

had messed up, her nerves screamed the truth. The few occasions she'd pushed the limits, Cassi had instantly reverted to defense in whatever method worked. It came naturally. And it was against every rule of boxing.

In a real match, things were different. According to what they'd studied, Ariana liked to get her opponents into the corners, in a clinch where she could cross the line with her elbows, punish them with jabs and punches they couldn't escape.

Except, Cassi had no doubt she could break loose using other styles of scrapping, ways that would disqualify her and embarrass Rusty. And... they would lose her the fight.

She only had three days to get her shit together. Three days to let Rusty work his magic without her confessing her misgivings. Three days before she made a fool out of herself and her oldest, dearest friend.

***

"Okay, now that we have a few minutes peace, I gotta ask. What's got you looking like you lost your best friend, princess?" Sam leaned against the back counter with his arms crossed and his attitude of concern clearly obvious.

"First a request, though, you won't be happy, I need Saturday night off work. You know I wouldn't ask if it wasn't super important." Cassi leaned next to him, her arms crossed too, their shoulders touching.

Glancing sideways, Sam's eyes narrowed and he nodded. "Fine. You got it. Now tell me what the hell is worrying you."

"I got myself in a bit of a pickle. Arlene, Rusty's fighter, got a cat bite, it's infected, and she's in the hospital for who knows how long."

"So..."

"She had a title bout on Saturday; remember I warned you I might be a bit late because I promised her and Rusty I'd be there."

"Yeah, I remember. You're her sparring partner. I've seen you two going at it at the gym. I'd be at the fight, too, if one of us didn't have to work." He grinned at her disparaging snort. "You still haven't told me why you're so upset."

"Arlene's in the hospital with an infected hand. She won't be able to compete for weeks. But if Rusty cancels the fight, he loses a bundle and Arlene could be blackballed from any title bouts around here for one hell of a long time." She went on to explain the finer details of the crazy mess.

Sam's long face showed his unease. "They got Rusty by the short hairs for sure. I'm sorry, Cass. But I'll say this; my money's on you. There's no other female can take you, and you know it."

"Sure, if I was allowed to use everything I've

been trained for. But..." She shrugged her shoulders and faced her friend.

He responded. "Ohhh! I see what the problem is. Christ, sugar. Isn't there some way to shut off the various defense moves and strictly use those allowed for boxing?"

"God, Sam. I sure as hell hope so. If I can't control my instincts, I'm going to look like a fool in that ring and poor Rusty will be jeered out of the place."

Unseen by the two in deep discussion, Dani approached the bar and slammed her empty beer glass down so hard it broke. "Fucking cheap crap." She sucked at a small cut on her hand and looked sickly when she saw more blood appear. Before Cassi or Sam had a chance to react, she yelled. "I'm not paying you two to hold little tea parties in the corner, assholes. You're paid to look after the customers."

Dani'd been in a piss-poor mood for days and both Sam and Cassi had tried to either dodge her or bend over backwards to keep her smooth.

"Sorry, Dani." Cassi hurried over with a fancy tin she kept under the bar for emergencies. She chose the bandage that would protect the wound, and she reached for Dani's hand. "It's not too deep."

Dani allowed her to fuss, but her pissiness

increased. "What're you two jabbering about back there? Christ, I can't get no one to do their jobs properly, don't know why I even bother. First Rodrigo's been a pain in the ass and Pete's a prick and now you two are messin' up. I'm sick to death of all of you."

Cassi looked at Dani and saw her enlarged pupils and red-rimmed eyeballs. Whatever shit she'd snorted or stuck in her veins was reacting badly. She figured Dani would hate looking bad in front of her boys. "Let me help you upstairs so you can rest on your couch. You're messed up, Dani."

"Here, I'll take her." Sam's warning glare made Cassi back off.

"No. Leave me alone, Sam. I want Cass to look after me. Come 'ere Cassi-girl. Help me to my office. We can have a drink together."

This time, Cassi knew better than to accept the offer, still sure her last drink with Dani had been spiked with who knew what crap. She backed off. "Sam will take you."

Suddenly, standing tall, her dictatorial attitude re-enforced, she slammed her hand on the counter again, this time the glass pieces still there cut into the side of her palm.

"Fuck-kk! Now see what you've done, you big jerk." She shoved Sam in the chest and almost fell when he stepped back. Clumsily stumbling to gain her balance, she whined, "Cass, come help me. I'm sick of this joint and these bastards." She swung her arm to encompass her observant men in the room. "I need to get away. Take me home."

Pete seemed to appear out of nowhere. "I'll take her."

"No. I want Cass." Her voice whined like that of a little girl. Without any forewarning, she slumped and Sam caught her, picking her up in his arms.

Pete's loathing for her behavior clearly visible, furious at being put in the ridiculous position, he answered, "Dump her upstairs. We have places to go. Come on guys, we'll take care of the delivery without her. Who knows why the bitch is acting so freaking crazy lately?"

Harry, one of the older members in the gang, stepped up next to Pete. "The previous boss is back in town and messin' with her head. She'll get it together. Just give her time."

Pete swore. "There ain't no time for someone who can't take the heat."

Bigger than Pete by a foot, muscles everywhere, Harry's harsh tone made everyone in the place stop. "Listen, prick. You might be second-in-command, but that woman took over our boys when the last boss lost his shit. She's pure dynamite and don't you forget it." He headed out the door and the rest of the mob followed, Pete trailing them.

Cassi watched Sam carry his armful to the second floor while she cleaned the glass off the counter. Seeing as how the place had virtually emptied out, she worked the tables, too, helping the waitresses.

By the time Sam returned, she'd made up her mind. If Rodrigo and Dani were on the outs, the time had come for her to put her plan in place. If she hung in later than Sam, just maybe she could get enough evidence of Rodrigo's involvement so he'd spill the works about Dani to save his own ass.

Chapter Thirty-one

Sam carried Dani upstairs, acting like a gentleman. Knowing he was being watched, he handled her with care. His druthers would have been to toss her out back with the rest of the trash but her men would have reacted and not in his favor.

He laid her on the sofa next to the far wall across from her desk. He'd nodded to the guard at the end of the hallway, knowing the guy had seen the action downstairs and wouldn't question the reason for Sam to be in her office.

Therefore, he used precious moments to rummage through her desk drawers and into the files. He spotted her laptop on the corner table and quickly pulled out the stick he carried with him everywhere for just such an opportunity.

Stopped by a password protected entry, he cussed. What the hell would the bitch use? Again, he rummaged into her drawers looking for a notebook or address list where he might find something to help him. His mind traveled at warp speed from one option to another. Giving up, he started trying the simplest options like *Armas Jovenes.*

Nope. It wouldn't be that easy. He typed in Lipstick and then Lipstick Club as one word and again got the message that the password was incorrect.

Shit! What the hell would she have used? He tried her name in various ways and still no luck. Then he used her birthday with the screen not letting him in. With time running short, his eyes saw a photo she'd slipped into a hidden alcove on the shelf above. When he slid it out, he saw she'd taken it of Cass behind the bar, laughing at someone who had been cut from the picture.

Worry kicked up his adrenalin, and distaste for what the image represented brought out his protective instincts. The bitch had the hots for Cass, he'd always known that. But could it go further. Wanting her as a sex toy was one thing but did Dani have an unhealthy fixation for his friend?

Fuck me, this is not good. Cass thought she could play this woman but she was a babe in arms when it came to just how low some people were willing to go to get what they wanted.

Suddenly, he knew, then hesitated. Could it be that simple? He typed Cassi and the screen lit up.

Yesss!!

He inserted his drive and downloaded the five files he found on the desktop. Considering the broad wasn't stupid, he didn't think they would contain too much evidence but any little bit would help in their investigation.

He took a few seconds to open the one that said "Deliveries" and instantly saw why she'd been comfortable leaving the file on her desktop. It was all in code. Shit! He grinned. This would give the guys back at the bureau something to bitch about.

Once he'd copied and pasted everything he could find, he shut down all traces of his meddling and properly extracted the drive. Then he cleared his trail from the computer's history.

Finding her office colder than the rest of the joint, he took a few seconds to grab a cover off the end of the couch that he could lay over the woman whose drooling open mouth and smudged makeup filled him with disgust.

From the beginning, he'd had a strange respect for the chick whose power had her men bowing every time she spoke. Seeing her looking like a woman who'd hit bottom, he knew she had no one but herself to blame. She made the decision to sully her body with that shit, and she'd pay the price.

Lately, she'd gone ballistic and he wondered what drove her.

Harry's words earlier came back to mind. He'd said that she'd taken over the gang when their old boss hit the skids. The rumors he'd heard were that the guy lost control because she'd made it happen, that she'd played him and then took over his position. Now that he was back, whoever the asshole was, could she be worried? Is this what was making her so jittery?

He noticed her hand still bled from where she'd smashed it on the glass. He'd send Cass up to deal with it. No doubt, she'd be safe with the boss out cold.

The door opening made him turn to the guard who'd come to see what was taking him so long.

"She woke up, blabbered something about some guy who was coming to get her. I had to talk her down. Crazy dame is bonkers, right now." Sam pretended to shiver. "It's like an Alaskan winter in here. I covered her."

The guard, one of the long-time guys, nodded and whispered. "She's a cold bitch. Lately, she's been keeping the temperature so low, we're freezing our nuts off. Us guys hate when we have to work up here."

Sam moved out of the office and the guard followed. They closed the door. "Did you see her earlier downstairs? She cut her hand. It's still bleeding. I'll send Cass up to bandage it for her. Dani'll freak if she sees all that blood. For a woman who handles a gun like a pro, she sure is squeamish when it comes to her own body." Sam chuckled and relaxed when the other joined in. One never knew how far to push when it came to loyalty with her crew.

"The old boss has been making a lot of noise lately. It's spooked her. She'll come around. After all, when she saw how he'd been cheating the gang for ages, she handled it. Knew how to get rid of him then, and she can do it again."

Sam's nerves bristled and glee began rearing its pretty head. Was this guy a blabbermouth? He'd tried plucking information from just about everyone at the bar. Most kept their mouths tightly shut. Fear of retribution could be a huge detriment.

"I keep hearing stuff about this guy, the one everyone calls the *old boss*. Yet no one ever mentions him by name. Can't figure it out."

"That's cause most of us never knew his real name. It was the way he wanted it. The few times any of us saw him; we called him boss and minded our own business, which is what I suggest you do."

"Message received, bro. Thanks."

"No problem, man."

Chapter
Thirty-two

As she made her way upstairs, Cassi carried a dispenser of antiseptic wipes that Dani kept under the bar, along with a small tin of bandages and medicated cream that Sam had for emergencies. The guard expecting her grinned. He was one of the fellows she'd gotten a bit closer to, a man who loved the fights and who she'd run into at the sports center and even the gym.

While drinking at the bar, he'd made a few comments about her prowess, and she always gave him a free beer whenever no one else was around.

"Hey, Doug. You working guard duty tonight?"

"Unfortunately, yeah. It's colder than a witch's tit up here."

Cassi shivered and laughed. "Man, you can say that again. Dani likes the air conditioner turned right up." She waited as he opened the door to the office. When he flipped on the light, she saw what Sam had seen, a woman who looked more like a lost cause than a leader of men.

Dani's small frame lay slumped over the cushions, one arm hanging down and the other cuddled to her chest, bleeding onto her customary white, see-through blouse.

Wine-red hair she wore spiked every which way stuck out like she'd had a bad hair day, a horrible example of what no woman ever wanted to see in a mirror. So did the smudged make up, mascara-thickened eye-lashes that had blackened her cheeks and the smeared bright crimson lipstick.

Cassi moved closer and saw that Doug had backed out to take up his post next to where there was another party underway, the kind that went on every night, but Cassi stayed away from.

Glad that Faith no longer worked in the place, she shrugged and knelt beside Dani. Lifting her arm so as not to wake her, she used the wipes to clean away the blood. Tiny pieces of glass were embedded into Dani's skin where she'd slammed her arm on top of the mess. She'd have to remove them or risk infection.

"Cass?"

Dammit!

"Yeah. I'm just cleaning the glass from your wounds, boss. I'll be finished in a few seconds."

"What happened to me?"

Dani's voice sounded like a little girl's and trickles of apprehension started breaking out all over. *What in the world?*

"Hold still. You banged your arm on the bar where there was broken glass, and then I guess you fainted. Sam carried you up here and sent me to put some bandages on it to stop the blood."

"I'm bleeding? Oh my God. Is it bad?" Dani jerked her arm away from Cassi and swiveled to sit so she could see for herself. Instead, she fell over, too weak to be able to stay upright.

Using her arm around Dani's back for support, Cassi reached out to steady her. Uncomfortable as hell at being so close, she had no choice. The woman needed help, and Cassi had too big a heart to ignore her needs.

"Slowly. Here, let me steady you." She slid onto the sofa next to Dani and kept her arm where it was so Dani could shift over without doing a face plant on the floor.

"You're a good person, Cass." Dani staggered upright, leaning her head on Cassi's shoulder. Rising it slowly, she added, "And you're beautiful. I'm nuts about you." Without any forewarning, Dani's strength suddenly emerged. She locked her arms around Cassi, forcing a kiss onto her startled lips. Her hand wound itself tightly in Cassi's hair so turning her head away would involve pain.

Shocked to her core, Cassi didn't resist... at first. Until Dani's tongue became persistent in gaining an opening between Cassi's closed lips. Using her elbow to break Dani's hold, she pushed away from the other girl and then stuck her forearm between their faces to stop Dani's from sweeping in once again.

She reached for Dani's chin, gripping it firmly and backing away until they could look into each other's eyes. "Dani, I've told you no before."

"You don't mean it." Again, Dani's voice sounded like a whiny little girl. "I can give you anything you want, baby. It would be so good. Let me show you." Her hand snaked out to Cassi's chest, her fingers squeezing the breast underneath.

Horrified, Cassi swept the errant hand from her body, leapt to her feet and backed away. "Christ, Dani. Can't you understand? I'm not into you. Look, I'm sorry but you already know I-I'm attracted to men."

"Like that prick McGuire?" All of a sudden, Dani reverted to her normal self, mean-spirited and harsh. "I know. I saw him kissing you, his hands all over you and you loving it. Made me sick." Dani's sneering expression revealed total fury, which radiated in waves from her shaking body. Spittle flew from her lips while she cussed words too vile to repeat. She struggled to stand, then crumpled as her muscles refused to follow orders.

Cassi reached over to help her up, only to get roughly slapped. "Get away from me, bitch. I don't need you. Fuck off and don't come back." By the time the last words left Dani's mouth, she was screaming.

Cassi couldn't get away from the twisted madwoman fast enough. She raced downstairs and shook her head at Sam when his eyebrow rose with questions. First, she had to bite down hard on her lips to stop them from trembling before she could speak.

He reached to take both her arms and stared her down.

Forced to answer, she said, "I'm okay."

"I heard her tirade. You still work here?"

Cassi backed away, put her hands on her hips and dropped her head so her hair covered half her face. Shaking and still shocked by what had just occurred, she answered him. "Shit, Sam. I don't know."

Chapter
Thirty-three

All day, Trace had worked like a son a bitch so he could get as much stuff cleared away as possible. His goal was to get that prick, Chief Hank Lester off his back, something he spent many of his days working toward and not succeeding. The man had it in for him.

With his new partner, Michael, also giving him a hard time, he got a kick out of loading the guy down with a bunch of the despised paperwork and making him suffer.

Taking a breather, he checked the time, and saw he'd lasted well into the evening. Leaning back in his squeaky chair with his feet propped on his desk drawer, he scanned the window that let him see into the outer room.

A bank of screens circled the far end of the main space where officers did surveillance of populated areas, kept an eye on street cams set up all over the city, and generally controlled the busy downtown core.

Trace let his mind wander back a number of hours to the last call from Cassi. Something was up. She wouldn't discuss it on the phone, but he could tell by her voice that whatever she had to say, chances were, he'd not be liking it.

Apprehension rode him hard, increasing his worry. After he'd talked to her, he'd been a bastard to anyone who came within ten feet. Not that it bothered him to have some quiet time and keep his annoying new partner from bugging the hell outta him. Though he didn't feel comfortable when people he'd worked with for years, guys he liked, circled around like he radiated a strong smell.

Guess you can't have it both ways, idiot. He'd make it up to them tomorrow, stop on his way to work for a huge box of donuts, pass out a bit of his normal sweetness. He grinned. That *would* make 'em suspect.

Just when he thought the day would end well, the call came. Multiple gunshots had been reported at the warehouse where Raoul Santino had been shot. Word was, a stand-off between two neighborhood gangs had broken out and the bullets were flying.

Trace banged his fist onto his desk. *Crissakes!*

Couldn't he grab a break? He listened before replying, "Ten four, copy that. We're on our way."

He jerked his desk drawer open to grab his gun, reached for the Kevlar vest he kept close and bellowed for Kowalski, his new shadow.

They'd need to calm this shit down before there was a media frenzy wanting a hot story for the late-night news. Those hounds loved describing heinous acts of violence and stirring up a city already on the edge. The mayor with all his bureaucratic bullshit rode Lester enough without another mass shooting taking place.

Once he connected his radio, the SWAT captain communicated their details. Being the lead detective, Trace knew as soon as he arrived, he'd be called upon to take control.

Just when he thought he'd be home free for the rest of the night, this shit had to happen. With disgust imprinted on his features, his glare froze the grin Michael wore when they met at the elevator.

Straightening his expression, Michael started his questions. "What's up, boss?"

"Swat's been called to a shootout going down at the warehouse owned by the *Armas* gang. They'll keep us updated. Let's just get there as fast as we can and see if we can persuade those young punks to quit playing with guns."

For once, Michael appeared sober, his grin disappearing, being replaced with somber disgust. "Hell, guns don't scare me near as much as their fucking AK47s. Kids playing with toys, thinking it's like a video game where 'shoot to kill' is the object of winning."

"Sad but true."

When they reached the car, Michael held out his hand for the keys and grinned at Trace's refusal to pass them over. He shrugged and got into the passenger side.

"I'm a good driver, man. You'll have to let me behind the wheel sooner or later."

"Yeah, never works best for me." The car took the next corner on two wheels and the siren's scream produced a kind of reality check every cop took as their sign to buckle up and get ready. If one believed in prayers, the time had come to get them said.

Chuckling, holding the grab bar above his head, Michael added. "Since I arrived, I've canvassed the city, and I'm up on most of the directions. One day, me being new to the place won't be a good enough reason. You'll have to give over."

"Okay, one day. Which doesn't happen to be today. See that block. The warehouse is at the end there." Trace stepped on the gas, urging the already speeding car around the next corner and screamed to a stop behind the last SWAT team's vehicle.

The SWAT leader stepped forward, lowered his rifle and shook hands with Trace, who then introduced Michael.

"What's the scoop?"

"From the info we have, seems the *Armas'* boys got a delivery here to the warehouse, first one in a long time. *Los Soldados*, Mandala's crew must have gotten wind of it happening tonight. I gather they were hiding outside when the vans arrived. Rather than just taking out the drivers and the few expected guards and clearing out, they got caught when a bunch more *Armas* boys arrived late and saw what was going on. That's when the war began."

"Have we got eyes inside?"

"Working on it. A few of my men have gained access to the roof. From what they can make out, they're reporting mostly younger gang members left. The bigshots must have flown the coop. I've got a couple of sharpshooters strategically placed. They're waiting for orders to shoot."

"I need to see for myself. Is there any way inside where we won't get picked off before we even get within a few feet?"

"Sure, follow me but stay low. I can take you through the back way. We've closed it off so no one can escape."

Trace and Michael crept behind the captain until they were at the back of the building where Raoul's murder had taken place. Being here in the same spot sent shivers of alarm racing through Trace's system. Already pumped with adrenalin, his pulse rate spiked higher than was healthy.

"Shit! They got one of mine." Enraged, the leader edged forward not taking the care he should have. Trace watched as the captain dropped to the ground where a dead body sprawled, the SWAT uniform splattered with blood, the man's eyes open and vacant.

Before they could find cover, a figure jumped out from behind the same fence where Cassi had hidden the first time Trace had met her.

"Hold it right there, cops. You stop, or I'll shoot."

The swat team leader turned slowly to face his attacker, holding out his rifle, intending to drop it. Before he could do so, the kid panicked and fired multiple rounds. The captain's body took the bullets like a puppet with no finesse. When the shooting stopped, the man dropped.

Both Trace and Michael dove for cover in opposite directions. Trace had his gun in his hand before he hit the ground. "Hey, asshole, stop shooting at us. We're here to help you."

Michael called out from his side. "You're scared.

We get that, bro. But if you drop your gun, we'll play nice. I promise."

Michael's answer was another round of rifle fire, this time in his direction. His agonized screams could be heard by both Trace and the panicked kid. *Shit, he's hit.* The bellowing seemed to hold a lot of power for a wounded man but his reaction shook Trace who couldn't just stand by and let his partner bleed out.

Fuck!

Coming out of hiding to get a cleaner shot, Trace fired continuously toward the fence. Just before a bullet clipped him, he fired one straight and true, hitting the sniper.

Then he collapsed.

Chapter
Thirty-four

Cassi worked till the end of the shift, waiting for Dani to appear, shrieking she was fired, but nothing happened. She still hadn't come to terms with Dani's attack. That woman was strong. There's no doubt, if she'd been at her best, Cassi might have had trouble getting away from her.

Thankful the boss hadn't reappeared, Cassi again blinked away tears that had threatened her since the episode.

Sickened by being forced to reject Dani so vehemently, she thought back over the last months. She'd never flirted or given the boss reason to think she was interested in a relationship, just the opposite.

Now, expecting she'd get her walking papers, it made her ill to think she hadn't gotten the evidence they'd need to frame Rodrigo into spilling the beans about the night Raoul was killed.

Suddenly, the lazy atmosphere behind the bar changed. Sam took a call, something he rarely did while working. His expression hardened. She wished she knew what he'd heard to make him so serious all of a sudden.

"Hey, princess, I need to get away early tonight. You want to close the joint for me. There's only a short time left. I'll go and hustle those last parasites to clear out."

"Sure, Sam. No problem."

Yes! Just when she thought she'd lost her opportunity to check out below, she caught a break. "Can I just run out to my car for a second? I left my purse there with my makeup bag, and I wanted to pretty myself before I meet Trace later."

He nodded but didn't grin. He'd normally have made a comment about her being a fussy female, and that kinda worried her.

"You okay, Sam?"

"Yeah. I'm good. Go get your girlie shit. I'll start the clean-up."

She ran out to the trunk of her car and retrieved her purse. Frantically, she searched for the parcel she'd bought some time ago and slid it inside her large bag. Then she returned to find Sam anxiously waiting for her.

"I'm off, Cass." Within a very short time, Sam

had locked the doors and disappeared, leaving her with the responsibility to count the cash and oversee the nightly cleaners. Wearing earbuds and glazed expressions, they worked to their own rhythm, seldom paying any attention to what she or Sam did in their area behind the bar.

Once she'd cleaned up, cashed out and had the money safely stored for deposit the next day, she edged closer to the back room, carrying a loaded tray of empties for the cleaners to take away when they finished.

Finding the hidden key so she could unlock the camouflaged passage downstairs, she grabbed the article she'd fetched from her car, a few miscellaneous items she decided might come in handy and her cell phone to use as a flashlight if needed. Then she tiptoed down the long flight of curving stairs.

She stopped at the first turn and listened, her pulse throbbing so hard she almost threw up. Deathly quiet, she took a few deep breaths. *Stop acting like such a wuss! What can they do to you if you're caught?*

Not liking the answer that came to mind, she wiped her hand on her pants and squared her shoulders. She came to the next bend and saw a lighted area ahead. Searching, she found the camera she expected to be there above her with the red light turned on that said someone was able to see what was happening in the room.

Listening, hoping the heartbeats roaring in her ears weren't heard by anyone behind the last twist, she took a few more tentative steps.

She ducked underneath the moving lens and scanned the area for another but found nothing. Quickly, she placed the piece of duct tape she'd thought to bring as a precaution over the lens.

Now she had a few seconds to set up her motion activated camera. Since no one appeared to be in the room, she surveyed the area for the best spot to leave her toy.

All she saw were tables for counting money in the middle of the large room and three huge safes against the walls at the far end. Stumbling, relief coming so fast it weakened her knees, she took out the device she'd bought that looked like an old clock. Configured, ready to go when she pressed the start button, she moved forward.

Trace's taping of his mother's death had given her the idea that just maybe, she could catch Rodrigo in the same way.

These fools felt totally safe in their little hidey-hole. They had no reason to think anyone could break in without them knowing. So, she didn't think they'd do any kind of sweeps to find taps or alien equipment that could be used by police to indict them.

After questioning Maria on her last visit to Billy's law office, a meeting discussing Mary Devin's defense, she'd pumped the woman for clues as to whether it was lawful to hide a camera and surreptitiously video people who were unaware that they were being taped.

Turns out, the video could be inadmissible as evidence in a court of law because it would be on private property and without the people's consent.

On the other hand, if she threatened to release the tape to the press, Rodrigo couldn't put the lid back on the opened can. And knowing how hungry the reporters were for just this kind of news about the hated neighborhood gangs, she knew it would make the evening news... as would Rodrigo.

Quickly, she found the best spot to hide the clock next to a bunch of miscellaneous, dusty junk on top of a cabinet with shelves full of what looked like broken-down old calculators and boxes of rubber bands. It needed to be in the right spot to be able to cover the main section of the room so it could pick up everyone who walked around the area.

Satisfied with her choice, she turned to leave. Ducking down, she ripped the tape off the camera and slipped it into her pocket. Heading to the stairs, she jumped when a voice she didn't recognize rang out.

"Stop there, bitch. Put your hands where I can see them."

She turned slowly and saw a youngish wannabe wearing a soldier-type outfit, his rifle aimed at her heart. Before she could say anything, another stranger joined him, and he was carrying, too.

Sweat broke out. She began to shake. How the fuck was she going to talk her way out of this mess?

Chapter
Thirty-five

Racing toward the hospital in the ambulance, the attendant replaced Michael's make-do pressure with proper bandages to stop the flow of blood gushing from Trace's wound. All during this procedure, Trace never quit grouching. Stunned at what his partner had just revealed, he repeated, "You screamed to throw buddy off and then you were intending to do what?"

The EMT grinned at the derision and disbelief Trace had used. Michael winked at him before answering Trace.

"I hoped he'd think I was no longer a threat. Figured to work my way around behind him. After he shot you the first time, he was hit but he wasn't done."

"I know. He'd recovered enough to try again. Never been so scared in my life seeing the prick standing over me and aiming. Fucker had the most evil smile on his face." Trace shuddered.

"Greaser didn't die easy. It took two more bullets to send him down to his maker."

"Hell, if you hadn't been there to take that first shot, I'd be your ex-partner."

"Hey, bro. You're the one who's the hero. He'd turned on me after I shot the first time. If you hadn't struggled for your gun and plugged him, I'd be lying next to you here instead of holding your soft little hand."

Trace tried to pull his fingers free and let out a loud groan that ended in a string of cuss words. Michael held on. "Hey. The medic says I need to support your arm. Quit being a whiny baby."

Trace knew when he was being played and this time, when Michael teased, Trace knew it for what it was. Not smart-ass bullshit, but a way of bantering that came natural to his partner. Instead of opposing, the time had come to play along.

"Okay, Mikey. Hold my hand if it turns you on. But I draw the line at kissing."

A guffaw broke from the technician who'd been quietly doing his job of setting up an intravenous. He grinned at Trace now and when their eyes connected, his were full of approval.

Chapter Thirty-six

Cassi's throat was so dry, she didn't say a word. She followed the orders not to move.

"What're you doing here, woman?" The taller of the dudes swaggered closer, his expression mean and yet interested. "Keep your gun on her, Al. I heard she's a tricky one. Works the bar upstairs. Don'tcha, sugar?"

Cassi nodded and stood ready. Her legs apart while her hands hung loose, breathing her way through the awful tension, calculating, watching. She didn't recall either of the two men. Thinking they probably spent most of their time upstairs rather than at the downstairs bar.

The one who walked around her too close for comfort, sizing her up with his enlarged pupils, his stenchy breath, and his gun propped over his shoulder, reminded her of a kid she knew in high school. He'd been bullied for years and it drew her sympathies. Until she found out that the weirdo had put up with it because it made him important, someone who got attention.

When Raoul tried to stop the bullshit, the kid turned on him instead. That's when she'd been forced to accept the sick truth. He'd told Raoul to leave things alone and mind his own business. Cassi had never forgotten that loser and for some reason, this dude reminded her of the poor slob.

The other man of medium height and build stayed in the background. She'd never seen another who so deserved the term – ordinary. His hair was shaggy, brownish, with no life, dull. So were his lackluster eyes and even the clothes he chose to wear. Beige and boring, they let him fade into his surroundings where he seemed most comfortable.

It was this man who scared her.

Yappy kept circling her, making a lot of noise and saying nothing.

"I thought I heard something odd so I came to investigate." She spoke the first lie she'd practiced while making her way down the stairs.

"Bullshit, bitch. It's quiet as a tomb down here. You couldn't have heard what never happened, could she Al?"

Cassi looked at Al. Even the name suited the

dude. He never spoke, just shook his head, his rifle never wavering from being aimed at her midsection. "Okay, I was snooping. I've been working here for months now, and I saw stuff. It made me curious." Maybe she could talk her way out of this mess.

"You'll have to try harder to convince us, right Al? We could be talked into letting you go, but only if you're willing to pay for your recklessness."

"I'm a bartender for crissakes. I have no money."

"Maybe not but you have a hot body, bitch. I'd be willing to look the other way if you decided to be nice to us, convince us of your innocence. We'd be open to discussing options, right Al?"

Al didn't move, and this time he didn't nod. But he did smile and it sent shivers rioting all over her. Okay, there was something not ordinary about the stoner. His yellowed teeth were sharp and twisted in front as if a childhood illness had destroyed his blackened gums.

Creeped out now, unwilling to let the conversation continue when she knew they'd have to kill her before she'd willingly let either one of them touch her, she braced for the first move.

"I don't think so, boys. Although the invitation is tempting, I somehow think my boyfriend would be disappointed in me if I agreed."

Deciding to get it over with while she still had

enough strength to make a play, she swiveled and reached for her adversary's gun. Using it as a device to yank him off balance, she crouched, flipping him over her back. Her elbow did a number on his face just before he rolled off the table and onto the floor.

Circling fast, she kicked out at Al's knee. Hesitating to shoot because of his partner being in the way was a mistake he'd regret. He flew backwards, dropping the gun so he could use his hands to break his fall.

Before she could get in close and finish him off, he'd leapt to his feet and had a total attitude transformation. There was life in his expression now, joy in his eyes and utter glee in his disgusting toothy grin. "Man, oh, man, I'm gonna love this." He crunched his fists, the crackling knuckles sounding like gunshots in the quiet.

Fuck! This dude scared her speechless. "You don't want to do this, Al."

"Yeah. You know, I kinda do." He cackled and started toward her.

He might be strong and wily, but thank God, he didn't have eyes in the back of his head. Plus, his hearing wasn't the best or he'd have heard Sam inching his way down the stairs behind him, carrying the gun he kept at the bar.

Her heart began slowing. She felt weak with

relief. Until hands suddenly snaked around her legs and toppled her over onto the floor. Slithering up behind and brutally choking her, the asshole she thought she'd dealt with forced Cassi to her knees. "Stop right there, Sam. I'll kill her, I swear."

"What the hell is going on down here? I came back to get the night deposit and heard a crash. Then I see you two messing with my bar partner. Dani's not going to like this shit, neither is Rodrigo. You better let her go."

"No way, man. She broke in down here, we caught her."

"Cass? What the hell?"

She looked at Sam and saw the message he didn't need to put into words. He expected her to take care of the situation. She dropped her face to her chin as if ashamed and felt the idiot behind her relax his hold slightly.

Giving no warning, she slammed her head backwards, connecting, hearing the crunch of a broken nose. Ignoring the expected resulting pain, she reacted before the victim behind even figured out what happened to him. Wheeling around, she slammed the bottom of her palm onto his chin, knocking him out cold.

Head pounding, she turned to see that Sam had taken care of Al, whose body lay sprawled on the floor. The gun he now held by the barrel used as a hammer.

"Seriously, sugar? What the hell were you thinking, coming down here?" He slid the gun into his belt at the back.

"I know, Sam. Dumb move. But I can explain."

"No time for that. The reason this place was empty tonight was because the gang had a delivery, this time at the old warehouse. Most of the boys were there."

Sensing he wasn't finished, she waited impatiently.

"That's the reason I left in such a hurry. I heard they had a problem with the *Soldados*. Those two gangs are always warring."

"Sergio Mandala's guys?"

"Yeah. You know about them?"

"I know Sergio. It's a long story." His expression worried her. As if her heart sensed the imminent pain, emotions controlled a few seconds earlier turned suffocating.

"I called your phone but you'd obviously turned off the sound. And that's not like you. So, I drove back here worried Dani recovered and she tried more funny stuff."

"How did you know I was down here?"

"José finished cleaning, and he and his crew were packing up to leave. He said the last time he noticed, you were taking the empties to the storeroom. I checked it out and it was pretty easy to track you once I heard the brawl."

"So, what happened at the warehouse, Sam?"

"You gotta stay calm, princess. Swear."

"Fuck. Okay, I swear, now tell me why you had to find me. And do it fast, because I'm losing it here."

Sam's fleeting grin disappeared. "Yeah, okay. The cops got called to the shootout at the warehouse. Trace was lead detective and ended up getting himself shot. Hell, girl. Don't faint on me." He dove to grab her around the waist and support her. "He's okay. Look, I need you to be tough."

Shaken, sobs building, she fought to control the urge to scream. "He's only wounded? Honest to God?"

"Yeah, took one in the upper arm, and he's giving them hell at the hospital. Says he's not staying. They need you to go and calm the crazy dude down."

"What about these two?"

"Don't worry. I've got some friends who'll deal with them. Go on now."

She rushed to bestow a swift kiss on his cheek. "Thanks, Sam. I adore you."

"Yeah, well, I kinda like you too, princess. Now fuck off and let me fix your mess."

Chapter
Thirty-seven

Cassi had promised Sam she would drive carefully but her need to get to Trace overrode her customary caution. Sweaty hands on the wheel, her body arched forward the whole way, her foot heavy on the gas, shaky, she prayed every mile of the way. "Please God. Please God. Don't let him be hurt badly. Oh, please..."

Once parked and running to the desk, she tried to calm down so they wouldn't turn her away. By the time they gave her directions to his room, she'd lied about her status as his fiancée and would have said anything so they'd allow her to see him.

When she arrived at his open door, it was to find a stranger, blood smeared on his shirt and pants, slumped in the chair next to the bed, and Trace lying with his upper body bandaged and appearing to be asleep.

As soon as he saw her, the visitor jumped up and grabbed her arm. For all his speed, his touch was surprisingly gentle. He forced her back out to the hallway. "Who are you?"

"Cassidy Santino. Detective McGuire is my fiancé."

"Nope. Trace isn't engaged. Try again?"

"You're Michael Kowalski, Trace's new partner. I'm his girlfriend. I work at the Lipstick Club. Sam, the bartender, told me that Trace had been shot. I came as fast as I could."

"So, you're the one that brings those goofy smiles to his otherwise poker face. Hell, honey, you're about an hour too late. They had to sedate the sucker. Talk about a horse's ass? He was determined to leave and get to you before you heard about the incident."

Her heart did a summersault and then settled into rhythm only slightly faster than usual.

"He's kind of difficult to persuade when he's made up his mind." She felt a silly smile light up her face and all her affection for Trace showed in her wobbling lips and her sudden tear-filled eyes. Now that she was here, her tight control started to wither and the shakes took over.

"Hey! Cassidy. He's fine. Come on, don't fall apart now. He needs you to be strong. Hell, I need you to be strong. You're the only one who can keep the big idiot in this bed where he belongs. He's weak from blood loss and madder'n hell at those *Armas* guys. He needs to calm down and let his body start healing. You tell him, okay?"

Liking this man more with every word he spoke, Cassi started to laugh with relief. Trace must be in better shape than she'd imagined on the hellish trip here. And this guy cared about him. She saw it, sensed it.

"Heck, you're his partner. You tell him. Me, I'm putty when it comes to giving him his way. Truly! No backbone. Pure silly putty."

"Well, hell!" Teasingly, Michael shook his head as if in total despair. "If neither of us can control the sucker, maybe we should just pull the plug."

Laughing, she stepped toward the door. "Can I see him?"

"Sure. I'll be right out here. Can you let me know when he comes to? I can't leave until I know he's good."

"Of course." Cassi reached out and touched Michael's hand. "Of course, I can."

She stepped back into the room and tiptoed to the bed. Standing next to it, her eyes greedily scanned Trace's face and body and her hands reached to touch and caress.

Less disturbed after meeting Michael and sensing his calm, she let her fingers soothe Trace's slightly bearded cheek and then travel through his soft hair and push it away from his tanned face. Leaning over, she kissed his lips ever so gently.

Suddenly, she felt weak, like the muscles in her legs had decided to take a nap. She sunk into the chair Michael had vacated and breathed deeply.

Scanning her surroundings, she stared first at the machines near the bed, a monitor and computer, a network of tubing, an IV which they had attached to Trace's arm and trays holding a plethora of instruments. She saw the oxygen breathing tube on the covers next to his pillow which most likely meant that he'd removed it.

She could hear beeping and see the numbers on the monitor above. Expecting that meant his readouts were activated, she knew very little about each number other than blood pressure and heart rate. Feeling reassured that his were fairly normal, she let her head drop to the bed near him and gave thanks.

His hand on her head stopped her from jerking upward. Instead, she let him stroke her and waited with her breath caught in her throat.

"I love the smell of your hair." His voice was weak.

"I'm sorry I woke you."

"Don't be. I willed you to come. Can't settle until I know you're okay."

Cassi slowly lifted her head so his hand moved to touch her cheek, to wipe away the tears she hadn't realized had fallen.

"No one could keep me away."

"I bet Michael tried." Trace grinned slightly.

"Yeah, I told him I was your fiancé."

"And he believed you."

"Not for a minute."

"He give you a hard time?" Teasing about her fighting abilities, he added, "Hell, is he a patient now, too?"

Cassi giggled, loving his humor. "Nah! He seemed to know who I was when I told him my name and where I worked. He was cool."

"Did he go home?"

"Nope, he's waiting till you wake up. Says he can't leave till he's sure."

"Sure? About what?"

"Why, I imagine, until he's sure you're good. At least, those were his words."

Cassi saw the gratification Trace tried to hide. This pleased him. It pleased her, too. "Do you want me to call him in so he can go home and get some rest?"

"Yeah. I better let the boy off the leash."

Cassi grinned. The fond way Trace spoke let her know a bond had been forged between the two men. Partners who worked together every day needed to trust. And liking each other certainly helped in that process.

Trace pulled himself upright as far as he could, probably so he wouldn't be at a disadvantage in front of the other man. She helped him up and ignored the cussing about bullets, stupid gangs, and hotshot kids that thought they were Bugsy Siegel. Finally settled, he reached for her, forcing her to bend over.

"Before you fetch the kid, I want to know about what you mentioned on the phone. It's been on my mind."

Suddenly her whole world flooded back and all the crap she had going on settled around her once again. The mess she'd left for Sam to clean up at the club, Dani, and even worse, the upcoming boxing match with Ariana Wilde.

She couldn't tell him about any of that now, not when he was lying in a hospital bed and needed to stay there.

Playing for time, she pretended to look confused.

"You know, the shit you wanted to share after work."

Fuck! Another lie. Her soul couldn't take it. She couldn't face him and bullshit at a time like this. Suddenly, she had the perfect story.

"After you say goodbye to Michael, I'll tell you.

And quit worrying, not all my shit is bad."

Chapter
Thirty-eight

Trace had needed time alone with Michael. To get Cassi out of the room, all he could come up with was to get her to tell the nurse he wanted something to eat. Truth is, he'd choke on anything right now.

But he'd had to give Michael the names of the files he should read over and familiarize himself with. The more information the guy had in his head, the better chance they'd have of locking up some of the offenders they'd brought down tonight.

Gathering crap on Dani and her gang to add to the growing pile would ensure a long stay for her one day in the state prison. Or, at least, it was what he planned. He explained it all to Michael and then added, "Any word on who might have pulled the trigger on Santino would be appreciated. And if

Bradford's one of the assholes we picked up earlier, I want to know about it right away. And be careful with the dude. He's dangerous."

"Yes, Sir."

"Don't mess with me, Mike. That guy scares the crap outta me. He's mean as they come and has a list of offenses pretty well from the time he was toilet trained."

"Gotcha! Mean sucker, watch out."

"Fuck! You're driving me crazy, man. Look, just keep me in the loop, Mike. I mean it."

"Shit, yeah! Otherwise you might decide to come back before we're ready for you." Joking his way through a lot of the conversation was acceptable for Michael. About this, he didn't. "I'll be calling in with every tidbit I come across, Trace, until you're fucking sick of hearing my voice."

"Hell, I'm a big boy now. I can take it."

Michael laughed and headed out the door, holding it open to let Cassi back in before he left.

Trace reached for Cassi's hand. "Thanks for telling the nurse I was hungry."

"You're not really hungry, are you? You could have just asked me to step out for a few minutes, Trace. I know you have important police stuff you need to talk to your partner about. I'm not a baby." Cassi's smile took the sting from her words, and he appreciated her tact.

"You're right. Next time, I'll do that, sweetheart. Now tell me your news."

Chapter Thirty-nine

Cassi settled next to Trace and held his hand. They kissed. Her breath caught from the wave of emotions created by his seeking, warm lips. Melting, oozing with adoration, it was all she could do to stay in the chair. Impulses of climbing into bed and nestling down beside him had to be controlled.

"Trace, behave."

"No." He moved in for another kiss, this one blistering. His lips were greedy and devastating in their attack on her senses.

"Stop. I can't. We can't. I mean it. Damn, you're a tease." Finding the strength to pull away, she grabbed the hand that had crept around her shoulder. "Behave."

She loved his hands. They'd protected her in some of the worst times she'd lived through recently. They soothed her soul whenever and wherever they stroked her body. And they lifted her to paradise every time they made love.

His hungry stare, zeroing in on her mouth, begged her to let him have his way. "You're driving me crazy, woman."

"Back atcha, bud. Don't make me go and sit by the wall." She chuckled at his disappointment.

"Then keep me amused. Tell me what you promised on the phone." He squeezed her fingers gently.

"Okay. Like I said, it's good to be able to share news that's not a downer. It's about Sunshine, you know Faith Whitely, Raoul's girl. Remember I told you about her losing Raoul's baby? Well, while she was recuperating from her concussion and knife wound in the hospital, she scared me. Talk about being depressed and lost, it seemed like she had nothing left to live for."

"I remember how sad you were about the situation. You wanted to help her."

"I was terrified. I had the impression she was suicidal, and I hated seeing her suffer. I knew it was impossible for her to return to the club. Even Dani agreed she should leave. Why would she want a girl working there who was so messed up? When I told Faith, I hoped she'd be happy. Instead, she couldn't care less."

"Darn shame. I remember her in the ambulance at the club before they took her away. She's quite a beauty."

"She is, inside and out. Surprising, considering the life she's led."

"So what's the good news?"

"Something fantastic happened while she was in the hospital. There was a newborn there abandoned by his mother, and the poor baby couldn't be soothed. Not by the nurses or even his father. When Faith came along a miracle happened. The little guy took to her, and she fell in love. The father, obviously being a very intelligent man" – at this point, Cassi grinned at Trace and got an answering smile acknowledging her joke – "he hired Faith to be the baby's nanny."

"Hey, that is good news. How did he handle her confession about her earlier profession?"

"She hasn't told him."

"Oh oh, not good. The guy deserves to know. Not that it should make a difference if she loves the baby and does a good job, but he has a right to make the decision with full knowledge of her background."

"I agree. Unfortunately, she refused to take the chance he'd back away. She needs to be with little Raoul right now. She's desperate."

"Raoul? That's the baby's name?"

"Since the mother ran off, the father didn't know what to call his son. When Faith suggested Raoul, he liked it."

"Whoa! That's kind of heavy."

"He accepted that the name belonged to someone she'd loved and lost. At least, she's been up front on that score. Soon, she'll be moving into his ex-wife's apartment. From what I understand, they were separated and not living together. He was going to pay her upkeep so she'd look after the baby. That's what he told Faith. I'm waiting to hear from her to let me know where she's at so I can visit."

Trace pushed her hair behind her ear and stroked her cheek. "You're like a mama bear when it comes to people who matter to you, baby, aren'tcha?"

His tender gaze made her insides melt. "I care about my friends, Trace. Isn't that what people are supposed to do?"

"Uh huh. But not a lot follow that rule. They tend to forget real easy when the going gets tough. Not you, though. Look what happened to Billy Duran? Street trash, and yet you took him in and cared for the loser."

"He wasn't always like that, Trace. He hit bottom, is all. I knew him when he was a student, working hard to get his law degree."

"And I knew him as a snitch, telling all for enough money to buy his next fix."

Cassi heard the growling tone and knew he didn't trust Billy after he'd found out the guy had come to her for help. "He's back from rehab and doing fine. Mary Devin's case has started now, and they're working it."

"They?"

"He has an assistant, Maria Delgado. She's the digger or so that's what he calls her. She's the one going through all previous cases for sources and strategy, finding precedence as defense for Mary. She's hoping they can clear this through the lower court rather than having a big trial. Billy says there isn't a chance, but if she's determined, he'll use whatever she finds."

"Has she found anything they can use?" Trace listened while his eyes roamed her face.

"Not yet. Thing is, any previous case, if used as precedence, has to be identical for it to apply, but Mary's case is unique in that she never actually killed anyone. It makes things difficult, and the judge is being extremely cautious because of the backlash from the media."

"That's totally understandable. What about the preliminary hearing?"

His hand still sifted through her hair, playing with it, turning her insides to mush. God, she loved this man. "It was today."

"Do you know the results?"

"Just what I saw on the news, and as far as I understood, there will be a trial."

"Not surprising. It's what I expected. I'll admit Billy's working the exposure, using public opinion to help win his case. There sure are a lot of people with varying opinions. I never imagined it would get so much coverage."

"I know. He's been on TV a lot, on talk shows and news stations. I didn't realize he was such a mover."

"You mean a camera hog."

"Trace!"

He chuckled at her expression. "Hell, as long as he gets Mary justice, I'll be happy."

"Me, too."

"I meant to ask you, how's Arlene doing? Is she ready for the big fight tomorrow night?"

Bus-ted!

Chapter Forty

Cassi squirmed, taking time to think of a way not to lie, yet not give away that she would be Rusty's fighter in the ring. Her eyes lit on Trace's bandage, and she knew exactly what to say.

"You never mind me and my stuff. What about you getting shot? You've been trying to change the subject to everything but the obvious?"

He had the grace to look sheepish. "Yeah, about that. A kid with a gun got lucky."

"Hell, Trace. In your world there're too many kids with guns. It scares me to death how many times you're in a dangerous situation, getting shot at or saving others who're in a shootout."

"I know, baby. But it's my job. You've always known that." He stiffened and dropped his hand.

She watched the fear on his face and knew her vocalizing her worry scared him. She'd heard that a lot of cop's families broke up over the stress from the job. And it made sense to her whenever she let herself think about the danger for Trace. She also knew that someone had to protect others and having the worry of a misguided girlfriend or wife to deal with on top of the danger wouldn't help the individual when they already had enough shit on their plate.

Time to soothe the big guy. "I'm proud of what you do, Trace. And since it's the career you've chosen, then I'm good."

His answering grin faltered, and then slid right off his face. "I wish I could say the same about your recent career." He grouched his comment and she had to laugh at the now sour expression that appeared.

"Well, quit worrying. After what happened tonight, I doubt I'll be there much longer."

He sat up too quickly and covered his cuss word with a groan. "What happened tonight?"

Shit! Would her tongue never check with her brain before it waggled? She thought fast and finally said, "You know." *Brilliant...That's all you can come up with? Think. Think!*

"Oh, you mean the warehouse debacle."

"Uh, yeah!" *Phew!*

"The *Armas* gang will hurt for a while. Between the Soldados and the police, we seized most of their shipment. From what I saw, we also took out a few of their boys, but they'll regroup like the slugs they are. Figure there'll be repercussions for Sergio Mandalas. He'd better start watching his back."

"Oh, I imagine he's been doing that for some time now."

"And you would know, right? He's another of your buddies."

She dropped her face into her hands. The giggle that burst forth couldn't be stopped.

"What's so doggone funny? Share, baby. I need a good laugh, too."

Merriment eased the terrible ache that had lingered in her head from her earlier showdown. A headache had ridden her scalp and the tension she experienced from the pain radiated through her neck and tight shoulders. "I'm just thinking that we make a good pair. Both of us live dangerously and try to protect the other from our everyday routine. Do you think we'll ever be able to openly share our news?"

"That's my dream, darlin'. To come home to you every night and live a normal life. You telling me about your day at the library and me grouching about the paperwork at the office."

"Sounds perfect, except for one thing."

He stiffened. "What's that?"

"I'll never go back to work at the library. It

wouldn't satisfy me now."

"I was afraid of that. Please tell me you don't want to be a cop. Please."

"I don't want to be a cop." She grinned and kissed his cheek. "I'd rather work with the FBI."

"What!" He jackknifed and cussed again.

Laughing softly, she held him in her arms and whispered. "I'm teasing, Trace. When this is all over, I want to go to law school."

Chapter
Forty-one

Spending hours sleeping in a chair next to Trace's bedside at the hospital had added to Cassi's discomfort. Kinks in her neck, stiff shoulders and a sore ass forced her to stretch every so often.

Trace finally talked her into leaving in the early morning hours, and she'd headed straight for the steam room in her basement. She followed that up with a good workout on her home equipment.

Keeping in mind that she'd need to be as limber as possible for the training session Rusty would be putting her through later in the day, she didn't push herself too hard. Heading upstairs for the kitchen, she turned on her cell phone and saw the calls waiting.

She accessed Rusty's voice message and noticed there was a flashing light on her home phone too. He must have called sometime after she'd shut off her cell on the way downstairs at the club. When she didn't answer there, he tried her here too.

"Cass, I bin thinkin'. I want you to be absolutely sure that you're not being blackmailed into doing something you'll hate. If you back out, I'll understand, kid. No pressure, I promise. Call me."

Rather than calling him back, she gathered her gear and headed to the gym. Until he saw her in person, he wouldn't calm down and she needed him relaxed for tonight.

The nervous fear in his voice came through loud and clear. She also heard the excitement that he couldn't hide. He'd always said she'd be his dream fighter. Now he was getting his wish.

All the way over, she fought the urge to head her car in the opposite direction and gun it. Crap! This was her worst nightmare. Getting into the ring with a pro and having to clamp down on everything she was trained for.

To win!

No matter how.

***

Once she was in the ring and sparring with a partner Rusty'd chosen to work with her, she settled down. Since she'd be fighting in the Featherweight division, he'd gotten one of the old Featherweight pros, a man who'd been around for years and often worked with Rusty's fighters. He was one of Cassi's favorites around the gym.

Adam had been a champion, still was, only he'd had to stop his career due to adult onset Asthma – can't fight if you can't breathe. But he could train and had been working with her and Arlene for a few weeks. Ever since Arlene had talked Rusty into signing her up for the title bout with Ariana.

Rusty let out another bellow. "Why are you clinching, Cass? You need to conserve your energy, stay out of the corners. You're always on to Arlene about that same thing and now you're the one pulling that shit."

Cassi backed away from Adam and lowered her hands as a signal to stop. "Sorry, Rus. I'm controlling my impulses to use my feet." The words slipped out before she realized what she'd revealed. Dropping her head, she hid her eyes so he couldn't see the worry.

"What the hell? Your feet... Oh! That's what's got you tied up in knots."

"What do you mean?"

"Don't play cute with me. Ya think I didn't know sumphin was eatin' atcha? What, you figure I'm blind? I don't know my fighters?"

"No, Rusty. I—"

"You gotta understand, little girl. I've been at this game since before you was a twinkle in your papa's eye. You're not scared Ariana will beat you.

You're scared you'll whup her ass but break the rules doing it."

"Man, I'm sorry, Rus." Cassi slumped. With her shoulders droopy, she confessed. "When I'm sparring with Arlene, I control my instincts because I seldom feel threatened. But tonight will be different. What if I forget and lash out?"

"So, what if you do? It's no biggie. There's no title on the line. As long as you show up, Arlene gets to keep her boxing stats and Ariana her title. And she'll get what's coming to her, mean little bitch that she is. God, kid, you had me worried."

Cassi felt the tightness in her chest begin to ease.

"Hell, now I can enjoy the show without giving a rat's ass about you taking a beating. All I'm gonna say is this. Don't let her work you over. She likes to beat her opponents into a pulp before she finishes them off. When you've had enough, do whatever it takes, doll, and I'll back you to the hilt."

Smiling, her world back in place, Cassi crouched down at the side of the ring so she was eye-level to her best friend. "You've taken a load off, old man. I was terrified to embarrass you tonight."

"You could never do that, Cass. Never in a million years." His gnarly fingers patted her cheek. That he hit her harder than necessary was just his way of emphasizing his words.

She stared him down, relieved that he didn't

flinch. "It's just a fun match?"

"Yep. They've featured you as the lead-up to one of the main events." Rusty's tuke was at the back of his head, and the white mop that always needed trimming stuck out everywhere. His one good eye, blue as a summer's sky and not clouded over like the blind one, twinkled now with glee. "Ariana can't put up her title because you're not a pro."

"True."

"Her manager put the kibosh to that as I would have in his position. The promoter still has all the bells and whistles in place as far as their TV exposure, and we both know she'll get the bulk of the coverage. So, she's not really putting anything on the line. She's a quality opponent, but for her to lose, it's no biggie. Well... except for her pride."

"And the purse?"

"That's not that big a deal either, kid. We get paid a portion of what they take in. I'll get my money back, don't you worry. She's a big draw and they've been highlighting you as a skilled amateur with guts and grit or some such crap they've added to the posters. You look hot by the way. That'll draw a crowd."

"I'm on a poster? Seriously?"

"Yep. Her fights get this kind of promo sh-stuff. They pictured you looking tough but played up on your looks. That'll be the real draw. I kept one of the best profiles for my office. It kinda warms my heart to see you there."

Cassi grinned at his teasing. "It's all about selling tickets, right?"

"Hell, girl, this is Vegas. It's all about the betting." He laughed at the face she made, and then lifted the ropes. "Come on, doll, get a hot shower and we'll spoil you with a body massage and some down time. I don't like to push a fighter on the big day."

"I guess a hamburger, fries and a milkshake are taboo?"

"Uh huh. But I promise to take you for the greasiest platter after you take this girl down a peg or two."

"You're on, my friend. And I want a pickle with my meal."

"Hey! Don't push it."

Chapter
Forty-two

Cassi totally enjoyed the spoiling after her workout. Rus did the massage himself, and he knew just how to dig into places that needed loosening.

Being in such good shape helped hugely, but he still managed to make her wince a few times and then called her a baby when she couldn't hide it.

Finally, he let her loose so she could visit Trace at the hospital. She also needed to catch up with Billy about the hearing they'd held at city hall.

Cassi had visited with Mary on the phone to give her moral support. If she could have appeared at the preliminary hearing, she would have done so, but it was closed to the public. She'd tried to call Billy, but all his phone messages were going to his voice mail, so other than a good luck text she had to step down.

Now, she'd like to know what the verdict was and what it meant for the case. So, rather than going straight to the hospital, she stopped off at Billy's law office on her way and found Maria at work, surrounded by messages, files and yellow lawyer's pads.

"Hi, Maria, where's Billy?" Cassi leaned against the edge of the desk.

"Hell, I don't know. He's so busy, right now, even I'm having trouble getting a hold of him. Just so you know, he did a brilliant job yesterday at the court house. No one could have worked the system better, but the judge wasn't having any of it. She's strong on jurisprudence and determined not to get appealed on this case, or to lose the popular vote from either side of public opinion. She's sticking strictly with the law. We're going to trial."

"Exactly what you expected."

"That's true. I've already done scads of preliminary work. Since Billy pushed for an early date rather than let it sizzle too long and lose the supporters, we lucked out. The judge, Ann Dover, an older, strictly by the book champion, agreed to slot this into her docket early since she had an unexpected opening. The prosecution didn't like it, but they agreed that the mass hysteria fueled by the media is best kept as short as possible."

"How did Mary handle the stress?"

"Like a trooper, as if all the squabbling was beneath her."

"She's something else, isn't she? You should have seen her with Detective McGuire's mother, Kathleen. Both Trace and his mother called her their angel. The night I met her, I had to agree. No one could have been gentler or more caring about the poor woman's horrible pain. Anyone with a heart could sense the affection between the two women. It gave Trace peace of mind, and I have no doubt, she gave the same relief to the families of her other clients."

"Let's hope they all remember this when we call them to the stand."

Cassi checked her watch and jumped up. "I have to run, Maria, but I'd sure like to be involved in the trial preparations. I know you're second chair, but I also know it's you doing most of the legwork." She grinned conspiratorially and liked that Maria returned it in kind. "If you could use some help, I'm your girl. In case Billy hasn't mentioned it, I used to work at the library and research comes easy to me."

"Oh, my God, yes. Absolutely. But I thought you worked nights at some bar downtown? That's what Billy said." Confused, Maria's big brown eyes revealed her state of mind.

"I do. It's a long story. Hell, after my crazy last

shift, I might not have a job. If so, then for sure I'll have plenty of time. Anyway, I'll get back to you on that score. Tell Billy I stopped by and—"

"Tell me yourself, sweetheart." Billy burst into the room and lifted her off her feet in a swirling embrace. He let her down slowly, ignoring her struggle to get him to stop performing. "I'm that happy to see you, Cassi. Did Maria tell you what happened yesterday? We're up for an early trial."

"That makes you happy. I can see it in your eyes. You weren't disappointed by Judge Dover's ruling?"

"Not at all. It's what I expected. Now we have a date, we can get busy and work on the issues. There's a lot to be done in a rather short period of time."

"Maria mentioned it. I offered to help out. You know I did a lot of studying with you for your exams. Plus, I'm experienced in researching so I may be of some help."

"Great. It's what I hoped you'd say. Before you leave, what time is the fight tonight?"

Stunned, Cassi stopped on her way to the door. She swung around, her eyes narrowed. "How did you know about that?"

Looking slightly abashed, Billy admitted, "I hang out at the casino every once in a while with some of my old buddies from law school. Don't look so scared. I'm a good boy. I drink soda water and the only stimulant I partake of nowadays is a slice of lime."

A tide of relief flooded her and she smiled with more warmth than she would have shown normally. "You are a good boy."

"Told you. I was there earlier. A small typhoon could have knocked me over when I saw your picture on the poster."

"Yeah, well, Arlene hurt her hand and Rusty had already put up a purse for her. When Ariana suggested I step in, I couldn't refuse." Cassi wouldn't admit that Ariana had forced the issue because something about Cassi's talent threatened her over-inflated ego. "I couldn't see him lose his money."

"Of course, *you* couldn't. I'll be there, Cassi, in your corner all the way."

"Me, too," Maria added. "Maybe we could go together, Billy." Her eyes beseeching, her face alight, Maria now standing, swayed closer to him and lit up like a firefly when he put his arm around her shoulder and agreed. "Sure we can. I'll pick you up here."

Cassi waved at them both before leaving, his words still in her head. He'd taken for granted that poor Maria would be staying that late. After all, the fight didn't even start until eight.

Chapter
Forty-three

Trace waited for Cassi to visit all morning. The time passed slower than a watched pot. Till it finally dawned on him that she wasn't answering her phone or showing up because she'd be at the gym. No doubt, they'd be working with Arlene and getting her ready for her big fight tonight.

Damn, he wished he could see it, be there for Cassi and Rusty. He'd become fond of the cranky old man who treated his lady with such affection. She needed someone in her corner and that codger adored her. Anyone could see it shining when he looked her way. And though he came across as gruff and snarly, he cared about his fighters. Even bitchy Arlene.

Truth to tell, whenever Trace thought about Arlene, he kind of got a warm feeling too. After all, she'd rescued Cassi from Juan, the crazy with the gun who'd had big plans for payback. No telling what he'd had in mind for Cassi.

In Trace's world, when someone did you a biggie like that, you were in their debt. One day, he'd be able to do something for the fighter but for now, as soon as Michael got back, he'd get him to place a bet on her being the winner.

A warm feeling erupted and he found himself grinning like an idiot. Lying, with his bandaged arm hurting like a son of a bitch, he forced himself to his feet and stumbled into the bathroom. Dizzy, hurting, he bitched and cussed but didn't let up. He had to get out of this hellhole as soon as he could, which meant exercise and moving.

According to his boss who'd visited briefly that morning, he was to consider this a holiday. He had a week off whether he wanted it or not. They needed him healthy and not taking chances that he'd push things too quickly and end up back in here with infection or muscle damage.

What the fuck else did he say? The man ranted, waved his arms around and stomped to the bed, surprising the shit out of Trace when he grabbed his good shoulder and gave it a squeeze. He'd stared him down and gruffly added, "Goddammit, Trace. Do you have to stop every bullet that comes your way with your body? Ever heard of ducking, man?"

Touched, speechless, Trace grinned. It took a

few seconds before he trusted himself to say the words, sorry boss, without being embarrassed by a wobbling voice or damp eyes. He just hadn't known the old guy gave a shit. The thought hit him and wouldn't ease off. Goes to show, man – sometimes a person can get the wrong impression if they don't pay enough attention.

Eventually, Michael appeared and they got down to work. He might not be allowed in the office, but there was nothing wrong with his brain, or his memory. A couple hours later, Michael had the gist of what needed to be done and followed up on.

One thing they'd surmised, Pete Bradford had been at the warehouse but had split the minute things got rough. They figure he'd made off in one of the delivery trucks which meant they hadn't seized the whole shipment.

Chances were that the attackers, the *Soldados*, ripped off a fair share. The word on the street was that Sergio's gang wanted the *Armas* gone, for good. They'd previously controlled the market until Dani and her gang had arrived with the crappy shit they sold. Now they were cleaning house.

Just before Michael left, Sam stuck his head in the door and cautiously slipped into the room.

Trace hadn't expected a personal call. He understood why Sam liked to keep his distance and was stoked to see the agent who'd become a pal in such a short time. "Hey, man, thanks for coming. Meet my new partner, Michael Kowalski."

Sam nodded at Trace and shook hands with Michael. "Yeah, no problem. Not too sure you're gonna be happy after I tell you the latest."

Trace's good hand automatically went to rub his head as it tended to do in moments of stress. "What the fuck has she done now?" Trace had no doubt Sam was there to tell stories on Cassi. It's what he did. Why they colluded... to keep her safe.

Sam grinned as if he couldn't help himself. He slouched in one of the visitor's chairs and lifted his feet to perch on the wooden bed rail.

Michael headed for the door, waved his good-bye, and once Trace saluted, he left.

Sam's gruff voice held a smile. "Hold onto your cool, okay? She's fine, bro, but the little monkey is up to something. Last night, I caught her downstairs in the counting area, pissing off two dudes who don't play games."

On full alert, Trace slid his feet out from under the covering, his intentions clear.

"Get back into bed, you prick, before you fall flat on your face. If you're gonna react to everything I say, I'll keep my mouth shut. Cass will kill me if she figures I upset you."

Trace noticed the door opening and tried to

signal to Sam but it was too late.

"You're right, Sam. About now, I'm contemplating where to hide your body."

"Cass, what the hell!" Sam jackknifed so fast his chair tipped over. If the guy wasn't so fast on his feet, he'd of ended up on the floor. "You don't sneak up on a guy like that."

***

Cassi leaned against the open door, her arms crossed. "I didn't sneak as you so delicately put it. Michael held the door open for me but you two old crows were too busy gossiping to notice it hadn't closed."

Trace quickly got back under the covers, a pathetic appearance suddenly appearing. "Sam just dropped by to see how I was. He was worried about me."

"It's timely, don't you think? Since I'm seriously contemplating doing some major damage."

"Aw, sorry, babe. We were just shooting the shit about—"

"I heard everything, Trace. You got Sam spying on me and running tales." She stepped into the room and marched up to Sam who had just righted the chair and looked about ready to flee. "What were you going to say, Sam? Please don't let me stop your flapping tongue."

Looking slightly abashed, and not happy being

in the spot he'd found himself, Sam's orneriness kicked in. "Hey, princess. You're the one taking the stupid chances. I can't talk sense into you so I hoped the guy you're sleeping with might have some clout and get you to back off whatever you're planning."

She made a silly face as if to downplay his statement. "I'm not up to anything as you so delicately put it. I was curious. I knew most of the guys had left and decided to investigate. No biggie, Sam. So, let's drop it." Her warning glare couldn't be seen by Trace but she knew Sam had gotten her message loud and clear.

He nodded. "Right, sugar. I'll drop it for now as long as you promise to stay in the bar where you belong."

"Far as I know, Dani canned me last night. So, I don't think it will be an issue any longer."

Trace, tired of being ignored, let out a loud yesss! And both Cassi and Sam turned to watch him playing at being a teenager, pumping his fist and grinning.

It totally lightened the tension and Cassi started laughing. "Seriously, dude? It makes you that happy to know I got fired?"

His face straightened, the playfulness disappearing. "Baby, you have no idea."

Cassi turned to Sam. "Did the boss say anything

to you?"

"Dani? Nope. Haven't talked to her or Rodrigo. I took tonight off, so I could go to your fight. Guess we'll have to wait until tomorrow to find out for sure."

Trace groaned. "They won't discharge me for a few more days but I'll be watching it on TV. Tell Arlene I'm in her corner. I even got Michael to place a bet for me."

Cassi scowled at Sam, her sharp nod enough to warn him to shut up. Which he did. And if his glower was any indication, not willingly.

"Gotta go, kids. You behave now. I'll see you later, Cass." The way Sam said the words didn't sound a warning, but the look in his eyes when they sent his message spoke much clearer.

Shit! Cassi felt overwhelmed. She couldn't catch a break.

Chapter
Forty-four

Once Sam left, Cassi breathed a sigh of relief. If she could just get through this visit without any more secrets coming out, she'd be home free. It wasn't so much that she wanted to be sneaky, or keep Trace in the dark, but she knew she couldn't deal with his misgivings and stay positive.

And today it was imperative that she keep her cool. The battle tonight loomed, and withdrawing, even after Rusty gave his permission, still festered and provoked. The thought of seriously pounding the shit out of another person just for the sport didn't ring her bell, never had.

Of course, she hadn't thought far enough ahead to realize that Trace could watch the fight on TV. But there was nothing she could do about that now. She guessed she'd have some explaining to do later.

Ya think?

She had full intentions of coming straight to the hospital when the fight ended to grovel, that's if she didn't end up in here herself. It was a fact that Ariana Wilde fought like a machine switched to kill. She was a tough cookie, mean and serious as a bullet.

Over the last while, Cassi had watched a lot of videos that likened the fighter to an out of control robot. And that was where Cass saw herself benefiting.

The other girl lost focus when she moved in for the kill. Her body worked ferociously but it was clear that her mind became incensed with the need to hit hard and win with no strategy whatsoever. Therefore, Cass had to keep her cool and box the other woman, right to the end. She had to be focused, at all times.

"Baby, don't be mad. Come closer so I can give you a proper hello."

Trace thought she was angry. "You were talking about me."

"'Cause we care about you, honey. We want to protect you."

Emotions swelled and her resentment dissolved. She rushed to sit in the chair she'd left just that morning and leaned over. Their lips met, and with very little effort, her blood started to boil and her breath caught. Passion that always lurked close by whenever this man's lips touched hers burst wide open.

His sneaky hand roamed under her T-shirt to stroke and caress before he wrapped his fingers around the silk-covered breast that swelled at his touch. She moaned, needy and aching.

"Trace, stop! Don't start what we can't finish. You're a wicked tease."

"Hell, baby, I'm not the tease here. You're so blasted beautiful, you're the temptress. I'm just the poor sap who's crazy in love. All I want is for you to get naked and join me here in this son of a bitchin bed so I can taste your skin and feel you next to me."

Stunned by his vehemence, she repeated the one word he'd never actually directed at her before. "You love me?"

"You're kidding, right?" He took her hand and guided it to the bulge he didn't even try to hide. "See how much I want you, darlin'? Not being able to fix that situation is a hell of a lot more painful than my bloody injury."

Not sure why the argument came to her, nonetheless she voiced it. "You can have that problem with any woman. It has nothing to do with love."

"Trust me, baby. There's never been another

woman who could make me feel the way I do whenever we're in the same room together. This hard-on isn't attached to my sex drive. It's connected directly to my heart. You gotta know it's true."

Stunned by his male explanation but buying every single word, her body softened with exaltation and her heart beat triple-time. Sure, that he could see the love shining in her expression; she leaned over to stare into his sultry blues and then she kissed him for a long time. Exploring, searching, finding, loving...

She pulled back, shame on her face. "You're hurting. And I'm messing with you. I'm sorry, love."

He leaned toward her, his features wreathed in misery. "No, you're not hurting anything I don't want you to. Be a good girl, Cassi. Go lock the door."

"You're kidding, right?"

"Not even for a second. I want you so bad, lady. You're gorgeous and seeing you makes me ache."

"Trace McGuire! There is no way I'm going to crawl into that bed with you and have you rip out your stitches. Behave, or I'll leave right now." The twinkle in her eye belied the harshness of her words. But it sent a signal she knew he'd received. She liked that he wanted her so badly that he'd be willing to defy the rules and accept the pain.

Like a little kid denied a treat, he pouted playfully. "Big meanie. It would have speeded up my recovery."

"Do you think kisses might help?"

"You mean there. Like, yeah!" He pointed at his erection.

"No. I don't mean there." She pointed at his face and laughed at his silliness. "I've got to head out now, but I'll be back after the fight. Maybe we'll get away with a bit of playing around then, big guy? What do you think?"

"I think you're on, little girl!" He winked and left her lips scorching from a last kiss that felt as if he'd drawn the very soul from inside her heated, quivering body.

Good lord, she loved this man.

***

On the way out of the hospital, she went to Arlene's room so she could let the other girl know where she stood as far as the upcoming fight. Only Arlene had left.

The nurse on duty explained the situation. "Her aunt picked her up earlier. Against doctor's advice, I might add. She discharged herself, talked them into letting her come back as an outpatient for her antibiotics."

"Okay, thanks." Cass knew it meant she'd have

another helper in her corner later. The weight of her biggest fear settled over her once again.

Would Arlene understand if she lost her cool and threw the fight?

Would it matter?

Surprisingly, the moody girl had edged into being someone she cared about. Therefore, yeah! Losing her respect would matter.

All the burdens hanging over Cassi's head began to feel like insurmountable weights wearing away her grit and determination to stay focused on her main goal.

What was it again?

Shit!

Chapter Forty-five

Rusty had gotten their dressing room organized and all Cassi had to do was bring her outfit and her guts. No biggie! Calm down and stay focused. Now she understood how Arlene felt before her fights. Why she hummed with energy and tension every time.

Cassi felt it thrumming through her system and knew she needed to get into the zone. She watched Rusty setting up and knew he wouldn't say anything to upset her before a fight but something ate away at him and she couldn't relax until it had been dealt with.

"Rusty, talk to me. What's wrong?"

He stopped unpacking the big black carry-all and dropped it onto the bench. His short, wiry body stiffened, his tuke perched at the back of his head. He knuckled his eyes, the bushy white brows messy from his mangling. "Your daddy would be so proud today, brat. I can't get him out of my head. He dreamed of Raoul taking his place and shit if it didn't turn out to be his baby girl."

Cassi swallowed the huge lump in her throat and stared Rusty down.

"Papá would never have believed I could be a fighter. He treated me like a brainy little girl whose biggest accomplishment was to be pretty, cook, bake and keep a clean house. Oh yeah, and praise the big strong men in the family."

"That's bull, Cass. Your daddy loved you."

"I know that! So did Raoul. And I adored them both which is why I played the role they set for me. I've come to realize it's in my nature to please the people I love."

"You sayin' you're taking this fight to please me? Cause that ain't necessary. I told you that."

"So you did. Therefore, you can relax. I've grown up from being that sad little girl. This is my choice."

Rusty mumbled. "Your daddy and Raoul would still be tickled, just sayin'."

Cantankerous old softic. "You know this is a one-time deal, right? We're good with that?"

"Sure. Of course. It's just a thrill for me to see something I never thought would ever happen... me training another champion."

"Rusty, are you okay? We both know the title's not on the line here." Cass began to worry about Rusty's words, that he had things all screwy somehow.

"Yeah, yeah. I know that. What'cha think, I'm losing it or sumphin? Let's just say, that no matter if you win or not, it should be a title fight and I'm proud to be the guy who's behind ya. So, don't get yourself in a big tizzy, okay?" Belying his rough tone, his hand gently pushed her hair behind her ear, and he pinched her cheek just as he'd done so many times when she'd been a little girl. Her heart swelled with love, and her happy world settled back into place.

She left Rusty to change and tightly braid back the right side of her hair. Taking time to meditate in the washroom, she loosened up with some yoga poses, concentrating on balance and clearing her mind.

The practice mentally kicked in and automatically, her body relaxed. It was some time before Arlene arrived to break up her routine. "Cass, can I interrupt?"

Cass unfolded her legs, rose, and put the towels she'd used as a cushion back on the rack. "Sure. Figured I'd see you here tonight. I went to your room at the hospital. They said you'd signed your own discharge form and an older woman came to get you."

"I called my aunt."

"Strange, at Mani's funeral, I got the impression you two didn't get along."

"We didn't, until my uncle got sick. For his sake, we had to behave. We're friends now."

"I'm glad. In today's crazy world, we need all the friends we can get. Sure you're okay to be here tonight? They said you discharged yourself against doctor's orders."

"No problem. I'm a bit weak but my temperature's normal."

"Well, I'm glad you're here." Cassi grinned.

"Are you kidding me? I feel like a Class A bitch for having conned you into doing something that you hate. I couldn't let you go into the ring without telling you. God, Cass, I'm sorry. I had no right to lay this shit on you."

"So you break out of the hospital, take a chance with your health, just to tell me what I already knew. You're a goofball, you know that?"

"You don't hate me?"

Cass walked closer, pleased that it mattered. Ignoring Arlene's typical hard expression that contradicted the tears gathering in her eyes, she grinned. Now serene herself, she sensed the turmoil Arlene suffered, and she couldn't stand it.

"You didn't force this on me, pal. Don't blame

yourself."

A soft sob, quickly extinguished, broke the silence. Arlene's mouth quivered. It took a few seconds for her to gain control. "If I hadn't known you'd win, I'd never have asked you to go in that ring tonight. But it wasn't my choice to make and goddammit, Cass, I'm sorry. That's all I wanted to say."

Cass held out her hand and waited for Arlene to take it. She kept hold and said the one thing that started a smile on Arlene's face.

"For Rusty."

***

"Hell, kid, I thought you'd snuck out the back door. Sent Arlene in there to get you, so I could wrap your hands. Time's moving on."

Cass took off the robe she'd donned after working out and saw him survey her outfit and nod his approval. That morning, he'd given her Arlene's gear with the gym's name on the back. The red silk looked good on her and it fit perfectly.

She saw the counter where he'd laid out some of the preparation paraphernalia: her gloves, mouthpiece, handwraps, gauze, knuckle padding and first aid stuff.

Arlene had the Vaseline ready and she worked it on certain parts of Cass's face and body while Rusty did her hands. As a pro, he knew exactly how they needed to be done. When he finished, they felt perfect.

She did a bit more shadow boxing, the strategy her and Rusty had worked on earlier firmly planted in her mind. She knew exactly what she needed to do. Now it was a matter of following through. The time had come.

While walking to the fight area, she said one last prayer and had a final mental check-in with Raoul. *"Bro, if I ever needed you in my life, I need you tonight. Watch over me. You too, Papá. Help me so I don't make Rusty look like a fool as my coach."*

***

The crowd was huge and noisy, nothing like the ones at City Center. This was a major Vegas casino with all the bells and whistles one would expect to see.

Entering the arena, a shadowy figure stepped close to her, enough for her to see his face from under the black hoodie. The number of guys surrounding him should have given her a clue that Sergio had decided to take a chance and be there for her tonight.

Appreciating his support more than she could reveal, not aiming to bring him unwanted attention, she furtively touched his arm for a split second before moving on.

As she appeared to more of the crowd, the

clapping and calls ramped up. Accepting that Rusty, and even Arlene had a number of fans, she didn't take any of the adulation to heart.

Still overwhelmed, Cassi and Rusty, followed by Arlene, made their way to the center stage, where the ring was situated under the floodlights. She fought down the clawing panic building inside her. Muscles in her stomach struggled to clench. She forced them to relax.

Rows of seats were filled on both sides of her. Though she scanned the audience, she saw nothing. A hand grasped hers and gave a squeeze, which drew her attention. She looked into Sam's encouraging gaze and instantly relaxed. He mouthed his usual comment when a brawl started in the bar, "You got this covered?" She nodded and grinned her thanks.

They slowly made their way forward toward the ring, people watching her and some whistling. Until a skirmish to her left caught her eye.

Dani and Rodrigo were walking down the aisle. Billy and Maria were ahead of them and stopped to turn into the row toward their empty seats. Cassi saw Dani react with fury and reach behind her until Rodrigo caught her arm and stopped her from retrieving her weapon. Or at least that's what Cass imagined she was going for. She'd seen the same thing happen more than once.

After Dani'd shoved Billy, likely to get his attention, Rodrigo forced the redhead to stop whatever shit she was starting and to keep moving. He'd broken up the altercation smoothly. Most of the people around them hadn't even noticed the problem.

Because she was standing, Cass had seen it all.

What the hell?

Why would that crazy woman go after Billy?

Chapter
Forty-six

A roar from the crowd got her attention and arriving ringside, she saw Ariana playing the diva for all she was worth. It didn't bother Cassi; in fact, she kind of liked taking the lesser role and staying out of the limelight.

When they called her to center stage for the introduction, she thought about Trace, how sorry she was for misleading him. All the longing inside her for that man could be seen in her eyes as she sent him a loving glance through the eyes of the camera. The expertise of the cameraman kicked in and he quickly zoomed in on her face.

That's when the world fell in love with Cassidy Santino.

***

Trace couldn't believe what he was seeing. His Cassi in the center ring, dressed like a boxer, ready to take on the Featherweight champion of the U.S.

What the fuck!

Stunned, he listened as the announcer stated what he'd already suspected; she was the fighter against Ariana Swift, one of the dirtiest boxers in the woman's game. Ever since he'd known Arlene would be her opponent, he'd followed Ariana's career, watched videos and read articles.

Frozen, he saw the camera zoom in on Cassi. The quirky, adoring smile she sent him through the screen, full of loving softness, got his attention like nothing else could have. It wasn't that he thought she'd smiled just for him, he knew it. That was the exact same look she'd left him with earlier.

Flipping the covers aside, he flung out of bed and sank to his knees. Shit, the morphine they'd fed him through the tubes had made him weak enough to drool. He'd refused to give himself the pain relief by pushing the button, and so they'd force-fed him intravenously.

Struggling to his feet, he stopped to let the adrenalin settle, carefully edged his way to where they'd piled his clothes and then into the bathroom. The exertion had been worth the effort; soon he had everything on but his shoes. They took again as long as the rest of his clothes, but finally, he'd finished.

Regaining some of his clearness, he headed for

the night table beside the bed and bent over to fetch his wallet, phone and the rest of his belongings. Totally focused, he didn't hear the door opening. Nor did he see the two white-coated misfits who came up behind him.

He did feel the needle they jabbed into his throat and knew they'd shoved him into a wheelchair. After that, everything went blank.

Chapter
Forty-seven

Cassi felt shock at the attention the crowd showered on her when the announcer called her name. They'd screamed for Ariana, dressed in black with yellow trim, but many had given her a rousing cheer as well.

She noticed Dani as one of the loudest, whistling and waving her arms, and even Rodrigo clapped. Her gaze automatically flipped to Billy who'd risen and was also making a bit of an ass out of himself.

She waved at the crowd rather than play the fool like Ariana was doing, strutting, working the screamers like a pro and boosting her own confidence at the same time.

Before heading to their corners, the girls were called to center stage to be announced and afterward, Ariana gave Cassi a shortened, pretend hug but ended it with a shove, a way of disrespecting her opponent and belittling her. Cass held her cool and let her get away with the dissing. In her mind, when the other girl lost, she'd have that much further to sink.

It all worked into her game plan, to let Ariana get over-confident so she'd make mistakes. Either that or piss her off so much, she'd forget her training and react with pure anger uncontrolled.

Arlene started talking her up as soon as she sat on the stool in her corner. Rubbing grease in spots that would get the most punishment, she worked the muscles to loosen them. Rusty gave her last minute instructions, as she'd expected and soon had her mouth guard ready for when the bell rang.

Rising, she watched her opponent bounding toward her and stepped out of reach. Circling, playing, getting into the rhythm, she took a few punches and threw a few, nothing serious, nothing deadly and sensed every which way that Ariana liked to play.

Watching videos had given her knowledge but nothing taught a person like really being in the ring and sussing the other person's moves, their strengths and more important their weaknesses.

If she fretted easily, the knowledge she gained would have given her a panic attack. Ariana Wilde didn't make a lot of mistakes. She wanted the win.

And she had full intentions of making it happen.

Cass also saw that the other woman wasn't taking her too seriously. Not yet. She threw a punch she knew would get her attention. Ariana's head flung to the side from the weight of Cassi's force and the other girl woke up.

She let out a roar of fury just as the bell rang. Hesitating, her body arched to go after Cass until at the last second, her coach's whistle got her attention, and she stepped down.

Smiling to herself, Cassi headed for her stool and let Rusty's words penetrate. "You rocked her good, Cass. She's awake now. And she's gonna turn up the heat. You okay with that? You gotta watch that right center hook, kiddo. She's wanting to plant it between your eyes."

Arlene turned on Rusty. "She's fine, you old shit. In her heart, Cassi's a fighter. She's not gonna let that bitch get away with nothing, are you, brat?"

Brat? Arlene using Rusty's pet name grabbed at Cassi and gave her a lift. It helped to know that, in her mind, Arlene cared and already had the match won. Her positivity eased the stress. Cassi winked at her, opened her mouth for a spray of water and said nothing.

Once the bell rang, she started back into the fight and watched the other girl shoot toward her. She waited until the last minute and veered away, constantly moving, swaying, and protecting her face and body as best she could.

Ariana, wanting to show who was boss, had ramped up the pressure. She kept on the attack. Cassi played with her, making her crazy, the same way she did while sparring with Arlene. It worked. Made the other girl expend a lot more energy. Still, through every skirmish, she watched, her brain constantly re-evaluating. Rusty had worked on her to keep her legs under her and sense where the attack was coming from. That training kicked in.

She watched the other girl's shoulder and sure as shit, she had a way of dipping when she planned to get in close. And when Ariana had her in a clinch, she'd swing them both away from the referee, and like pistons, her elbows managed to find a rib and do plenty of damage.

Fuck! Rusty had warned her. Still, it hurt like hell. Some in the crowd jeered their disapproval but more cheered.

The ringing announced the end of the second round and Ariana's knee snuck in a final dig before the referee pulled them apart.

Rusty's good blue eye, filled now with black flames, stared her down. "Pump that jab, brat, and stay the hell out of her clinches." His short body vibrated with rage as he spit the words he couldn't hold back. She saw his fury and grinned at him to show she was fine.

Arlene's wrath couldn't be cooled so easy. She yelled her indignation with a blue stream of cussing that helped blow off steam and strangely lifted Cassi's spirits. "Keep your chin down, Cass. You're making the bitch look bad."

Settling into a steady rhythm, Cassi played the game, got in her shots and egged on her opponent. Mental stress could be as effective as physical punishment and Cass had one thing working for her. Ariana had to show the world she deserved her title because she was the best.

All Cassi had to show them was that she could fight. She threw a series of punches she'd practiced with Arlene and knew they'd scored.

Cassi sensed the other flagging, her breathing becoming labored. To combat her waning energy, she kept forcing Cass into the ropes so she could land even more of her sneak attacks with her knees and elbows.

The judges weren't calling her on her bad behavior because this fight was just casual entertainment, a kind of start-up to the main event. Having a title holder involved, had gotten a lot of attention. And the more nasty shit that happened, the better the crowd got worked up. A guarantee the folks would enjoy the show.

At the beginning, the cheering had started off

muted, but after Ariana's last string of violations it had become ear-splitting. Though Cass didn't allow herself to focus on such trivial matters, it was hard not to pick up on the tumultuous jeers and the deafening applause.

They continued to throw punches; Cassi's well placed and deadly while Ariana's wild, yet lucky. When the bell rang, Cassi pushed the other girl off her, the referee helping. But Ariana swiveled around behind the referee and came at Cass. If she wouldn't have side-stepped, the last jab would have done damage.

Son of a bitch!

The crowd was on their feet. The judges were smiling and the referee shook his head, accepting that to end the fight would be frowned on. This was turning into a no-holds barred match.

Cassi saw the whole thing in the few seconds it took her to sit on her stool. In her mind, the words "bring it on" began to clamor.

Rusty, more pissed than she'd ever seen him, had trouble climbing under the ropes. "You listen to me, Cassidy Santino. You get back in there, and you win that fight. I don't care if you fling the broad over the ropes or stomp on her freakin' head. The bitch has got it coming." He was spitting with righteous rage. Cassi could see he was so wound up, he'd lost control. While he mechanically worked on the cuts and bruises on her face, she nodded soothingly.

"Got it, Rus. Finish it. Okay."

Arlene's voice kicked in also. "Cass, if you don't finish that wacko whore, I'll get in there and do it myself. She's playing dirty with you, girlfriend. Bring her down! Do it!"

Cassi knew they were in her corner, on her side. She appreciated their faith in her abilities but she wouldn't ruin Rusty's reputation for the world. On the other hand, he looked like a pending heart attack victim if she didn't do something to end this charade. With that in mind, she headed back into the fight.

The referee had determined they were both okay to fight and admonished Ariana to watch herself. She brushed past him like he meant less than nothing and came at Cassi full boar, her fists flying.

Veering, swivelling, watching for the opening, Cassi felt the other's fists sliding off her body, leaving little or no damage. She pulled off some fancy feet-work and was able to catch Ariana off guard.

Her fist plowed into Ariana's side. She felt it connect and knew she'd scored points that time. Then she came in low and used her uppercut to sneak in another good jab that had Ariana's head jerking to the left.

Before she could follow up, Ariana grabbed her and pushed her toward the corner. Her elbow dug into Cass's neck and it hurt like the devil.

Done! Fed-up, she shoved the other girl away. Pivoting, and using the corner post, she ran up it, flipped high in a somersault to land in front of her opponent. Then she drove her fist into the side of Ariana's head.

Game over.

Ariana hit the pads and didn't move until her coach, yelling foul, rushed over with the smelling salts.

Rusty charged into the ring. His arms wrapped around her thighs, lifting Cassi high, he swung her around and around.

On their feet, waving, screaming, joyful for the fantastic ending, the spectators were shouting her name and showering her with admiration.

Unfortunately, Cassi knew she'd be disqualified. The judges had no choice. Considering how happy Arlene and Rusty were, now high-fiving each other, she realized it didn't matter. They felt like winners, and that was the only reason she'd played along.

Chapter
Forty-eight

Trace came to on a disgusting, grubby mattress in a dark space he sensed was little more than a long narrow closet. Stonework, like one might find in a basement of an older home, surrounded him.

Whoever kidnapped him; the sons of bitches had cuffed his wrists. The handcuffs had a foot long chain separating them. And they'd run another chain under the handcuffs, which passed through a steel ring bolted to the wall and was padlocked. This arrangement gave him a very small area to move around.

The pale lightbulb, high above, threw shadows everywhere. But once he could assimilate between where the floor ended and the walls began, he saw that the room was darker in his end. Wincing, concentrating, he could barely make out a handle-less, discolored, plastic bucket next to a bottle of water. They were the total furnishings in his palatial suite.

Lurching to sit up, he held his head in his hands to let the raging headache ebb. He groaned and gritted his teeth to stop the string of obscenities seething. Once he could open his eyes again without the pain stabbing brutally, he took in more of his surroundings.

He felt the cold and sensed the lack of fresh air, which made him think he was underground, in the bowels of some older building. Trying desperately to remember what had happened after his attackers had overwhelmed him at the hospital, all he could recall were male voices and cruel hands.

After they'd wheeled him out of the hospital, they'd thrown him onto the floor of a vehicle, likely a van. He'd passed out again, only to wake up when they carried him down a staircase.

His transporters hadn't been gentle. Not only was Trace a large man, he was solid muscle and heavy. He remembered his head getting bashed into a wall and his legs being dropped while the carriers had bitched about how much he weighed, cussed and then kicked him as if he'd been to blame.

Struggling to gain his feet, he stumbled to the bottle of water. Leaning against the cold, damp stone, he allowed himself a small amount. No telling how long before someone came and replaced the bottle.

Playing with the steel chain, needing to see just how much leeway they'd given him, he realized that they'd been careful to leave him room to get to the side where he could use his shitter, but not enough spare to get anywhere close to the stairs.

Bastards!

Who the hell would kidnap and imprison a Vegas police detective when the penalty was life or worse?

And what the hell did they want?

More important – why him?

Chapter
Forty-nine

Back in their dressing room, voices high and full of glee, Rusty and Arlene were still giggling like kids and recounting the fight, complaining about what a bitch Ariana had proven herself to be.

"You worked her good, kid. Played with her like I taught you."

"Did you see that last punch, Rus? Cass flipped over like an acrobat and wham." Arlene acted it out. "Done, baby. Light's out."

Cassi laughed. "It wasn't as dramatic as you're making it sound."

"Trust me, Cass," Rusty positively glowed. "I'm sure the boxing world never saw a fight end in quite that way. They'll be yapping about it for a long time. It's already shown up on the news, and they're milking it for all they can. You were the long shot so a lot of people who bet that way, are crowing about the money they made. I'm one of them."

"But I didn't win the fight."

"That's true but there are all kinds of bets. One was who might score a knockout punch."

"Seriously? Okay, I don't want to know. I'm just happy if you're happy."

Scads of people had come to the dressing room and were turned away by the locked door and Rusty's admonishment that Cassi would give the press a few moments in the bar area just outside the arena. Right now, she didn't want to talk with anyone.

But the last time he opened the door to say his spiel, he turned toward her instead. "Cass, there's a hooded guy at the door who's kinda pushy and says you'll talk with him. Want I should let him in?" Rusty looked at her. She knew if she refused, he'd tell Sergio to leave.

Since that wouldn't be healthy, she went to the door herself and opened it so Sergio could slide in and be out of view. She saw his bodyguards were obstructing the way for anyone else to come into the hallway.

Both Rusty and Arlene fussed around with the equipment at the far end of the room to give them privacy, but she sensed they had no intention of leaving her alone with this obvious criminal.

Sergio's hand gently stroked the bruise forming on her cheek. When he saw Rusty start to rush over, he dropped his hand and stepped back.

"Hey, babe. You did real good tonight. I was proud of you for not taking any more shit from that skank."

Not sure about the tag but guessing its meaning, Cassi grinned and reached for her friend's hand to let Rusty know he didn't need to worry. She held it tightly. "It meant a lot to see you there, rooting for me, pal. But you shouldn't be putting yourself in danger."

"Like I could stay away? I was there to replace Raoul. And just so's you know, he'd have been proud of his little sister tonight... real proud."

Tears gathered. She blinked to stop them from overflowing and embarrassing her visitor. Softness appeared in his dark eyes, and they shared the moment until a frown took over. Oh, oh. She knew that look. It meant he had something important to tell her, and she'd better listen.

"Saw Billy Duran here tonight with his honey. I thought I told you to ditch that prick."

"And I explained he's a family friend. You know he's Mary Devin's lawyer, and I'm helping with the case. But I promise, I haven't invited him to the house again after your last warning."

"He's poison. So are the people he hangs out

with. You still got my number?"

She pointed to her head, nodded and smiled, hoping to soothe the savage beast. "Got it."

Up till now, adrenalin had kept most of the pain from attacking, but suddenly, she felt every punch and dig her poor body had suffered. Sergio, sensing her discomfort, started to turn for the door.

Before he could step outside, Cassi held his arm, moved in front of him and checked that the hallway was safe before giving the all-clear signal.

Smiling, pleased, Sergio gave her head one last awkward pat and then he disappeared.

Rusty, knowing the signs, spoke up. "Arlene, help Cass to the shower and turn the water on hot. Call when you're ready, and I'll give her a massage. She's going to be aching for a few days but we can tone it down enough so she can move around."

Ten minutes later, fresh from the hot shower, she relaxed on the table and let Rusty work miracles on her poor muscles. Knowing she had people waiting to see her, and not looking forward to the attention, she sighed and let herself enjoy the pampering.

All too soon, they were done and she could get dressed in her regular sweats. Thankfully, no doubt sensing her need for quiet, they hadn't said much while she'd rested. But once she was ready to meet the world, they both moved in.

Rusty's face, still wreathed in grins, pushed close so he could make eye contact. "I'm freakin' proud of you, brat."

Arlene nodded and added, "I can't wait for my hand to heal so Rus can get me a fight with that bitch. Now you've got her number, you can train me. I'll take her down good. Then it'll be me wearing that fucking fancy Featherweight belt."

Cassi stopped dead. She let the words sink into her head and played with them before she overruled her protective instincts and answered. Her first reaction had been to say – no way. Ariana's deadly and she's dirty.

But it dawned on her that Arlene was the real fighter. Unlike her, the girl had the desire and drive to win in the boxing world.

She turned Arlene's way and grinned, her words earning her a huge smile. "It'll be my pleasure, brat."

Chapter Fifty

Once she appeared, the press surrounded her, everyone with questions. There were so many pictures taken, the flashes went on forever. Turns out, they'd researched the story of her father, José Santino. How he'd won the Middleweight Championship years back. The media hoped she'd share so they could tie it to her fight tonight.

She refused to go into much detail, and disappointed for losing such a great scoop, they quit asking. She wasn't a pro and never intended to be one. In fact, she preferred to pass the limelight to Rusty and Arlene. Every chance she could turn the conversation around, she happily promoted Rusty's gym.

Rusty fielded most of the reporters, explaining that Cassidy Santino had stepped in to fight at the last minute because Arlene had hurt her hand. But the real fighter they needed to watch for was Arlene Montgomery.

Suddenly, Cassi noticed a good-looker at the edge of the crowd and forced her way to where Michael Kowalski stood; a huge bouquet of flowers in his hands.

"Trace called and asked me to pick these up and take them to Rusty's girl after the fight. At that time, neither of us knew you were 'starring as the feature attraction' – his words, not mine – but he wanted you to have these."

Touched to the point of tears, her heart fluttering crazy-like, Cassi held out her arms for the huge bundle of colorful, mixed blooms. She swallowed and forced her mind to mundane questions so as not to appear rude. "Thank you. They're beautiful. You were at the fight?"

"I got here a bit late but in time to see the fantastic finale. You rocked the fight world. I made a bit of a fool of myself, yelling along with the rest of your glee club."

She laughed. Had to. The man was funny and his expression invited her to enjoy his humor. Arlene strolled over and stood next to her, as if she might need some backup. She knew about Trace and yet here was a handsome stranger handing Cassi flowers.

"Arlene, these are for you." Cassi passed them

over.

"For me?" Arlene opened her arms, looking stunned.

"This is Trace's new partner, Michael Kowalski. He's here on Trace's orders, to deliver these flowers."

"He's your man. Why the hell would he send me flowers?"

Michael interrupted, his voice soothing. "He thought you were Rusty's fighter tonight. I guess he wanted to show his support."

Arlene forced them back into Cassi's arms. "Then you deserve them, not me. Far as I'm concerned, you're the true winner."

Arlene turned to Michael. "Hi." She would have settled for nodding her hello, but not knowing about her hand, Michael reached to shake. Forced to do something, she held out her left hand instead. Then she seemed shaken when he took it and didn't let it go as politeness decreed.

"What happened to your other hand," Michael seemed truly interested in the small bandage wraparound she'd used.

"An infection from a cat bite. It's much better now but not good enough to box. Otherwise, I would have been the one getting my ass kicked around the ring tonight."

"So I heard." Michael angled his head toward

where the last of the reporters still questioned Rusty. "You're the fighter Trace told me about, the one he hoped would win. Guess he got quite a shock when you showed up on his TV screen tonight, Cassi."

Arlene had finally tugged her hand free. The man's cheeky grin flashed in her direction and Cass watched the interplay. If she didn't know Arlene better, she would have thought cupid and his bow had made an appearance.

Suddenly, Michael's cellphone rang, Hawaii 5-0 being the goofy ringtone. Cassi grinned at Arlene and got a lifted eyebrow and a snicker in return.

When he first answered, Michael's face was still wreathed in smiles. Within seconds, he'd stiffened, his face no longer relaxed. Instead a frown took over and then anger. He turned his back.

Something had upset the man and Cassi sensed the news affected her. She waited until he finished listening and barking the few questions he'd asked, like when and how, and then stepped into his path.

"What happened?"

"Gotta go."

Arlene blocked his way and Cassi closed in. "Something's wrong."

"It's police business."

Cassi stared him down and saw the way his eyes slid away from her searching gaze. "It's Trace. I heard his name"

"I'll get back to you when I know more. Right now, I have to leave."

"Hey, Michael, if you want to walk out of here with both legs working, you'll answer her questions." Arlene had now stepped forward.

He looked from one face to the other and then conceded. "Yeah, it's Trace. He's been taken out of the hospital."

"You mean kidnapped?"

"Since it appears they drugged him and forced him into a wheelchair to get him out, I'd say that's probably what happened."

"They? Do you know who *they* are?" Cassi pushed the panic down. She had to know. "Can you find him?"

"That's my goal. Let me go now. I promise I'll get back to you with every detail I can share." He copied her cellphone number and even got Arlene's. "No doubt, there'll be questions for you to answer. As I said, I'll call."

Chapter Fifty-one

Sam had been watching the byplay from the edge of the room where he'd stayed with his back turned so as not to be seen. He'd planned to congratulate Cass right up until he saw Trace's partner with the flowers.

Knowing they were fully engaged and paying no attention to anyone else, he inched closer. Overhearing their exchange, he recognized Trace's new partner, Kowalski, from meeting him earlier at the hospital. He was the guy who'd driven Trace crazy at the beginning but who'd earned his approval during the recent warehouse shooting.

After the dude got a call, he sensed a change in their discussion. Cassi looked like someone had shot her and Arlene appeared shaken. A few steps closer, and he heard the shitty news.

Snapping into action, he waited until Kowalski

left the distraught girls. Following him to the underground parking, he approached him there.

"Hold up, man. I want to talk to you." Though Sam had briefly met Michael earlier at the hospital, he was pretty sure Trace's partner didn't know he was FBI. He decided to go slow. "I overhead your conversation with Cassi and wanted more information. Trace and I go back a ways. I hoped you could tell me a bit more about what happened at the hospital tonight."

Michael's hand shot out and gripped Sam's. "Hey, good to see you, man. Guess you were at the fight tonight too. Look, I got a call so I gotta scram."

"Just a sec. I overheard some of it. First, did Trace tell you anything about me?"

Looking slightly annoyed, Michael stiffened and inched closer to his vehicle. "Nah! We talked job. I really gotta go, man. Sorry."

"Yeah, I know. Look, I'm on the job, too. But I'm undercover with the bureau, working narcotics at the club. I need you to tell me what happened to Trace."

Respect for Sam's badge replaced Michael's annoyance, and he willingly shared. "All I know is that Trace was removed from the hospital in a wheelchair by two medical attendants. Someone found the abandoned wheelchair flipped over at the edge of the driveway. They have some videos waiting back at the office. I'm on my way there now."

"If I was you, I'd run those two through face recognition. If you don't get any hits, you might want to forward them to me so I can clear them through our International database. Bet you a C-note they have records."

"Nah, that's a sucker bet. I'm sure you're right. Unfortunately, they wore surgeon-like face masks. It's made ID-ing them impossible. If you wanna ride along, I got no problem with it."

"Can't. Boss'd kill me for blowing my cover. But Trace and I are friends so keep me informed. I work with Cassi at the Lipstick Club, been keeping my eye on her. That chick is dynamite with a short fuse. Not sure if Trace mentioned anything about her quest but she's determined to find out who shot her brother. She's been raking the cesspool and her involvement could be tied to Trace's disappearance."

"You think? Trace brought me up to speed with the case, says they caught three killers yet Cassi believes there's a female witness who still hasn't been identified."

"And I'm beginning to think she might have something. Problem is, the one woman, who I have no doubt could be the shooter, was at the club at the time Santino was killed."

"You're talking about Dani Andino."

"That's right."

"No chance she could have left without you seeing her?"

"I wish the fuck I could say yes, but she didn't leave until sometime after he was shot. I watched her and the boys heading out and checked the time." Sam's hands gripped his hips, strain obvious.

Michael scratched his bald head and ran his hand over his short beard, straightening it, a habit that many had with face hair. "Just so you know, with all the overdoses lately, and other crimes that have escalated, Trace's been shaking up any number of the gangs over their drug dealing and other illegal shit. He's riding them all pretty hard. Not only did we pick up a bunch of losers from the recent warehouse debacle, he's been personally putting out a warning that we're closing in. There're a lot of people pissed off at him right about now."

"You figure it's related to one of the gangs?"

"Hell, man, I have no fucking idea. All's I know is he's been working on that nonstop, trying to clean up the streets. Stands to reason someone wants him gone."

"If they wanted to kill him, why not shoot the bastard in the hospital and save themselves all the trouble of kidnapping."

"Hell, I don't know? But I intend to find out. What I do know is the boss has been riding him hard. Lester's retiring soon and wants his record as clean as possible before he hands over the department to the next captain. " Michael handed Sam his cellphone. "Add your number, man. I'll keep you in the loop."

"Appreciate it. I'll snoop around some, too. If I come up with anything that looks like a clue, I'll get back to you."

"I need a favor. Can you take Cassi home and stay with her until either I, or some of my men, arrive to get her statement? She was one of the last people he was with so they'll be questions."

"Sure, will do."

Sam watched the taillights as the car drove away and his stomach took a dive.

Could Cass be connected to Trace's disappearance?

Nothing popped, but he'd lay down his next paycheck there was a link.

He'd taken care of the two slime balls last night, made them disappear. About now, they'd be locked up in the hull of an overseas liner headed for China. He'd called in a favor, a trucker he knew who had a load heading for San Francisco. He and his driving buddy had been perfectly comfortable adding two unidentified parcels to their consignment when the time came for them to load the cargo.

It paid to make friends with lawbreakers who rode the legal fine line, not quite crossing over to force an arrest. He'd owe them but what the hell. Some occasions called for strong measures. And protecting Cass would top the list.

Now, to find out what the hell she was really doing last night down in the dungeon. He returned to the empty room where only Rusty and Arlene flanked a distraught Cassi. As soon as she saw him, she approached, her face drenched with tears and her arms crushing the mangled bouquet of flowers.

"Sam, someone's taken Trace out of the hospital, kidnapped him."

Sam wrapped his arm around Cass's shoulder. Her pale face and devastated expression broke his heart. He glanced at Arlene and knew she was aware of what this could entail. Whoever was serious enough to take a Las Vegas police detective hostage, they weren't playing games.

They meant serious business.

Chapter
Fifty-two

Devastated, numb, her heart broken, Cassi lost all feeling in her aching, sore body. With just a few words, her whole world had collapsed. If Arlene and Rusty hadn't of been close by, she'd have curled into a ball in a corner and lost it. When Sam appeared, it was as if a merciful god had heard her pleas.

Arlene approached him with the news. "Sam, Trace's partner Michael got a call that someone's taken Trace from the hospital. They figure he's been kidnapped."

"I overheard and followed him to the parking lot to get more info, except he didn't know anything yet."

Cassi put into words her greatest fear. "Oh, Sam, do you think Dani could be responsible?" Cassi watched Sam's face and saw the closed expression, the hardness and knew worry when she saw it.

"Let's not speculate at this time, princess. But I would like to talk with you alone, Cass. Do you mind leaving us Rusty? Arlene? Just for a few minutes."

Rusty looked like someone had kicked him in the balls. His face matched the whiteness of his messy mop of hair. "Sure. Arlene and me will get the equipment out to the car. If you want to drive Cass home, we'll meet you there."

"Good idea, thanks, man."

***

As soon as the other two left, Sam gathered Cass close and led her to his vehicle. It broke his heart to see her follow him like a child. Once he'd helped her into the passenger side, he went around to the driver's seat. Then he turned her way and gathered her twisting hands into his to hold firmly. "Cass, I know you're worried, but remember, Trace is a cop – a good cop – one of the best, right?"

Penetrating her grief, his words seemed to make sense. "Yes." She nodded. "Yes, he is."

"So, whoever's holding him, he's their worst enemy. Thing that gives me hope is this, if they wanted him dead, they'da killed him in the hospital. Therefore, they want him alive. And as long as that's the case, every cop in the city will be on their trail."

"They will?"

"Of course. Plus, the FBI will be working the case; they usually get involved in kidnappings, especially for an officer of the law." He pulled on her hands, forcing her to look at him. "You were probably the last person to see him, other than the two kidnappers, right?"

"I stayed for a while after you left, so I probably was the last visitor."

"Therefore, the police will want to talk to you. In fact, I have no doubt they'll be waiting for us when we get to your place. Will you be okay with that or would you rather go to the precinct?"

"No. Take me home."

Tears sprouted and her body started to shake. He'd seen misery before, but hers tore at his hardened heart. Hating to see her suffer, he spoke words she needed to hear. "Cass, you can't go weak now, princess. They'll expect your help with the investigation. Be strong, darlin'. For Trace."

***

His words penetrated the mist of pain she'd begun to sink behind for protection. How could she survive such agony? Losing Raoul had taught her well.

About how relentless the pounding grief was.

How each new day opened with the horrible

awareness waiting – he was dead. He would never come back.

Oh, God, not again!

Afterword

Thank you so much for reading the 3rd book in *Her Sweet Revenge Series*, **Resolution.**

I loved writing this story and I hope you enjoyed reading it. If so, I would ask you for a favor. Wherever you purchased this book, please take a few minutes and leave an honest review. Authors enjoy hearing that readers like their stories, and hopefully, others will read your words and choose to buy the book because of your sentiments.

My website at **http://mimibarbour.com** now has all my books listed with links to the various publishers to make it easy for you to return to where you bought the book and to find my other work.

While you're there, I'd really appreciate it if you would sign up for my newsletter so I can keep in touch.

http://mimibarbournewsletter

I only send out newsletters approximately once a month and you have my word that your address will never be shared.

Hugs, Mimi

Endings

AMAZON

Her Sweet Revenge Series Book #4
by
Mimi Barbour
NYT & USA Today Best-selling author

***IMPORTANT!! Her Sweet Revenge Series –
must start from Book #1

The challenges that Cassi faces in this last book
are enormous. Trace has been kidnapped, and
every passing day destroys her hope that he's alive.

The US Featherweight Champion seeks revenge
in a rematch that Cassi refuses to even talk about.
But she worries how her rejection will affect Arlene
and Rusty.

The female witness of her brother's murder is
still at large. Always in the back of Cassi's mind
is the craving to learn the truth and finally get her
revenge.

The Vegas mob she works for is entangled in a
gang war, and patrons of the Lipstick Club become
even more dysfunctional. She's forced to hide
from the crazy-assed, she-devil gang boss who
wants her and is closing in.

All Cassi yearns for is that Trace will soon come
back to her – alive.

Trace faces his imprisonment with an intense

determination to break free – but how? His cell is impregnable. Every waking moment, he's filled with the need to get back to Cassi. Though the girl fights like a hellion, she's as soft-hearted as an angel, and he can't stand the thought that he might die before ever seeing her again. Visualizing her world of turmoil and danger, he won't give up.

How can he?

She needs him...

Endings - Chapter One

Surrounded by the people she most cared about, Cassidy Santino handled the police interrogation about Trace McGuire's disappearance as best she could. Considering her heart was shattered into small painful fragments, she held her cool rather than following her instincts to crawl into a corner and scream out her pain.

Detective Michael Kowalski, Trace's new partner, cared about her anguish. She could tell. But the gleam of seriousness in his questions belied his gentle tone. Another Vegas officer she didn't recognize, totally businesslike, stood taking notes. The two men had arrived at her house after her boxing match with Ariana Swift.

Unable to think cohesively, she'd let Rusty and Arlene play hostess for her, passing out coffees, showing everyone to chairs, shielding her as best they could.

Hurting, bruised, the punishment her body had taken earlier finally catching up with her was nothing compared to the utter devastation of her thoughts, her fears. How could she focus on their stupid questions when all she wanted was Trace?

Here.

Now.

Holding her.

Protecting her from the horrible pain.

Michael, bald and oddly handsome, leaned closer. As Trace's new partner, a Polish man with a reputed sense of the ridiculous, he wore a serious expression. It gave no clue to the quirky personality Trace had earlier described. Perched on a chair next to her, he reached for her hands to stop them from mangling each other and to gain her attention.

"Cassi, I'm sorry for your distress, but we really need you to answer these questions." His green eyes searched hers, providing support and strength. "Okay?"

"Okay. Yes. What do you need to know?" She connected with him and her eyes focused on his.

"I was at the hospital to see Trace and left before you arrived. In between, he had a visit from Sam." He nodded at the man slouching in a tipped chair next to the wall.

"Yes, Sam Smith, my co-worker at the Lipstick Club downtown."

"Right. Sam told us that he spent a very short

time in the room after you arrived."

"I caught him telling tales to Trace and scared him away." Her sad grin toward Sam let everyone know how well they got on. "After that, Trace and I were alone." Her mind fled back to the wonderful moments they'd shared when Trace had told her for the first time that he loved her, had put it in words. "*You're so blasted beautiful, you're the temptress. I'm just the poor sap who's crazy in love. All I want is for you to get naked and join me here in this son of a bitchin' bed so I taste your skin and feel you next to me.*"

A sob broke. Wrangling her hands free, she lowered her face into them, shaken, distraught... terrified.

Arlene Montgomery, Rusty's protégée, leaned forward from the other side of Michael. Her harsh tone was anything but cordial. "Look, you moron, she's upset and you're questioning her? Man, you guys suck. She just got the crap beaten out of her in a ring by the US Featherweight Champion, and then she finds out her boyfriend has been kidnapped. Give her a break."

Michael responded quickly, his face was only inches from Arlene's. Sparks ignited between them. His expression became deadly serious.

"Look, lady. Trace is my partner. I care about the guy. And I need to know whether Cassi saw anyone loitering or hovering around when she went into his room or when she left. It's important. So, either sit back and be quiet, or I'll have Officer Grady escort you out."

Rusty, who'd been the coffee maker, interrupted and saved the day. "Arlene, come into the other room and help me make up a bed on the couch. I'm not leaving Cassi here by herself, not when there's crazies around kidnapping people. Christ knows who's next."

Cassi heard the exchange and Rusty's words filtered in. The older man still looked as shaken as he'd appeared in the hotel's bar area after they'd left the dressing room. Now she had a suspicion as to why. He thought she was in danger. The sweet idiot wanted to protect her. She adored the old man for putting her welfare first.

"I'll be okay, Rusty. You don't need to stay."

"Ain't no discussion going on here, toots. I didn't ask, did I?"

Cassi saw his lip jut out and caved. "I'm fine, Arlene." Without realizing she'd touched the prickly girl, she patted her arm. "Please go and help Rusty."

Her dark-haired sparring partner scanned her face to see if she was telling the truth, and it still took a moment before her defender stood down. With a last glare at Kowalski, she followed Rusty and disappeared down the hallway.

"I'm sorry, Detective Kowalski. I'm a mess."

"Please call me Michael. I understand completely, Cassi, but we need this information. If there's anything you can think of that will help us, any lead you can give us, I'd appreciate it immensely."

At this point, Sam coughed to get her attention. The telling look he sent vocalized better than words that she needed to get it together. She nodded at him and turned to Michael who held a small pad in his hand, waiting.

Her mind drifted back to the hospital. She'd been in a daze. Her thoughts absorbed with the coming fight. Plus, her determination not to lie to Trace had been a paramount worry and had kept her from focusing on the world around her. Trace had still been under the impression that Arlene would be in the ring.

"No, I'm sorry. I had just a short while with him. Rusty expected me to get to the casino early, and I wanted to stop and see Arlene first before leaving the hospital. Turns out, she'd discharged herself, and so I left."

"Trace told me that he'd given Dani Andino a fairly strict warning that he would be coming for her. Any leads there?"

Fuck! Her heart dropped to the floor and lay

there quivering like a dying goldfish escaped from its bowl. *Dani!* Her mind whirled.

"Cassi?" Michael didn't miss a thing.

"She was at the fight. I saw her. You said Trace was taken during that time? She couldn't have been two places at once."

"Since it was two men who wheeled him out, I didn't suspect she'd be there. Just wondered if any of her men might have been hanging around the hospital, and you recognized them."

"How do you know there were two men?" Cassi shot the question at the surprised detective.

"We have it on video. But the men were dressed like surgeons with face masks, hats, and gowns so they can't be identified."

She shook her head, then stopped because the crushing torture on the inside of her scalp pounded unmercifully. "God, I wish I could help you but I truly don't remember anything. I was kind of focused on the coming fight."

Dani!

"No doubt. Look, is there anyone else you think might have had reason to kidnap Trace? Has he mentioned anything to you about being worried or followed?"

"Trace didn't talk about the job. And he only worried about me and my working at the club. But you're correct about one thing. He did have a run-in with Dani Andino there a few days ago. Plus, he was shot at the warehouse, right? So, he must have made even more enemies when the police interrupted their drug delivery. Did he hurt one of their members and now others are getting retribution? It's what they do, you know. They're all about payback. You can ask Sam about that. He's been around them longer than me."

Michael glanced briefly in Sam's direction but turned back to her. "A good suggestion, we're looking into it. One of the *Armas* members was killed in the shootout when Trace was wounded. We're talking to anyone who knew him and his family."

"Which member?"

"We haven't been able to identify him, just his gang name, Gunner."

"I don't remember him."

"Another man also died before we got there, shot in the back. Harry Sneed. Did you know him?"

"A little. He stood up against Pete for being disrespectful to the boss. That was the last time I saw him. And it was the night of the warehouse shooting."

"We heard about that. Talked to Pete yesterday but got nothing. Certainly not enough to lay charges, but some hinted he had it in for Harry and could have shot him in the confusion. Ballistics has the bullets at the lab and we'll try to match them to Pete's gun. Of course, there's no witnesses who'll step forward."

The chatter finally got to Cassi. She stood and hovered over her interrogator. Angry and frightened, her voice rose. "You've got to find Trace. Who knows how long they'll hold him as a prisoner? Oh God, they'll kill him, won't they?"

"I don't know, Cassi. I'm thinking if they wanted him dead, they'd have killed him at the hospital and saved themselves all the effort of stealing him away in a van."

"Not if the person who wants him dead intends to do the job herself."

Dani! It has to be Dani...

***If you wish to continue reading this story, click here for my Amazon Universal Link: http://myBook.to/sweetendings

***All 6 book in the series are Free in Kindle Unlimited

The Vegas Series

AMAZON

Romantic Suspense at its best
by
New York Times Best-selling author,

Mimi Barbour

This sizzling box set for the Vegas Series starts off where we meet up with hardworking, hard-assed Detective Aurora Morelli. Attempting to arrest a rapist who attacks her colleague then continually thwarts her attempts to bring him to justice—to a horrific nightmare where her new baby is kidnapped—this scrappy detective does everything in her power to control these events. Kai Lawson, a partner she doesn't want, fights against and in the end accepts (in her job and in her bed) is the hero in these first few stories. The bald-headed, purse-carrying hotshot knows just how to pull her crank and the outcome is entertaining. Their blockbuster story will get you totally invested in this series.

In the last three books, along comes Lisa Jordan, a kick-ass kinda gal who loves wearing the shield as a Vegas detective and enjoys the more strenuous aspects of her job. She steps in for a while as Aurora's partner while Kai is MIA. Her story begins here and ends the series as she fights her attraction for wealthy casino owner, Jeff Waters. After one wild night, the charismatic charmer digs his way into her heart and that of the three-year-old nephew in her care. The fact that he leaves her speechless, literally, detracts from his appeal for Lisa since as a self-professed chatterbox, it's the first time ever. On the other hand, everything else about the man is fascinating. She can no more fight her memories than stop herself from rescuing him from two killers holding him hostage in revenge for the mistakes of his father.

~*~*~

Praise for the Vegas series:

"Cops & drama, absolutely loved this series!" ~ reviewed by luvbooks

"Good action and great stories. What a bargain!" ~ reviewed by Johnny Rotten Apples

"Great story lines, wonderful characters!" ~ reviewed by Rachel Larson

"Bloody fantastic!" ~ reviewed by Bernadette Boyce

Special Agent Booker

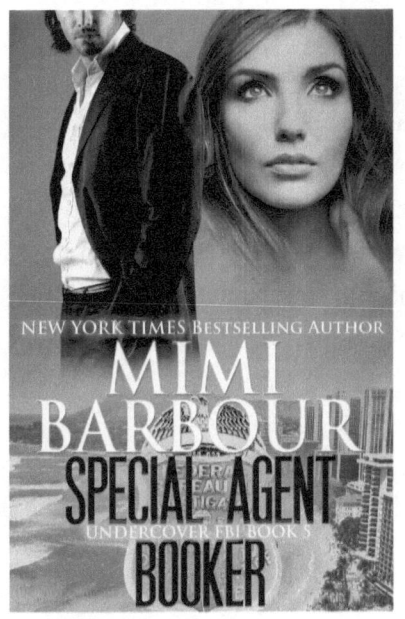

AMAZON

Undercover FBI Book #5

by
New York Times Best-selling author,
Mimi Barbour
~*~*~

Suspense lights up in every page of this fast-paced blockbuster of thrills!

When Sloan Booker's father dies tragically, he has no other option but to give up his job as an FBI agent and take over his family's vehicle restoration business in Oahu, Hawaii. Giving up his badge is difficult but having Homeland Security and his old boss request the use of his house in a stakeout, spying on his Muslim neighbors who they suspect are terrorists, is just too damn much for a man already frazzled. It makes no difference that they've offered him a partner to be in charge of the surveillance... until he meets the gorgeous divorcee.

Special Agent Alia Hawkins might look more like a model than a cop but looks can be deceiving. Not only does she rescue street kids, fights their battles and transports them to safe homes, but since she lived many years in Pakistan and speaks their language, she's a sought after agent. So far, she's kept her personal life and job separate. But when Alia's slimy ex-husband threatens to steal her eight-year-old son, she has no choice but to bring the kid along on her latest undercover assignment – living with a hotshot, sexy as hell agent under the guise of his long lost stepsister. Her life suddenly takes some drastic swerves and she wonders if things will ever slow down.

A word about the author, Mimi Barbour

Mimi is an incredibly busy New York Times, USA Today and award-winning, best-selling author who has nine series to her credit.

She lives on the beautiful east coast of Vancouver Island and fills most of her day with writing and promoting her work. The rest of her time is spent in her garden, doing minimal housework, enjoying her puppy and getting enough exercise to keep her brain working.

"The favorite part of my job is meeting the characters from each new book. Creating them the way I want and having them act however I think they should. It's thrilling. Especially when most of my make-believe folks are interesting, witty and in most cases, people I would love to know."

Contact Me:

Write to me, I truly love hearing from my readers!

~ ~

My website: http://www.mimibarbour.com/
Follow me on Twitter, Facebook, Pinterest
Amazon, Goodreads, BookBub, LinkedIn

www.ingramcontent.com/pod-product-compliance
Lightning Source LLC
Chambersburg PA
CBHW030549180626
46816CB00005B/1471